DREAM CHASER
Awakening

P. Christina Greenaway

Dream Chaser
Awakening

ISBN-13: 978-0615947235

girl by the sea publishing

PRAISE FOR CHRISTINA GREENAWAY AND DREAM CHASER: AWAKENING

"I was totally drawn in to something different than I've ever read before. I couldn't put it down. I felt like I was in a deep meditation with my mind open to a million different possibilities."

—Lisa Smith, *Big Blend Magazine*

"Your beautiful spirit comes shining through especially in the main character. Magical and mystical!"

—Gayle Johnson, host of *Chaklet Coffee Books*

"Awesome read! Amazing writing and well-developed characters."

—Brian Sandell, host of *Before Bedtime*

"I loved Greenaway's new book *Dream Chaser*, a fascinating tale of the soul's journey to experience the power of forgiveness and everlasting love."

—Richela Chapman, author of *Through the Veil* and *One Speaks for mother*

The wound is where the light enters you.

—Rumi

PROLOGUE

August 1944

Ed flew his Spitfire head-on and fast toward the Messerschmitt. He opened fire. Bullets pounded into the German's left engine. Ed pulled back on the throttle. The Spitfire shot into a swift climb, dodging the enemy's fire. At 7000 feet, Ed plunged into a dive and fired at the Messerschmitt's right engine. The German rear-gunner shot back. Bullets ratcheted against Ed's fuselage. The Spitfire buffeted. Ed rocketed into an upward roll. He glanced down. Sheets of flames licked out from the German's engines and swept back over the fuselage. The aircraft dove vertically to the ground. Flames exploded in the field below Ed. Black smoke trailed through the skies.

"Blue 2, this is Blue Leader. Enemy behind you at nine o'clock."

"Blue Leader, this is Blue 2. Message understood."

Ed looked behind him. A great wedge of darkness came out of the moon. A bloody squadron of German bombers—mostly Heinkels—flying in rigid formation. A fighter patrol of

Messerschmitts flew some distance behind them—a little late for the party. The bombers headed north, for England, no doubt. "Oh, no you don't!" Ed climbed and rejoined his squadron.

"This is Blue Leader. Let's go. Take what you can. There's plenty for everybody!"

The squadron fell out of the clouds and swarmed into the German formation, looping and curling around the bombers at a terrific speed. The mass of fighters scattered all over the skies.

A pair of Messerschmitts came at Ed on his left side. He put the plane into a dive and flew beneath them, so close he glimpsed oil streaks on the bellies of their fuselages. He pulled up and found himself beside a German bomber. In a beam of moonlight, Ed saw the pilot's head and the dark shape of his oxygen mask. Ed gripped the stick and melded himself to the steel bird. "Come on, Spitty, dance for me." The Spitfire, with her speed and elliptical wings looped through the sky as agile as a ballerina. Ed revved the engine, shot forward and up. He hovered above the bomber. Enemy tracers tore into his left wing. The Spitfire rocked and dipped to the side. Ed's left knee trembled. He glued his eyes to the gun sights, lined the Hun up and fired. Another Spitfire swooped down and hammered the Kraut from the other side. The Heinkel went down—a blaze of fire and smoke.

Ed stuck up his fingers in a V for victory. In the beginning, he had felt a pang of sorrow when he killed another human being. No more. Too much carnage on the home front.

His limbs ached, sweat rolled down his cheeks, and his oxygen mask clung to his face. Another Heinkel headed in his direction. Ed's adrenaline pumped. The fat bomber flew alone—the other German fighters all busy battling Spitfires. Ed pulled the stick back, climbed and looped around the bomber. He laughed. "All the world's a little mad except for you and me, and even you're a little mad, so that leaves only me." Ed leveled off and unloaded all of his eight guns into the German craft. The bomber shook as the pilot over-boosted his engines in an attempt to get away. Dark smoke trailed from the aircraft's exhaust.

"Oh, you want to go home, do you? Well, you can forget that." Ed eased the stick forward, opened the throttle and chased after the German, firing. The tail of the Heinkel split off and fluttered toward the earth, looking frail as an autumn leaf. The fuselage snapped in two and plummeted through the air. The strings of someone's parachute tangled in the wreckage. The poor bugger rode to death in a sea of flames. Ed closed his eyes and swallowed hard. *Straighten up, Ed.*

The whole sky buzzed with aircraft. Some fought wing-over-wing, others crashed into the fields of The Fatherland. A few limped away, hoping to regroup.

Ed's helmet pressed hard into his forehead. Sweat dripped into his eyes. A plane shot past him, falling in a blaze of fire. A Hun, he hoped. No time to check. He had another Messerschmitt on his tail. Bloody hell! He sometimes thought Hitler knocked his pilots off an assembly line like automated pogo sticks.

Ed climbed to 7000 feet. The German trailed him, his tracer bullets pelting against the Perspex hood of Ed's cockpit. Ed looped to the left, then came up behind the German. The rear-gunner in the Messerschmitt opened fire. The German's bullets seemed to travel in slow motion and veer in a wide outward curve. Ed laughed, forgetting time could be a trickster. "Bloody Kraut. Can't even shoot straight!" The next instant, the Hun's bullets came straight at him.

A massive hail of fire ... bullets pounding on metal. Shrapnel sliced into Ed's arms and legs. Blood ... warm ... thick ... seeped through his trousers. "Damn!" The world wobbled. *Pull her up, Ed!* He fought to grip the stick. His fingers froze. The Spitfire spun and spiraled down.

Spinning ... darkness ... *Bail out, Ed. Can't. My arms won't move.*

"Lord, thank you for a wife so loving ... so beautiful in the morning when you shine the sun on her. Lord, look after her."

Trees ... fields ... farmhouse ... Christ! Was that a woman running across the fields?

Nose up, Edward! Glide! Steel bird glides like a ship on a glassy sea. Over the rolling greens of fields of Suffolk. Soft … moist … gentle England. Onto the flare path of the aerodrome.

The Spitfire walloped on the ground, bounced up and crashed down again. Bounce … crash … skid … belly to earth on the German soil.

Ed slumped over the stick. A woman sang.

> *We'll meet again,*
> *don't know where,*
> *don't know when,*
> *But I know we'll meet again,*
> *some sunny day.*

Silence … darkness … the luscious darkness of the Dutch Masters … darkness brimming with light.

CHAPTER ONE

Sara rifled through a drawer in her desk, searching for her checkbook. She slid her hand beneath a menu for Chinese takeout food. Her fingers brushed against a sheet of heavy vellum notepaper. A fiery energy swept up her arm. Sara gripped the edge of her desk. A long-forgotten promise flashed back to memory. Her heart raced as if trying to keep pace with the fleeting nature of time.

Sara ran a tentative finger over the knife-like crease in the fold of paper. She flipped it open.

I, Sara Elizabeth Jensen, age 22, promise myself that I will be a woman of capital before I am forty. I will head my own company, and I will help anyone around me who aspires to a leadership role for themselves.

I dedicate this goal to the memory of my father, whose favorite saying—a dream come true puts hope in the world—inspires my life.

Sara E. Jensen

Sara stared at the bold, straight up-and-down handwriting of her younger self. Her hand shook. Blood rushed through her arteries and pounded in her ears. She collapsed on a sofa and cuddled a cushion against her fast beating heart. She had written that goal on the day she landed her first job after college—as a production assistant with Grey Advertising. She recalled how carefully she had chosen the words. Words never to be altered. Never, because her father had said hope was an energy that passed from one person to another as they achieved their dreams, and that hope existed the moment it had been written into a promise. It would be better never to commit a promise to writing than to break faith with the seeds of its hope.

Sara felt a desperate need to touch something of her father's—to reconnect with the feel of him. She got up and hauled a photograph album from a shelf above her desk. She looked no further than the first page. In an old black-and-white picture, her father stood in front of a cottage with a thatched roof—a gawky boy of about thirteen. A wistful smile shimmered on his face. Sara laughed. He had smiled like that as a grown man. She lifted the photo from the album and turned it over.

Visiting Sussex, England. 1952. The cottage where Elizabeth lived.

Sara wondered what he had being doing in England and what Elizabeth had meant to him. Her father had been born in Denmark, but Sara knew little else about his early life. Sara gazed back at his young face. Her longing for him melted into his smile.

2

The background noises of the city fell mute. The air filled with a vaporous shadow. She sniffed the fragrance of bergamot and cedar—cologne her father had splashed on his face after shaving. A cool essence brushed against her cheek. Sara closed her eyes. Her father glided toward her in a haze of golden light. She heard his voice as clearly as if he stood there beside her.

"Everyone you will meet on the way to your goal already waits for you, Sara."

"Daddy!"

Sara drifted back into the seamless days of her childhood. Her father tucked her into bed. "Dream big, Sara. Never believe anyone who says you can't do what you've decided to do. Never let anyone steal your dream." Magical futures rushed to life at Sara's command. She reigned as prima ballerina of the New York City Ballet. She orbited the planet as an astronaut. She competed in the U.S Open tennis tournament and won.

The loud buzz of the intercom interrupted her fantastic achievements. The aroma of burnt toast yanked her back to the present. Sara dropped the photo and dashed into the kitchen. She popped the bread from the toaster and pressed the TALK button on the intercom. "Yes."

"Your driver's here."

"Thanks. I'll be a couple of minutes."

Sara steadied herself against the fridge. The vision of her father unnerved her. Her skin shivered over her bones. Sara did a couple of yoga breaths, inhaling deeply, filling her lungs to capacity, then releasing the air in short puffs. The day came into focus. She had a meeting with her creative team in half an hour. Sara returned to her desk, fished her checkbook from the drawer and placed it in her briefcase. She picked up the note and headed for the door.

In the foyer, Sara hauled her coat from a closet. How had her goal slipped her mind for all these years? *Easy.* Her rise to senior vice-president and creative director of the most prestigious ad agency in the world had demanded every ounce of her inventive energies. That, plus being a single mom, had left her no time to ponder the dreams of her youth. She had transferred those to her son—to his shining future.

That revelation shocked her. Two days ago, she had celebrated her thirty-seventh birthday—hardly an age to settle for anything. Sara looked in the mirror on the closet door. She had inherited her father's Viking coloring. Her hair tumbled to her shoulders, a heavy curtain of light and dark gold. Her eyes sparkled blue. Sara searched them for the glow of a woman at peace with herself. Not there.

Her thoughts fell quiet. The dream she had for her life all those years ago shone again in her mind. Sara Jensen, entrepreneur, striding forth, her sleeves rolled up—her gut burning with enthusiasm. Sara held the note to her chest. No fire this time. A sheltering stillness enveloped her, and then her future stretched before her, as vibrant and thrilling as only the pursuit of a dream could be.

Sara tightened her grip on the note. She would run her own company. She would meet the people waiting to meet her. She would put hope in the world, whatever that meant.

Ideas raced to mind. Sara strode to the door, making mental notes. The phone rang. Sara stopped. Had the forces of her goal unleashed already? Could the person calling be a major player in the next phase of her life? Sara backtracked to her desk. Vicki's name appeared in the ID screen. Sara gulped a breath. Surely fate would not be so wicked as to thrust Vicki on her. Vicki could be brilliant but mercurial. Vicki had trodden where no true girlfriend would, and Sara could not forget it.

She pressed the receiver to her ear.

"Hey Sara, have I got a gift for you? You must be living right. Are you sitting down?"

"Uh-huh."

"Remember Jonathon Hoffman from college? Sure you do. No one forgets the heir to a billion-dollar fortune."

Sara tried to focus as Vicki rambled on about how she'd kept up with Jonathon over the years. No news here. Vicki regularly called anyone she met with a minimum net worth of ten million. "The promising," she labeled these carefully researched people—possible investors for her next big idea.

"Anyway." Vicki laughed. "Guess what?"

"What?"

"Jonathon has agreed to back us in our own agency … as in advertising agency! You and me, babe. What do you say?"

.

CHAPTER TWO

Sara strode into Vicki's office. "What's so urgent that I had to give up my morning run and beat it down here?"

The metallic click of Sara's heels bounced off the plum-painted concrete floors as crisp as her annoyance with Vicki. Vicki had called at six o'clock this morning and insisted Sara get to the office as soon as possible.

"Don't ask why," Vicki had said. "I can't talk about it on the phone."

Until then, Sara had begun to think Vicki had overcome her reckless disregard for others—and the law. She had worked for three months without a single objection to the many legal ramifications of setting up a new business or Sara's choice of key employees.

Vicki sat in a plum leather chair behind the pink marble expanse of her desk, her large but solid body draped in a tiger-print shawl dotted with sequins. Her dark brown hair hung to her jaw straight as a plumb line. A harsh frame for a harsh face. She pointed to a plain brown shoebox—a lone object placed in the middle of her desk.

"Our ticket to the big time."

"Manolos? Jimmy Choos?" Sara's mood improved with the thought of a closet filled with strappy sandals, given in gratitude for a dazzling ad campaign.

Vicki shook her head. "What account is in play that belongs at this agency?"

"Come on, Vicki. I'm not in the mood for games."

Vicki tapped a finger against the lid of the shoebox, then flipped it off. "Tah-dah!"

Sara took a step back. A brilliant iridescence shimmered off the seal-gray leather of the running shoes. A flutter whooshed across her chest—soft like that of a page turning over. Sara pictured herself running in the shoes. She was naked except for a rainbow of lights that glittered over her body like a second skin. She raced flat out as if thrust forward by some unstoppable power coming from the small metal wings studded into the heels of the shoes. She chased after something. Something so precious, she wouldn't stop running until she found it. A collage of images flashed one upon the other. An old fighter plane. Two men, their faces blurred beyond recognition. Bolts of swirling black silk. Another whoosh, and it all vanished.

Vicki clapped her hands. "You've seen the ad. I knew you would."

Sara knew she hadn't. The vision had been about her, not the shoes. Sara picked up one of the athletic shoes and turned it over. The bottom had been soled with thick rubber treads shaped like bolts of lightning. Lumina Studios had been stamped at the arch. Sara's alarm antenna hit Mars. "For God's sake, Vicki, where did you get these? All the big agencies clamored to get this account, but Lumina only invited Y&R and Faircroft-Owen to—"

"Fuck invitations. We're crashing the party." Vicki pointed to a stack of files perched near the end of her desk. "Info on Lumina Studios. Ross DeLuca, president, is flying in from L.A. today."

"Wait a minute." Sara raised a hand. "The shoes are top secret … exclusive only to the agencies invited to pitch an ad campaign. Where did you get them?"

Vicki eased herself from the chair behind her desk, wrapping her voluminous shawl around her shoulders. "This is our mega break, Sara. This is where we knock the big boys on their asses … where we show them that we can rock the scene. This is you and me giving a hundred and ten percent of ourselves. No one can match that. So, I'll get to the details later. Here's how we're going to scoop the account. Ready?"

Sara folded her arms across her chest in a stance that said pass-it-by-me-if-you-can.

Vicki plowed on. "Ross DeLuca will stay at The Meteor, that new hotel right down the street from your apartment. Ross runs in the mornings, just like you. So there you are, you've got it going on with him already." She flipped her hair behind her ear. "Tomorrow, Ross will run in Central Park at seven. You will too. As you always do. After, Y&R, then Faircroft-Owen will present Ross with their campaigns to launch these shoes. But he won't be impressed with either agency, because earlier that morning, he will have met you in the park. Where you, shod in the Lumina shoes, will have wowed him with your legendary on-the-spot smarts. Is that a fantastic idea or is that a fantastic idea?"

Sara studied Vicki's triumphant smile and felt the challenge rousing in her. Mention of Sara's on-the-spot smarts further excited her. Those came from her muse. Sara knew the muse to be some highly creative aspect of her own consciousness. However, she preferred to think of her as a contrary being living somewhere beyond Sara's control. Creativity needed space. Her muse dozed dreamily, keeping her ideas to herself—sometimes until the last minute—sometimes never to reveal them at all.

Sara looked down at the shoes, lying so pristine in their box—waiting to be linked to their dream image. She recalled her vision of herself running in them. The blurred images of the two men preyed on her thoughts—floated between them like a memory just beyond reach. Sara's curiosity fired up. She had to wear the shoes. Running cleared her mind. She might unravel the mystery of the men. Sara glanced back at Vicki. Her conscience returned. "We're partners, Vicki. You've got to tell me—"

"Come on Sara, we're back at square one here. With Jake in college and your mother's medical bills on top of that, we've got to score an account like Lumina. You need to make the hefty income you're used to."

"I also need to stay out of jail, so I can earn that hefty income."

Vicki walked to her desk and glanced down at her computer. "Jonathon's father had another heart attack last night," she said.

"Oh, I'm so ..." Sara stopped short of expressing sympathy for Jonathon. He was their backer. "Exactly how does Jonathon's father's heart attack affect us?"

Vicki tapped on the space bar of her keyboard. "Jonathon called a while ago. He said investing with us was his last chance to prove to his father that he's not the irresponsible dilettante that he is ... that he's worthy of inheriting the Hoffman fortune."

"Are you saying he could be disinherited and without that ..." Sara's voice trailed off, the consequences too awful to imagine.

"Loft space in Chelsea." Vicki waved her arm in a wide circle. "Gratis Hoffman Holdings. We've got to do something or we could be on the street."

"Loft space be damned. What about our employees?" Sara flopped into an armchair, reeling like a boxer after a knockout punch. She had checked and double-checked every aspect of her contract with Vicki. Suspicion raged. Vicki had slipped something under the radar. "And this is the first you know of this condition with his father?"

"Look, we land Lumina, and it won't matter how Klaus Hoffman's will reads."

Sara noticed Vicki swing her jaw to the side, the way she did when she was caught in a deception. Sara fumed, but it was no use interrogating Vicki. She'd claim to have been born by virgin birth if it advanced her cause. A few minutes alone with Jonathon, and Sara would know the truth, but she'd have to wait until things settled down with his father. "And what if we don't land the account?"

"We will. The shoes are a dream product. No one can compare with you when it comes to creating an image for them." Vicki removed the shoes from the box, placed them on the floor beside Sara's feet and began pacing back and forth across her office.

She dodged the fringed edges of antique carpets and the metal arms of abstract sculptures, while reciting the high points of Sara's career. At times, her oratorical skills took Sara back to when they had first met at Columbia University. Back to when Sara stood in awe of the mogul-minded woman with her flagrant abandon for authority. Before Vicki had done something that changed the nature of their friendship forever. Sara cautioned herself, as she had when she agreed to open the agency with Vicki, not to visit old wounds. Success followed positive thought.

She glanced down at the shoes. Enthusiasm started to burn like a sun at the core of her being. Her imagination lit up. Women ran across it—women of all ages—wearing the Lumina running shoes. Wings glittered at their heels. Campaign ideas spun in Sara's mind, but before she could catch one, Vicki swooped to a halt in front of her. She nudged the Lumina shoes closer to Sara's feet.

"They're your size."

"Where did you get them, Vicki?"

"I borrowed them."

"B o r r o w e d?" Sara dragged the word up a scale of disbelief. "From whom?"

"You want me to betray a confidence?"

Attack the integrity of your accuser—vintage Vicki. Sara might question her for hours, but Vicki's possession of the shoes would only escalate into the most magnanimous favor ever bestowed on her by a deeply valued friend whose identity she would take to the grave.

"So," Sara sat up straight. "What do you suggest I tell Ross DeLuca when I turn up in the *borrowed* shoes?"

Vicki grinned. "Ross is Hollywood. He won't care about that. You flatter him. It'll be easy. He's twenty-five and a real pretty boy."

"Twenty-five! Oh, *please*." Sara scowled.

"You kill him with your golden girl thing … you know … blink your baby blues and tell him you love his movies."

Vicki trailed her fingers through her hair and raised her shoulder up and down in her favorite come-on mode.

"For God's sake, Vicki, I'm thirty-seven. I don't do girly things."

"Hah! You've got more flirty moves than a line of Vegas showgirls. You've always got some guy in tow. You haven't been without one since you divorced Jack a hundred years ago." She leaned back against her desk. "But don't fuck Ross. You know, never fuck the client. It never works out. Right?"

"You ought to know."

Vicki pressed her lips in a thin, dismissive smile and pointed to the files on her desk. "There's a bunch of CDs in there. They'll tell you everything you need to know about Lumina, their movies, TV shows and products."

"And I am to study them, track down Ross in the park, catch him, wow him and reel in the Lumina account. Is that all?"

"I'd do it if I had your talent."

"Did you steal the shoes?"

"Borrowed … Sara … borrowed."

"Why do I have to wear them?"

"Why? Because you've told me umpteen times, you can't create an image for a product unless you've got it in your hot little hands."

"Did I say that?" Sara snapped her fingers. "Damn! And you went to all this trouble."

The flicker of fear in Vicki's eyes lasted a mere second, but it helped to appease Sara's need to punish her for her deceptive business practices—at least for the moment.

Vicki glowered. "Bitch!"

CHAPTER THREE

Sara yawned as she knotted the laces of the Lumina shoes. She had stayed up until two this morning, cramming her head with facts about Lumina Studios and its president, the twenty- five-year-old Ross DeLuca. She studied reports on the buying habits, careers, education and hobbies of Lumina's prospective customers. Still, she hadn't a clue what she'd say to Ross when she landed on his heels twenty minutes from now. She flew on the edge of terror and excitement—the place where she waited for her muse to deliver.

Sara left her bedroom, careful to look away from her son's room, and hurried down the hall where once the sounds of heavy metal music had assaulted her senses. Jake's departure for college had cut a hollow in her heart, deeper than she bargained for.

She swung through the living room, thinking of the morning when her father had appeared to her in a haze of golden light. Sara had gazed at the old photograph of him several times since then, willing him to return. Apparently, it didn't work that way.

Sara swiped a fleece jacket from the hat stand in the foyer. The sprawling piece of Victorian furniture was like an old friend. She'd bought it at auction years ago, at once falling in love with its tortoiseshell arms, shelves, drawers, and holes for umbrellas and walking sticks. The antique had cried out to belong to a family. Now it had only her coats to bear.

"Sorry," she whispered. Broken relationships paraded across her mind. "Look at me," the men said, "if you hadn't been so caught up in your work, chasing dreams ...."

Sara cut that tape short and tugged her hair through a rubber band at the base of her neck. She slipped on a cap her mother had knitted her for Christmas, tilting it low on her forehead, covering "Shoe Thief"—a sign which surely glowed there in neon lights.

In the elevator, she mingled with the early-to-work set. Huddled in winter coats and designer scarves, they kept their eyes down, guarding their anonymity—a hallowed right among New Yorkers. Prizing hers, Sara assumed a similar stance. The doors opened onto the lobby. She stalked across the white marble floors, readying herself to hunt down Ross DeLuca.

Pedro, the doorman, tipped his cap. "*Buenos dias.* You run today? You brave. She is going to snow."

"*Perfecto.*"

Pedro swung open the glass doors. The sunshine of his native Puerto Rico danced in his smile—a smile that had greeted Sara almost every day since she moved into the building thirteen years ago. She had invested her first big bonus check as a down payment on the condo, choosing the Upper East Side for its selection of schools. Jake had been five. Sara blinked a tear, remembering the feel of his little hand in hers as she had walked him to kindergarten.

"I get you a taxi. You ride to the park in this weather." Pedro followed her outside.

"Don't be silly." Sara nudged him off in a friendly way.

The dappled gray and purple light of predawn hung over the city like a veil for a somber event. An icy wind cut across her cheeks. She lingered at the curb, imagining cops hiding in side alleys, handcuffs glinting. A siren wailed nearby. Sara took a couple of steps back.

"Something wrong?" Pedro edged up to her.

"No! Oh, no. Not a thing." Sara turned right and jogged toward Central Park. At Lexington Avenue, the light changed from red to green. Sensing the pulse of the traffic, she sped across the street. Cars charged off their marks, tires screeching, horns blasting as if saying, try that again, and we'll mow you down. Sara pounded onto the pavement. Her adrenal glands pumped. Steam hissed up through iron grates at her feet. Subways rumbled below. She bumped into a man carrying a Styrofoam cup.

"Bitch, watch where you're going!"

Immune to angry comments, Sara strode through the steamy air. A police car had been parked halfway down the street. Her body tensed. She pulled herself up to her full five feet eight inches and jogged on. She caught the light at Park Avenue and dashed across the wide boulevard.

The glass tower of The Meteor soared into a sky bruised with heavy clouds. The new hotel had become a favorite of the Hollywood set. On the dot of seven o'clock, Sara halted outside its revolving glass door. The black-clad doorman rolled a suspicious glance down to her feet.

Sara sprinted to the corner, turned right on Madison and hid in a doorway, wondering if Ross had put out word of the stolen shoes.

Two minutes past seven. She wriggled her fingers inside her mittens and rubbed her arms. Her breath fogged the air. Five minutes past seven. Had the California man decided to stay in his warm bed? Seven minutes past seven. Sara peered around the corner, searching for a young guy, six foot two, with dark hair. Perhaps she'd missed him. She walked over to Fifth Avenue. Ross would either enter the park by a small path at Sixty-Sixth Street or at Seventy-Second, a major cross town artery. Sara jogged to the park side of the avenue and kept her eye on both entrances. The roar of buses, the shrill whistles of doormen hailing cabs, the flurry of New York waking up energized her.

Runners filed past her. The trim and the strong. The overweight and the out of shape. The pros and the amateurs. Then she spotted him—a lanky young man sprinting across the avenue, his dark hair flying on the wind. Her glance went to his feet. He wore purple running shoes with white zigzags on their sides, the same shoes worn by *The Purpose*, the main character in Lumina's highly successful TV show of the same name.

Sara hurtled into the park after Ross and followed him onto a trail veering north. Long-legged and lithe, Ross steadily gained distance on her. Sara picked up speed and stumbled through runners bunched together, combining morning exercise with social exchange. Ross streaked into oblivion. Sara ran flat out, her legs scissoring until she almost split in half. The trail curved left then forked in two directions. Panting, she came to a standstill. Damn! She'd lost him. Vicki's info on Ross said he ran for thirty minutes. She decided to take the right fork and run another fifteen. If she didn't catch him, she would head back and wait for him near his hotel.

She pounded on. Blood thundered in her veins. Sweat beaded on her brow. She wiped it on the sleeve of her jacket and raced on. Energy surged up from the earth and propelled her beyond her own effort—into the zone—the high of running. Her mind became a blank screen. She watched it, waiting for her muse to paint the dream image of the shoes. Nothing. *How about another look at those two mysterious men?* Not that either.

Sara glanced at her watch. Thirteen minutes had passed.

Walkers and joggers straggled behind her, none with the gangly loose-jointed grace of Ross. She turned back. Nearing the hotel, she glimpsed Ross crossing Madison. She spurted forward and leaped into the revolving door of The Meteor, one partition behind Rossano Giancarlo DeLuca.

Sara spilled into the lobby, gasping for breath. The doorman swept a skeptical glance in her direction and beckoned to a man in a black suit, obviously the house detective. He stepped from the shadows behind the reception desk. Ross sauntered through the atrium of glass and steel, heading toward the elevators. Sara bolted after him and tugged on his arm with the gusto of someone finding a long lost friend.

He looked down at her. The hollowed beauty of his chiseled bones and the cornflower-blue of his eyes dazzled her. Ross was not a pretty boy. Ross was disturbingly handsome. She smiled her brighter-than-bright toothpaste smile. "Hi."

He arched a brow. "So, you're better at picking up men in hotels than on the street."

She wanted to belt him. Instead, she belted a laugh and clutched at her ribs as if he'd said something of side-splitting amusement. Over his shoulder, she watched the house detective step back into the shadows. The doorman retreated to his post outside. She disentangled herself from Ross. "You run fast."

"Or else I would be caught."

He exuded the impenetrable air of someone who would not be known, let alone caught. Add to the chiseled cheekbones an elegant Roman nose, wide brow and strong jaw, all in perfect proportion to one another. He looked like someone from another race—a people where every irregularity had been expunged from their genes.

"Sara Jensen." She extended her hand.

He ignored it and stared at her with a bored expression. Her glance went to a small scar above his right eyebrow. It was shaped like a quarter moon lying on its back—a perfectly beautiful scar—too perfect to have been accidental. Had someone marked him?

Ross took a step back and glanced at her feet.

"I can explain about the shoes." Sara smiled. "I—"

"I'm already there."

"It's not what you think. I'm with Hoffman Mills Jensen. "

"I know about you and your agency. You're not for us."

"Let me prove you wrong."

He continued on to the elevator. Sara followed. The steel doors parted. Ross stepped in. Sara slipped in beside him and hugged her arms about her, taking as little space as possible. He inserted a key into a lock marked *Penthouse*. Sara relaxed her grip on herself. An elegant Japanese couple slid in before the doors closed. Spicy perfume wafted off the woman.

Ross dropped his head a little and sniffed the air above the woman's head. Sara caught his glance. He mouthed, "*Her* by Armani." He mouthed the *Her* with such ardor that his breath traveled on the word and fell on her cheek intimate as a lover's sigh.

An exquisite softness floated over his eyes, an almost unbearable sweetness. Sara felt herself drawn into another place, another time. A man sang *I'll Be Seeing You,* the song that seemed to dog every World War II movie. The soft fluttering started in her chest.

The elevator stopped. The Japanese couple got off. Ross stared at her like a man under hypnosis. His transformation from brusque and remote to soulful romantic astounded Sara. To break the spell between them, she said, "You were right about the woman's perfume. You're a nose."

His eyes hardened. "I'm a man with fifteen minutes to get showered and make my first meeting of the day. You're a woman who wants to sell me on your agency. How hot can you take the water?"

Sara laughed, thinking he was kidding. His mouth slackened, giving him the satiated look of a man without boundaries. Sweat rolled down Sara's back. She had been naked in that vision she had of herself running in the shoes.

Not going to happen, Sara.

The elevator stopped. The doors opened directly into the penthouse. She tilted her chin up and stepped into the foyer.

Spatial music floated on the air—seemingly random notes, elusive like the man who occupied the suite. Ross shed his jacket and hung it in a closet, sliding the overcoats aside and placing it neatly next to a windjammer. Sara flung her jacket and hat on a peach silk bench. With a look of horror, Ross whipped them up and laid them on a shelf in the closet far away from his coats. He took off, loping across the foyer in long, lazy strides.

Sara strode after him. They wove through a sumptuous blend of flesh-colored furniture in a room that towered into a sky of heavy, menacing clouds. From her neck to her tailbone, she felt taut as a piano string. Another offbeat pluck from Ross, and she might snap. Sara focused on her mission. The running shoes were for a new female character in *The Purpose*, an intergalactic saga. She needed to know which planet the character hailed from and where the shoes might take her. While Ross showered, she would think of ways to ask him these things.

Ross stopped abruptly. Lost in thought, Sara bumped into him. Her face brushed against his sweat-soaked T-shirt. She shivered with disgust but forced a smile. She had followed him into a hallway. "I'll wait in there." She pointed to the living room.

He gripped her arm and opened a door. Sara faced a palatial

bathroom of green marble and mirror. He gestured for her to enter.

She scoffed a nervous laugh. "We can talk after you've dressed or on the way to your meeting, if you like."

He waved his hand like a cop urging traffic forward.

"I can come back later, any time. You name it."

"There's only now."

"You expect me to shower with you?"

"I expect nothing."

His voice sounded flat, and his expression appeared vacant. He couldn't care less if he heard her pitch. She thought of the people she had hired away from top jobs at other agencies, brandishing the security of the Hoffman name. Her gut twisted. If she got in the shower with him, he'd surely make a pass. Maybe not. She wasn't so young anymore. Ouch, that hurt. Anyway, he didn't strike her as a man getting a thrill out of controlling the situation. He didn't strike her as a man who could be thrilled by anything. She gritted her teeth. She was here to win the agency a chance at the Lumina account, and she wasn't leaving without it. She slid past him, scanning the hot tub area for signs of needles and dope. All appeared shiny and clean. Either the maid had already scrubbed the glass sinks, wiped them dry of water stains and placed his toilet articles back in a cabinet, or he had not yet brushed his teeth. *Ugh!*

Or, considering the scene at the coat closet, he could be a neat freak.

Ross opened a glass door and reached into a shower big enough for at least six people. He turned on the faucet. Water spurted from the cool green marble walls in a dizzying crisscross of jets. "After you."

Sara eyeballed him. "I can—"

"Twelve minutes." He tapped his wristwatch. "The next five of those are yours."

She tightened her stomach, glad she worked out on a regular basis.

Navel to spine, Sara.

She imagined herself as Joan of Arc tied to the stake. Courage burned in her breast. She peeled off her sweats, yanked the rubber band from her hair and shook it loose. Naked, she stood tall with her chin up. "Your turn."

He kept his gaze locked on hers. "You're still in your shoes."

Nakedness vanished. The thrill of challenge took over. "I don't take off my shoes."

"Why not?"

"I'm a cosmic woman. My shoes are my wings."

He rubbed his ear. "Is that the campaign theme?"

"If you like."

He pulled a wicker hamper out from beneath a vanity, stripped and tossed his clothes into the basket. Sara kept her gaze eye at level with him, until he stepped into the shower. Then she explored the ripple of his shoulder muscles, the narrowing of his hips, his buns—the all of him— suntanned—seamlessly suntanned.

Steam cloaked the air in the shower, dressing them in robes of mist and shadows. She thought of herself as a cave woman. Man comes home from hunting. Woman and man get clean, all very natural. They've done it for years—for so long that woman is no longer fascinated by the way water plasters man's rich black pubic hair against his skin. *Eyes up, Sara.*

Ross squeezed liquid soap on his hand and lathered his torso. "So, the cosmic woman doesn't take off her shoes. What else doesn't she do?"

"She doesn't use sex to get what she wants."

He snorted water from his nostrils. "Why not?"

"She's smart. She doesn't have to."

"She doesn't think getting naked with a guy will lead to sex?"

Sara sponged soap onto her arms. "She's not naked. She's wearing her shoes."

He sloshed his face and drew his hands over his eyes, clearing them of water. "You think this will fly on prime time?"

"Should the cosmic woman take off her clothes in prime time, she'll be covered in a glittering skin … iridescent like her shoes."

He massaged shampoo into his scalp. "Why aren't you covered in a glittering second skin?"

"I'm thinking on my feet, aren't I?"

He stilled his hands on his head. "Explore that."

Her pulse raced. Water pummeled onto her shoulders.

I'm thinking on my feet.

She said it over and over to herself, waiting for her muse to kick in. Bad ideas stormed into her thoughts, tossing up labels like "buy one and get one free." Her mind ran with this, and a one-legged woman hopped into the picture. She wore a Lumina shoe and waved the free one above her head, barking out the value of the purchase. It was a near-career-death moment. Sara imagined herself swiping a cart from the grocery store, throwing in a few possessions and living out her life, tin cup in hand. All the while, Ross kept his hands on his head, his fingers splayed in a luscious mass of foaming shampoo. His blue eyes steady on her.

Sara's heart leaped to her throat. Then, in a blink, her muse awakened from slumber and reached her long, elegant fingers into the ether and lured the mythical essence of the running shoes into life. A sweet flush of ideas kissed Sara's mind. "I see a series of commercials featuring women from varied walks of life. Each is in a chaotic circumstance and on the verge of losing her cool. Then she sees the shoes. The music rises. She dreams of freedom— freedom to run and explore. She hauls on the shoes and dashes into the street. The wings at her heels spread open. She's transported. She views her problems from a different perspective. She knows how to solve them. She's a thinking woman ... she thinks on her feet."

Ross leaned his head back, rinsing shampoo from his hair. "Is she young, beautiful and sexy?"

"You said, you knew my work."

He slicked his hair back with hands. "How real is she?"

Sara laughed. "Everyone is beautiful when they're truly themselves. Physical effort clears the mind. When the thinking woman runs, she frees herself from worry. As her mind clears, she becomes her own best advisor. A luminous glow radiates in her eyes and shimmers on her skin. She's beautiful. The shoes take her there."

Ross moved away from the water jets and stood but a few inches from her. He tilted his head as if studying her from a new angle. Sara felt more naked than naked. She wanted to run. She looked him straight in the eye. Water dripped into his. He blinked.

"You suggest using women from varied walks of life. Do they

have any one thing in common?"

"Yes. She will always be a loveable, quirky misfit." Sara laughed. "After all, deep down most of us feel like that."

"But is that something we want to be reminded of?"

"Yes. It makes us feel unique."

"Are you quirky and loveable in your uniqueness?"

Sara grabbed a bar of soap and lathered her hands. "Qualities are a matter of perception. I'm good at what I do, Ross. I'll create a character who will seduce the audience into an intense desire to own a pair of the shoes ... to sink their feet into them and run. A customer touched by her will likely be a customer for life."

Ross rolled his torso under the pulsing waters, then squeezed soap onto a small brush and scrubbed his nails. "Want me to wash your back?"

She searched his eyes. Inscrutable. *For God's sake, tell me what you're thinking.*

Water splashed off his shoulders and onto hers. He placed the nailbrush on a shelf and wiggled his finger, indicating that she should turn around. She nixed her annoyance at him and followed his directive.

He rubbed a sponge in small circular movements, moving it down her back, into the small of her spine, over her buttocks and down to her calves. Her nerves caught fire.

Never fuck the client.

"Turn around. I'll do your front."

"My front is already clean."

He swiveled her around by the shoulders. "Does the thinking woman make love with her shoes on?"

He had an erection. That unmistakable hard-on energy crackled off him. "You haven't got the time to find out."

"I'll make it."

"No."

He looked beyond her. The hint of a smile flickered on his face. She sensed him retreating into another place—perhaps into a secret life—a life richer than this one. The air around her felt sensuous— heavy with intrigue. Without thinking, she ran a finger over his scar. The second she touched his skin, a sharp pain struck her between her shoulders, a pain so specific it could have been shot by an arrow. Danger oozed off him. If she were writing a symphony or an opera, she'd have to sample it—swallow it whole and let it thrust her into something compelling enough to complete a great work of art—but not for an ad for a pair of running shoes.

No, Sara. No.

Sara took a step away from him. "When do we present you with a campaign to launch the shoes?"

He turned the water off, wrapped a towel around his waist and draped another around her. Knotting it above her breasts, he raised a mysterious brow.

CHAPTER FOUR

Slivers of moonlight stole through cracks where the blackout curtains didn't quite meet. On the wireless, Frank Sinatra sang, "I'll Be Seeing You." Sara danced in the arms of a tall, handsome man, the image of Ross DeLuca. He wore the dark blue uniform of an officer in the Royal Air Force. She gazed into his eyes, soaking up the exquisite softness of their deep blue light. They moved as one.

He said, "I, Nicholas Arthur want you, Elizabeth Sara, to be my wife."

She said, "What if Ed is alive?"

A voice came over the wireless, interrupting their song. Air raid sirens moaned into the night, interrupting their love.

"I've got to go." He pulled away.

"Nicky." She clung to him. "Oh, Nicky, please don't die."

Sara blinked into sunlight spilling through the shuttered

windows. The love and the fear from her dream dominated her thoughts.

Dan squeezed his body against hers. She rolled away. Dan tumbled after her. "Come here, you."

Sara faced him. "Not now."

A hurt expression crossed Dan's face. They had been dating for a couple of months, but this weekend in Colorado was their first trip together and, of course, sex was expected at every opportunity. Sara met Dan over the baked tofu at the salad bar at her neighborhood Korean market. He'd struck up a conversation, telling her he was an architect and had just moved into the city. He had the lost air of a newly single man—the kind who should not cut his dating teeth on her. However, he carried a bunch of pink roses—to brighten up his apartment—he'd said, which was a bit bare at the moment. Ah, a sensitive man! Sara had immediately imagined them wandering through the Egyptian wing at the Met, exploring the artifacts with shared admiration and scintillating dialogue. This fantasy perished when Dan arrived for their first date. "Where do you want to have dinner?" he'd asked at seven o'clock on a Friday night in the height of the fall season.

"I had a disturbing dream." Sara yanked the blankets over her shoulders. "I can't shake it off. Sorry."

"A dream about what?"

"Oh, I don't know. I guess about war and death."

Dan swung his great hulk off the bed and padded to the bathroom. He treaded heavy and resigned like a man accustomed to sexual rejection, which Dan had been—according to the sad tale of his recently failed marriage. Sara regretted hurting his feelings, but her dream lingered behind a veil so thin it could disintegrate at any moment and become her waking reality.

She pulled on a robe, opened doors leading onto a terrace and walked outside. Pine-soaked air rose off forests that sloped away from the hotel. They lodged in Mountain Village, a resort high in the Rockies above the charming little town of Telluride. She thought of her meeting with Ross. He had liked her Thinking Woman idea. Vicki worked with his assistant in L.A. to set up a date for them to present Lumina with a campaign to launch the shoes.

"Yes!" She waved a winning fist. Yes was her favorite word. Yes and success were soul mates. Indivisible.

She inhaled the sharp clean air and pondered her dream of last night. How strange, her names had been switched around. This man she called Nicky, who looked like Ross, called her Elizabeth Sara.

"What are you doing out there?" Dan stood at the door, huddled in a terry-cloth robe. "Freezing air is blowing in. I could feel it all the way in the bathroom."

"Sorry." Sara strolled inside. Dan slammed the terrace doors closed and stormed back to the bathroom.

Her gaze fell to a book on the coffee table, *Love Interrupted*, by Sean Granger. Dan had designed the author's house in Telluride and had come with plans for a solarium and pool Sean wanted to add on.

Sara picked up the novel. The jacket showed an old fighter plane plummeting to earth—a Spitfire, she thought. The pilot hunched over the controls, gritting his teeth in a grim battle with death. On the ground, a young woman in a floral print dress ran toward the plane with her arms open as if she hoped to catch it. Sara turned the book over and studied a photograph of the author on the back cover. He sat on a bluff above a beach, his sandy hair blowing in the wind. He wore thick, black-framed glasses. His hazel eyes seemed unnaturally bright. That fluttering sensation flurried across her chest, but it wasn't gentle. This time it felt as if all the pages of a book were being flipped backward and forward.

"Ed." The name flew out of her mouth.

"Who's Ed?" Dan sauntered toward her, pulling on a sweater.

Her heart raced. She had looked at a photograph of Sean Granger and called him Ed.

"What if Ed is alive?" I said that in my dream.

Sara placed the book back on the table. "Are you meeting Sean at his house?"

"No, Sean's picking me up. We're going to his contractor's office."

"What's Sean's like?"

"Why? I thought you couldn't stand him. You won't even read his novel."

"Damn right I won't. You can't turn on a talk show without hearing some woman speak of how she's emulated that sickening, do-good healing-woman character."

Dan grinned. "Makes perfect sense to me. A guy who gets his heart broken by one woman deserves another to come along and help him get over it."

"Yeah, right. So, what kind of a man is Sean?"

"He's a writer. He's crazy. In fact ..." Dan paused as if to stop speaking but plunged on. "After he finished *Love Interrupted*, he became convinced he had been Ed Harroway, the hero, in a previous life. He spent months in a psychiatric hospital."

Ed Harroway? What if Ed's alive?

"I should be back in a couple of hours. We can ski then, or whatever." Dan rolled blueprints and stuffed them in cardboard tubes.

Sara ignored the hopeful ring to his voice.

Sara handed the valet at The Peaks Hotel a five dollar bill, then climbed into the Ford Explorer Dan had rented at the airport. Guiding the car up the steep driveway of the hotel, she glanced at her directions to Sean's house. The car skidded on the slick ice. She shifted into low gear. The thrill of adventure tickled inside her ribs. She sensed a mysterious connection between her and Ross and the author, Sean Granger. A good snoop around Sean's house might reveal some clues.

Snowflakes swirled and rushed toward the windshield. Pines drooped under their weight. Aspens reached skyward, their naked arms swaying like elegant silver skeletons. Sara checked the odometer. She'd driven nearly two miles. The next road should lead to Sean's house. She swung the Explorer left, navigated a series of hairpin bends and drove onto an apron of land in front of a sprawling house built of stone and glass—*Star Mesa*.

Sara parked and picked up a roll of blueprints. Dan had told her Sean was divorced and had one daughter away at college. He lived alone except for his elderly housekeeper, Molly. If Molly opened the door, Sara would say Sean had asked her to bring some drawings to the house. She would gain entry somehow and sweet-talk her way into a look around.

Trembling with anticipation, Sara got out of the car. Her feet sunk into deep snow, so deep that it cascaded over the tops of her boots and soaked her socks. She shivered and scanned the house. She spotted a telescope in a bay window on the second floor. The lens appeared to be aimed at her. She could almost feel it slit into her mind like a scalpel. She developed an uncontrollable urge to get up to that room and look through it, a sense that if she did she would see beyond the face of things, just as the telescope saw beyond the face of her.

She took a few steps back. Her heel slipped. She looked over her shoulder. The land fell away beneath her foot, plunging hundreds of feet into a ravine. A copse of tall aspens clung to the top of the slope. Sara gripped the bark of one for balance and dragged her foot back to safety.

Something rustled. Her heart thudded. An animal scampered into a thicket of pines. Wind howled through the leafless trees. Sara trudged up to the house and pressed the doorbell. A low gong reverberated inside. No one answered. She pushed the bell repeatedly and yanked on the door's brass handle. Locked.

Sara scudded through the snow. Spotting a side door to the garage, she traipsed down an alley. She turned the doorknob. Open. Luck? Or did fate thrust her forward?

Two of the three parking spaces in the garage were empty. Sean must be out with Dan. That meant the housekeeper would be out too, unless the racy black Nissan Z belonged to her. Sara doubted it. Anything other than a four-wheel drive would be hard to handle on the icy, mountainous roads.

She eased past a wall stacked with firewood and turned the handle of another door. Unlocked. She walked into the kitchen. Last week, she had chased Ross DeLuca in a pair of stolen shoes. Now she broke into Sean Granger's house. What next? Maybe a bank robbery!

Unzipping her parka, Sara took in her surroundings. The kitchen was a large square room with tiled terra cotta floors, butcher block counters and walls painted burnt orange. Shiny copper pans hung from hooks over a center workstation. Light poured in through triple-story windows—snow-white light reflecting off a mountain that towered up behind the house. The air seemed thin and quiet—still as a tomb.

She heard a soft thud. A cat stalked into the kitchen—a Siamese with bulging ice-blue eyes. It stopped with one paw raised and stared at Sara, whiskers twitching. Relieved, Sara knelt. "Hi kitty," she said, although it wasn't a kitty kind of cat. She reached for a medallion hanging from a leather collar around its neck. The Siamese arched her back and hissed.

"Okay." Sara moved away.

The cold eyes of the cat made her uneasy. Leaving the kitchen, Sara closed the door, trapping the animal inside. In the front hall, she dumped the blueprints on a table and climbed a flight of pine wood stairs covered with a runner of burgundy carpeting. At the top, she turned right down a corridor. Except for a wooden railing on her left, it was open to the living room below and up to a wood-beamed cathedral ceiling. The house plans showed four bedrooms on this floor. Sara figured the one with the telescope had to be at the far end.

She prowled along the corridor. Her heart thumped in her chest. What if Sean had a house guest, and they resided in one of these bedrooms? She scrubbed the idea of bank robbery, this was scary enough.

Sara eased her shoulder against the door of the last room. It opened with a long, whining creak. She took a deep breath and stepped inside.

She passed a king-size bed, its red satin duvet strewn with balled up sheets of paper. Sara unraveled one.

> INT. HOSPITAL WARD—CHICHESTER, ENGLAND—DAY
>
> Nicky sits on a small hospital bed, cradling Elizabeth in his arms. She tries to raise her bandaged hand to touch his cheek, but it falls back onto the white sheet.
>
> ELIZABETH
> Nicky ... tell Ed I ...
>
> Nicky can no longer hold his tears back. He uses his finger to move a wisp of hair from Elizabeth's cut and swollen lip.
>
> NICKY
> Darling ... please ... don't. I can't go on without you.

Sara's mouth went dry. She recalled a trip she had taken to the West Country of England. She had passed through Chichester—a lovely cathedral city in Sussex. She thought of her father's writing on the back of the old black-and-white photograph: *Visiting Sussex, England. The cottage where Elizabeth lived.* Her mind leaped to her dream of last night. *Please don't die, Nicky?* What did it all mean?

Sara screwed the paper back into a ball and flung it into the mess on the bed. She wiped sweat from her forehead and headed for a stone fireplace flanked with shelves of books. Her eye roved over *Ulysses. The English Patient. The Tibetan Book of the Dead.* Now she shivered. Her attention fell to a table stacked with manuscript pages typed in screenplay format. A near empty bottle of Jack Daniels stood beside them. No glass. She moved close to a leather chair where she assumed Sean sat to read his work. She laughed, picturing him scrapping the pages and tossing them onto his bed.

Dark as it seemed, the author's private world intrigued Sara. She trod carefully over animal skins scattered on the polished wood floors, to the wide bay overlooking the mountains. The telescope stood before a bank of tall, naked windows—lone like an altar in a vast and vacant cathedral. The elegant probe beckoned. Sara hesitated. Solitude gave the instrument an air of being sacred to its owner. However, the telescope had already intruded on her.

Trembling, not daring to touch the slender object, Sara lowered her eye to the viewer. The lens had been trained onto the forest above the ravine where she stood minutes ago. The picture appeared fuzzy at the edges. Sara reached to adjust the focus when she heard the droning of an engine. At once, the scene through the telescope turned crystal clear and became hugely magnified, so magnified that she felt no separation between herself and the objects outside. In the distance, over the tips of the tall aspens, an old fighter plane sliced through the sky like a toy airplane through a paper backdrop. The aircraft looked like the Spitfire on the jacket of Sean's novel. It headed straight for the house!

Sara wanted to run, but her feet felt riveted to the base of the telescope as if cast in concrete. The plane hovered above the aspens. The smell of oily fumes filled her nostrils.

The pilot slid the cockpit open. A white silk scarf unraveled from his neck and flapped in the wind. Through his goggles, Sara met a pair of bright hazel eyes—Sean's eyes! The pilot shouted something, but she couldn't hear him above the roar of the engine. He banked the plane, lowering it dangerously close to the trees. One word whirled through the tube of the telescope and into Sara's head. *Elizabeth*.

The pilot leveled the plane and started to fly away. A wing caught in the branches of a tree. Flames blazed across Sara's vision. "Ed, bail out!"

She tilted the telescope and followed the aircraft as it spiraled down, trailing black smoke. The plane crashed into the depths of the ravine. A bloodstained scarf drifted up from the wreckage, waved briefly on the wind, then fell to earth staining the snow red.

A young woman in a floral print dress floated across the scene like a mirage. She retrieved the bloody scarf and looked up at Sara. A cruel smile curled her lips.

Sara's heart filled to the brim with sorrow. She hung onto the telescope with both hands until she regained control of her feet. She stepped back. Grief faded. She glanced into the viewer again. Snow fell and all was quiet and slightly out of focus.

The phone rang. Sara leaped as if someone had crashed through the windows, lunging for her neck. Heart pounding, she went to the desk. Her hand hovered over the phone. Photographs of Sean and a girl, obviously his daughter, caught her eye. In one picture, Sean stood beside a small, one-engine plane, resting his arm on the wing. He smiled, but it appeared a forced smile like that of a boy pretending to be brave.

Her gaze fell to Sean's diary open to today's date. Beside two o'clock, he'd written: *Fly to L.A. Meet Ross DeLuca. Take notes for screenplay.*

Sara studied the writing, half expecting it to leap off the page and solve the mystery of her connection to Ross and Sean.

The phone stopped ringing. She heard a click. A man's voice came on the answering machine—a voice laced with an Irish brogue—Sean's voice.

"Elizabeth Sara, I know you're there. Wait for me."

CHAPTER FIVE

It seemed colder in New York than Colorado, but Sara felt glad to be home. She ducked into her office building, shielding her face against a fierce wind whipping in off the Hudson River. In the old freight elevator, she obsessed over the message Sean had left on his answering machine. How had he known she was at his house? Why had he called her Elizabeth Sara? Why had she fled the scene in bone-shaking terror? The lift shuddered to a stop. Sara yanked the cage door open and entered the agency.

Zoey, their receptionist/girl Friday, leaned against the reception desk with her back to Sara, talking on the phone. Her plaid, pleated skirt barely covered her butt. She shifted her weight from one foot to the other, perching on red platform shoes thick enough to support the Brooklyn Bridge.

Sara swept past her. "I'm here, if anyone calls."

Spotlights flooded the large open loft, and soft fusion music rocked down from speakers sunk into the ceiling. The young toiled at drawing boards and computers, their ears and brows glinting with silver rings. Sketches of characters from *The Purpose* lined the walls. The atmosphere buzzed with excitement.

Jonathon's father remained on the critical list, and the perilous future of the agency remained a closely guarded secret—so far. Sara smiled at Peter Marks, their art director, sitting inside a cubicle of Plexiglas panels. She had hired him away from Ogilvy & Mather. Thoughts of his wife and four children nestled in their big Westport house tugged on her conscience.

Annie Martin greeted Sara with a warm hug. Her short red hair flounced about her face. Annie was a single mother of two, and one of the best copywriters in the business. Sara thought of last summer when Annie and her little daughters had visited Sara's cottage in The Hamptons. The girls played on the beach, so carefree and secure in their mother's care. If Jonathon was disinherited ... and if they didn't win Lumina ...

No ifs, Sara.

If could be a dangerous word. It could evoke the very disaster she wanted to avoid. However, "what if" could lead to constructive brainstorming. Whereas, "if only" should always be avoided. It implied wanting something that she did not think she could get.

Vicki charged up to Sara and drew them both to a halt outside Sara's office. "Remember our plans for decorating your space?"

"Aha, for when we're bucks up."

"Well, surprise!" Vicki steered Sara inside her office.

"Oh my God!" Sara looked at the new deep-cushioned chairs covered in textured fabrics of slate and magenta. "It's fabulous." Her eyes froze on a metal sculpture that careened across one wall like a bolt of lightning—the logo of *The Purpose*. "Isn't that a little premature?"

"Act as if." Vicki slid her hand over a long slab of rose-colored granite resting on blocks of dark pink concrete. "Santos made this for you … nothing but a unique work of art for the desk of the brilliant Sara Jensen." She waved a hand. "I don't want to hear any talk about money. I've got it covered."

Sara sighed and reminded Vicki they'd agreed they would not dip into their own capital, not that Sara's amounted to much. She'd invested in real estate, betting her house in The Hamptons and her condo in the city would appreciate more than stocks and bonds. They had, but selling them was not an option. Her homes were sacred.

"Just this once," Vicki said. "We've got to get the place fixed up for the Lumina presentation. Santos is here with a crew of his artist friends. They're turning that dead space at the rear of the loft into a conference room. I don't want you to see it until it's finished." Vicki eyes softened. "Santos is a genius. He needs exposure. Maybe someone from Lumina will like his work and get him a show in

L.A."

Sara relaxed. Vicki's efforts to help artists was one of her more endearing qualities. The phone rang. Sara answered.

"Hi Sara, it's Zoey. Ray O'Brian's here. He says he's president of the Owen-Faircroft agency. He insists on seeing Vicki … something about some stolen shoes. Shit! He's charging through the loft now!"

Ray loomed at the door of Sara's office before Sara could say anything to Vicki. He waddled in, his chins swaying beneath the set of his angry jaw.

He pointed a finger at Vicki. "You bitch! You spiked my drink the other night. I passed out, and you searched my apartment and stole the Lumina shoes."

"Ray, baby!" Vicki threw her arms open. "Why didn't I think of that?" She wagged her finger at him. "You know, we had sex the other night, and you didn't call me the next morning."

Sara sank into the chair behind her desk. The bagel she'd eaten for breakfast churned in her stomach as Ray threatened to have the police search their offices for the shoes.

Vicki pouted, sticking her face up close to Ray's. "Does this mean we're not going to see each other again?"

Ray shoved her aside and glared at Sara. "What do you know about this?"

Sara steeled her nerves. "I know we've got the talent to compete for the Lumina account. You shouldn't be surprised to find us in the ring with you."

"You're a smart woman, Sara Jensen, and I'm warning you, I want those shoes now or I'm going straight to the police."

"The police?" Vicki grabbed Ray by the collar of his jacket and yanked him back. "I don't think so. You don't want your wife to find out you fuck around. Isn't her daddy the major stockholder in Faircroft-Owen?"

"You leave my wife out of this."

"We'd like to." Sara smiled sweetly.

"You're a couple of whores, but you won't get away with this."

Vicki laughed. "Okay, I'll give you the shoes, Ray. Follow me." She sauntered from Sara's office into her own.

Sara followed Ray into Vicki's office, wondering what the hell Vicki was up to.

Vicki stood by her desk, one arm behind her back. "The story goes like this, Ray. Two nights ago, you returned to your city pad exhausted from working late at the office, but you felt creative. You ran yourself a hot bath, and you placed the Lumina shoes on the edge of the tub. You reached out to pick one up, but you slipped, and as you grabbed the side of the bath the shoes plunged into the water." Vicki swung her arm forward. The soggy running shoes dangled from her hand, their iridescence dulled to a dirty gray.

Ray's face creased in horror. He snatched the shoes. "That's what you think."

"That's what I know." Vicki moved closer to Ray. "And that's what your wife knows. Someone bumped into her on the street in Scarsdale and told her. She found the story amusing. That's my Ray, she said. Always working. So, by the time you get to your office this morning, your late night bath will be water cooler gossip."

Ray shook his head as if at a loss for words and stormed from the office.

Sara gaped at Vicki. "Tell me you didn't drug him and steal the shoes."

Vicki shrugged. "I didn't drug him and steal the shoes."

"God damn it, Vicki, how could you do such a thing?"

"You said it yourself, Sara, we have to do whatever it takes to make this agency work. We're up against the giants—"

"I know what I said, and you know damn well it didn't include this sort of thing."

"So, what's your version of how the shoes got so wet? Did you jump in the hot tub with Ross?"

Sara spun around and returned to her office.

Vicki followed. "How was your weekend in Telluride with Dan?"

Changing the subject—one of Vicki's tactics for catching Sara later with her guard down. Sara opened her briefcase. "Fine."

"That bad, huh? Did you meet the famous Sean Granger?"

"No."

"Dan was probably afraid you'd run off with him."

"What!"

"Come on, Sara, you're not into Dan. He's just filler, but Sean Granger ... well—"

"When are we making the Lumina presentation?"

"Next Friday."

"You're kidding! Can we get it together by then?"

"You bet. It's a blessing, since we haven't got the money to make a glossy commercial. Remember the comedy routine we used to do in college?"

"You're not suggesting—"

"I am. You and me, babe. We're the show. Annie's written some skits. Be in my office in an hour. We'll start rehearsing."

Vicki took a couple steps closer to Sara. "What really happened between you and Ross?"

"As I said, we sat in the lobby of his hotel and talked."

"Purleeze! With a hunk of man-meat like that?"

"Then I guess I just dazzled him with my on-the-spot smarts."

Vicki stood motionless, looking wide-eyed like a girlfriend expecting to hear a confidence. The penultimate "if only" struck Sara. If only she could trust Vicki. "I'll see you in an hour."

Vicki swept off, the jeweled fringes of her scarves tinkling in her wake.

Sara pulled up her e-mail. The Instant Message box dinged. Ross.

I'm thinking of you, he wrote.

Sara lowered her fingers to the keyboard. Her heart raced like a girl anticipating her first date. She typed, *Me you too.*

What about?

She cooled the excited girl. *The campaign.*

Come to my beach house after your presentation on Friday.

What for?

What do you want?

Your account.

What else do you want?

I don't know. What do you want?

I don't know either, but I want it.

Hummmmmmmmmm? She wrote.

Hummmmmmmmmm, yourself. Bye.

The phone rang. Sara didn't have time to ponder the ramifications of this exchange. Dan's name appeared in the caller ID. Her shoulders slumped. It wouldn't work with Dan, and she'd let it go on for too long. She had to end it.

"Hi." Sara leaned back in her chair.

"How are you, Sara? How about dinner tonight?"

"Can't. I've got opera tickets. You know, my season tickets with Brad."

"I thought you went to the ballet with him?"

"Both." Sara swung her feet onto the windowsill. "When you've been single for as long as me, you get into a routine with these things."

"Geez, you spend more time with a gay guy than with me."

"Brad's my *best* friend." Her voice rose with anger.

53

"What about tomorrow?"

"I promised my mother I'd visit her." Sara hoped Dan would pick up on her reluctance and initiate the breakup conversation. He didn't.

"I'm showing Sean the revised plans for *Star Mesa* on Thursday. We're meeting for dinner at his apartment in Chinatown. Sean asked me to bring you."

CHAPTER SIX

Zoey looked up from the reception desk. "Looks like you had a late night."

"That's opera. It's long." Sara trudged into her office, the music of *Tristan and Isolde* still ringing in her ears. What a story. Love idealized to its highest level—love ending with Isolde holding the dead Tristan in her arms, dying of love for him—all that set to the soul-searing music of Wagner. After the performance, Sara and Brad had returned to her apartment, as they always did. They'd swigged ice-cold Aquavit from tiny frozen stem glasses and rehashed the opera, living vicariously through the characters until the liqueur with its complex mix of caraway and anisette loosened their tongues. Then they spoke of their old love affairs, for the umpteenth time, complete with the sobbing and gnashing of teeth.

She hummed the *Liebestod*, the glorious love-death aria and wrote the opening for the presentation for the Thinking Woman campaign. The last two chords of the opera remained with her—

the long, B-major chords that played as King Mark blessed the dead Tristan and Isolde. She worked nonstop for hours, then drove to Queens, her mind still captive to Wagner. The B-major chords died in the blast of an angry horn as she backed into the last parking space on her mother's street.

Avoiding the enraged driver, Sara bolted into her mother's apartment. A belch of hot air assaulted her senses. She itched to open a window and let out the smell of sickness, but a bitter wind howled outside, and Olivia was little more than a skeleton. Sara thought of her mother as Olivia. Mom had not passed her lips easily since Sara turned ten years old—since the night her father left them.

That night, she had been awakened by the sound of a door closing—a steely click with a frightening finality. She ran to the window. Her father hurried down the street, his collar up, his breath puffing in the cold night air. He clasped a suitcase in his hand. Earlier, he'd told her, he had to leave for a while to work on his dream. "I'll be back for you, Sara. Trust me." She had pressed her hands to the window panes. *Hurry Daddy, before Mommy catches you. Hurry, and come back for me.*

Two days later, he died in a car crash. Sara's childhood ended. To mark her independence, she began calling her mother Olivia.

"You're late," Olivia rasped—before breaking into a fit of coughing.

Sara dumped a bag of groceries on the kitchen counter. Her mother lay on a small bed in the living room. Sara glanced at her through the open partition. "Would you like an omelet?"

Olivia coughed and spat into a tissue. "I've had my dinner. Alice had to make it. You're late, you're always late."

Sara fanned through a new batch of bills and slid them into her purse. "Traffic was terrible." She fished the check for her mother's rent from her billfold and set it by the phone. Aunt Alice, her mother's sister, lived in the duplex next door. Unlike Olivia, Aunt Alice was sunshine itself. As a retired RN, she had taken on the job of caring for Olivia after her last round of chemo.

Sara sat on the edge of her mother's bed. The frail woman wore a pink fleece bed jacket and had been propped up against bolsters and pillows. A new dusting of hair sprouted on her head. Behind rimless glasses, her watery eyes took on the accusatory look that had settled in them on that night Sara's father disappeared. "How are you feeling?"

Olivia scowled and delved into the quilted bag where she kept her knitting. "I suppose you worked late. Work is always more important than me. Now that you've chucked the best job you ever had to start your own business, you'll have even less time for me." Olivia shook her head, muttering beneath her breath.

Sara tried to ignore her mother's whining. She wanted to make peace with her before it became too late. She needed to say, I love you, Mom. She thought if she could get those words past her lips, they would become true. But it seemed Olivia knew, and every time Sara came close, she floored her foot to the painful past. "What are you knitting?"

Olivia fished needles from the bag. An oblong of blue wool dangled beneath them. "A scarf to go with the hat I made you for Christmas."

"Great. I love the hat. I wear it when I run in the mornings."

Olivia poked a needle through a stitch, crooked yarn over her finger and slipped the stitch to the other needle. "How's my grandson? He never calls me."

"He's fine. He's busy with his college life."

"You've always given him too much freedom. Playing in a rock band, staying out till all hours. It'll lead to no good."

"Yes, well now his studies don't leave him much time for that sort of thing."

"Tell me about that nice man ... the architect ... Dan. Are you getting married?"

"I don't want to get married."

Olivia lowered the knitting. "You've broken up with him, haven't you? What did you do this time?"

"Why do you always assume I do something?"

"Because you always do. You were such a relentless child, you—"

"Please." Sara raised a hand. "Let's not get into that."

Olivia pursed her lips. Lines wrinkled around her mouth like dried up rivers. She resumed knitting. The clack of needles filled the silence, perhaps signaling a truce.

Her mother dropped the knitting and gazed at the ceiling. "Your father was so handsome. He could speak French and Russian as well as Danish and English. I was not pretty or clever but still, he chose me. Until you drove him away."

Sara's temper flared, and she bit the bait. "Daddy left to find a better job. He was coming back."

"Work, my foot. Your father was a dreamer and a—"

"Stop it! He's dead. Leave him alone."

"But he wouldn't be dead if you'd told me of his little scheme. I'd have talked some sense into him."

Sara clenched her fists and stopped herself from tearing into her mother and laying the blame where it truly belonged. Not that she hadn't done that before, but she'd promised herself she wouldn't do it again, at least not while the cancer was eating away at Olivia's bones.

"Sure your father drank." Olivia blinked. "You drove him to it.

Always wanting to know things. You with your dreams of fancy colleges … things he couldn't afford." Olivia picked up her knitting. Stitches flew from one needle to the other. Her cheeks flushed as if this war between them fueled her will to live. "Your father named you Elizabeth Sara after a woman who was murdered."

"What are you talking about? My name is Sara Elizabeth."

"No, they got it wrong on your birth certificate. Your father never told you that, did he?" Olivia smirked, and glee lit up her expression.

"Who was this woman?"

Olivia resumed knitting. "You father had an aunt who lived in England. He adored her, and she him. The aunt was quite well off. Having no children of her own, she often brought Lars down from Denmark to visit her. She lived in the village where Elizabeth Sara lived before she was murdered."

"In Sussex?" Sara's voice trembled.

"Yes. How do you know that?"

"From an old black-and-white photograph of Daddy. Was his aunt a friend of Elizabeth's?"

Olivia shrugged. "I suppose so. She told your father Elizabeth was beautiful, hauntingly beautiful. That's what he said about you when you were born. That's why he named you after her."

Sara gulped a breath. "What else do you know about Elizabeth?"

"She was murdered by another woman. It was over a man, shortly after the end of World War II." Olivia rested her head against the pillows. "I'm tired." She closed her eyes.

Trembling, Sara picked up her coat and bag and walked to the door. She bumped into Aunt Alice.

"Oh, my darling, Sara, look how lovely you are."

Aunt Alice wrapped her arms around Sara and hugged her tight. Sara fought to breathe.

"Is Olivia all right?" Alice asked.

Sara nodded, nuzzling her aunt's face. "Did you know I was named after a woman who was murdered?"

Aunt Alice gasped and covered her mouth with her hand. "I've not thought about that in years."

"Then it's true. Tell me about it, please."

Aunt Alice closed her eyes and frowned as if in some inner debate.

"I've got to know." Sara grasped her aunt's hands, fondling her short, stubby fingers.

"All right, dear. When your father looked at your birth

certificate and saw your name had been recorded as Sara Elizabeth instead of Elizabeth Sara, he took it as an omen that you shouldn't know about Elizabeth Sara." Alice brushed a tear off her cheek. "He made Olivia and me promise we would never tell you about her. Now we've both broken that promise." She dug a tissue from her bag and blew her nose.

Sara kissed the woman she'd always wished had been her mother. "Don't cry. I'm all right."

"Are you, dear? You see, your father thought if you found out about your namesake … no … it's too silly."

Sara gripped her aunt's shoulders. "Tell me!"

"Don't shout at me, dear."

"Sorry, but I've got to know what Daddy thought."

Aunt Alice closed her handbag. "Your mother put up with a lot, you know. It's easy to idealize the dead. When Olivia married Lars, she thought she might one day be the wife of an ambassador. Your father worked at the Danish Consulate when they met. Oh, dear!"

Aunt Alice sighed as if the weight of Olivia's broken dream rested on her. Sara pulled her aunt into a small den off the living room. "What did Olivia put up with?"

"When your father's post ended with the consulate, he'd been due to return to Denmark. Your mother was beside herself. She had fallen madly in love with him. The next I heard, Olivia called and said they had married." Aunt Alice's eyebrows shot up.

"Are you saying Daddy married her to stay in the U.S.?"

"No." Aunt Alice shook her head. "Olivia had many wonderful qualities, as did your father. However, I suspect your mother pushed for the marriage. No doubt, it seemed like a good idea at the time, but it might have been better if Lars had returned to Denmark and sorted himself out. He seemed lost after they married. He worked at odd jobs, and then he suddenly took off for England to stay in the village where Elizabeth had lived, leaving your mother alone and pregnant with you."

"It must have been urgent. Olivia told me Daddy had an aunt there, and he used to visit her as a boy. Was she sick? Did he go to help her?"

"No. His aunt had died some years back. What a colorful character she was." Aunt Alice tossed off a loud laugh. "Your father told us, she used to speak to the dead … you know … she was one of those Ouija board people."

"She was a medium." Sara felt defensive toward Daddy's aunt. After all, Sara herself had seen her father's spirit and heard his voice.

"A medium … oh yes." Aunt Alice clapped her hands and her eyes lit up. "I love that show on TV, but you know, dear, you never see that pretty blonde actress sitting in a spooky room, spinning a Ouija board. She's—"

"True." Sara cut Aunt Alice off before she wandered into a long diatribe about the TV show. The spark went out of her eyes. Sara felt awful. She squeezed her aunt's hand. "We'll have dinner soon and hash over our favorite shows, but right now I need to know about Daddy. "Why did he go to England?"

Aunt Alice patted Sara's hand. "That's all right, dear. I know you're busy." She sighed. "You know, my memory isn't what it used to be, but let me see. Oh yes, your father told us that Elizabeth's spirit had appeared to him and his aunt several times when he was a boy. He felt very connected to her. He longed to see her again. Then, right after Olivia told him she was pregnant with you, he told your mother that Elizabeth had visited him in a dream and asked him to come to England to be with her. So off your father went."

Sara felt stunned. "Why? Could Elizabeth only appear to him in England?"

"I have no idea, but that's the sort of thing your mother had to put up with."

Aunt Alice stared at Sara, her brow raised as if expecting a sympathetic response. No luck there. Sara would argue her mother did not *have* to put up with her father. That sounded like a lame excuse for not having the courage to take control of her life. Sara buttoned her lip on that one. "How long did Daddy stay in England?"

"Three months, and don't ask me what happened during that time. I don't know."

Three months with a dead woman! Now Sara's brow shot up. "Does Olivia know what he did during that time?"

Aunt Alice laid her hands on Sara's shoulders. "You must not interrogate your mother about this. It will only upset her. I forbid it."

Sara smiled—her sweet little-girl smile. "Can you tell me why Daddy didn't want me to know he named me for Elizabeth Sara?"

"Honestly Sara! You should have been a detective."

Sara widened the smile. "Why, Aunty?"

"He thought Elizabeth would haunt you."

CHAPTER SEVEN

Sara dashed up the stairs of the Canal Street subway station on her way to Sean's apartment. Her conscience prickled over her foray into his Telluride home. Suppose he had an elaborate security system with hidden cameras. Suppose her whole escapade had been videotaped and Sean meant to confront her.

Sara veered onto the pavement outside the station. She unbuttoned her coat. Warm air had surged up from some southern climate and melted the snow. She turned onto Canal Street. Open-front stores spilled onto the sidewalk displaying gaudy goods. Silk robes, scarves and beaded slippers from India. Sara swerved between street vendors, their suitcases bulging with fake Louis Vuitton bags, Chanel sunglasses and Rolex watches. People swarmed in and out of small ethnic food shops.

Sara crossed the wide avenue, thinking she might enjoy living here on the border of Chinatown and Little Italy. She loved both cuisines. She walked for several blocks then found Sean's building.

A couple of Chinese men sat on the steps of the entrance, talking. They wore white chef's jackets and white hats. The door to a nearby restaurant swung open. Sara sniffed the aroma of toasted Szechuan peppercorns. *Yum*!

Sara trod between the two chefs. "Nice evening." She pressed a bell with Sean's name beneath it.

"Who is it?"

The man's slight Irish brogue sent shivers down Sara's spine. "Sara Jensen."

"Three flights up."

A click told Sara the front door had unlocked. She pushed it open. Orange light bathed the narrow stairwell. She mounted the stairs. A row of orange paper lanterns hung from the ceiling of the second floor. Sara paused by a set of double doors.

Ming Zhao. Acupuncture and Chinese Herbs. Infertility. Arthritis. Anxiety.

Sara wondered how long it took to fix an anxiety attack. She climbed two more flights, her chest tightening with apprehension. Maybe she should call Ming Zhao and make an appointment for later this evening. She leaned against the banister on the third floor. A gleaming red-painted door swung open. The sandy-haired author squinted at her through thick, black-framed glasses.

"Ah!" He dragged the little word up a scale of surprise.

"Hitchcock knocks on his coffin lid."

"Excuse me?" Sara peered over Sean's shoulder into a dimly lit foyer, hoping Dan had already arrived.

"Alfred." Sean waved her inside. "Master of suspense. You're his type … cool, blonde, with piercingly clever eyes." He glanced over the tops of his glasses. "Good. You've got the requisite vulnerability too." He smiled. "I'm Sean Granger."

Sara shook his hand and relaxed a little. The author didn't seem hostile. Eccentric, of course. She expected that.

The Siamese cat Sara had encountered in the author's Telluride house, slunk around Sean's ankles. He scooped her up. "This is Pussy." He dangled the animal in front of Sara. "I don't go anywhere without my Pussy." He grinned, obviously expecting some reaction to the remark.

Sara kept a neutral expression, while the Siamese stuck her head out and sniffed her cheek.

"Look at that." Sean laughed. "Pussy seems to know you."

To Sara's relief, she heard Dan's voice. "Is that you Sara?"

Sean tilted his head. "Well, is it you, Sara Elizabeth? Or is it you, Elizabeth Sara?"

Sara's throat went dry.

"Naughty girl. You haven't read *Love Interrupted*. I can tell. I can always tell." He lowered his voice. "You should, you're in it."

She scoffed a laugh. "That line is wasted on me. I don't have time to read fiction."

"It's not fiction. The characters are based on real people. I changed their names to protect their families, but only their surnames. No one knows that but you and me."

A ghostly hush followed the author's secret revelation. At a loss for words, Sara ignored Sean and smiled at Dan as he lumbered up to her.

Dan slid her coat off her shoulders and handed it to Sean. "I guess you've met each other."

Sara caught Sean's glance, and a loaded look passed between them. The kind that transpired between people who had prior knowledge of each other. She shuddered. The author, slight and fast on his feet, scurried to a closet with her coat.

Dan led her though a wide arch. "Remember, Sean spent several months in a psychiatric hospital."

Sara glanced back at the author. "Maybe they let him out too soon."

"I sometimes think so." Dan huffed. "He's a high-profile client. I need him. Otherwise—"

"Why all the whispering?" Sean scooted up to Sara. "You must be talking about me."

Dan laughed. "Give me a moment with my girl, will you?"

"No." Sean took Sara's arm and whisked her into a huge room. "I have the whole floor from the front to the back of the building. I knocked down most of the walls. I need space. I like to dance." He slipped an arm around Sara's waist, gripped her hand and spun her around and around at a dizzying speed. He stopped suddenly. "See, doesn't that feel good?"

Sara caught her breath. Dan rushed up and drew her away from Sean. She felt like a possession up for grabs. Sean sped off to the rear of the apartment. Sara laughed. "He is different."

Dan leaned close to her. "We'll break away right after dinner. Okay?"

"Okay." Sara took in the colors and design of the room. A massive gold Savonerrie rug rolled over bleached hardwood floors, its swirling patterns of pink and peach worn thin by time. Glass tables nestled between large leather sofas. Copies of *Love Interrupted* had been piled high on a long trestle table.

"Hi, Sara. I'm Arielle."

At a small mirrored bar across the room, a girl waved and tossed ice cubes into a martini shaker. Sara walked over to her, recognizing her from photos in Sean's bedroom in his Telluride home. The girl's hazel eyes glowed in a paler shade than her father's. She was pretty in her youth and bubbly personality.

"How about a martini?" Arielle pointed to the pitcher. "We're a round ahead of you."

"Thanks. Vodka. Straight up. Olives."

Dan nudged up to Sara. "I haven't seen you all week. Are you living at the office?"

"Almost, we've got a lot going on."

"Excuse me," Sean tapped Dan on the shoulder. "While Sara's waiting for her drink, I want to show her my garden."

Dan looked disgruntled but nodded and joined Arielle at the bar.

Sean led Sara toward the rear of the apartment. They passed a kitchen. Sara glimpsed counters of black granite and rows of bleached wood cabinets. A stout woman stood at a stove with her back to Sara. Steam rose from a large saucepan and vanished into a big stainless steel hood. The smell of grilled parmesan cheese drifted up Sara's nostrils. *Yum.*

They entered a hallway. Sean pointed to the left. "My bedroom and the study where I work." He pointed to the right. "Arielle's bedroom."

The door to Sean's room stood ajar. Sara nearly choked on curiosity. Did he have another telescope in there? Just as well, she didn't know. She'd be itching to have a look through it.

"Here we are." Sean released his grip on her.

They stood before a row of windows looking out onto the fire escape stairs. Sean unbolted an iron-barred door and stepped outside onto a small platform. Sara followed. The crisp cool air felt good on her skin.

Sean pointed down to a small walled-in garden. Tiny orange lights glittered on the branches of trees. A small bamboo structure stood beneath them. Wind chimes filled the air.

"I share the garden with Ming Zhao. You passed his acupuncture salon on the way up. He's a lovely man. When the weather's nice, he uses that bamboo pavilion for treatments, but I can't write when he's working on someone in there." The author leaned over the railing and shouted, "Close up, Ming! All my characters are turning up in orange robes with needles stuck in their foreheads."

Arielle charged outside and pulled her father back into the apartment, "*Daddy!*"

She scolded him sweetly like a mother to an errant child. Her kindness impressed Sara. She felt an instant fondness for the young woman. Sara followed them back to the main room and sat beside Dan on a dark-green leather couch.

"How's it going with Xenon Oil?" Dan asked. "Did you

convince them to become a client?"

"No, but I'm close. I—"

"Bloody hell, Dan." Sean loomed over them. "Why are you talking business with a beautiful woman?"

"Because that's what she's all about."

"Nonsense." Sean lowered himself into a recliner chair and swung his feet up. "Someone broke into my house in Telluride and stole a piece of my soul."

Sara's heart lurched. She prepared for the worst.

"Lighten up, Daddy." Arielle squeezed her father's shoulder, then handed Sara her drink.

Sara swigged a big gulp. "Yes, actually Dan's right about me. I'm very focused on my work. Every man I've been involved with has broken up with me over it."

"I'm not complaining." Dan squeezed her hand.

"Not yet." Sean chuckled.

Sara grimaced. His chuckle irritated her.

"How sweet you are, Dan." Arielle bent over and kissed Dan on the cheek. "We women need men like you … men who support us in our careers."

"About my house in Telluride." Sean tapped his fingers on a side table. "The intruder looked through my telescope. I see the past and the future through my telescope. The intruder saw something that belongs to me. She stole a piece of my soul."

"She?" Dan leaned forward a little. "How do you know it was woman?"

"My Pussy told me."

Dan let out a great guffaw of laughter. Sara sunk a fist into the sofa, trembling with relief. Obviously, she'd not been filmed by security cameras. She sipped her martini, grateful for the soothing buzz of the vodka.

"Did you call the police?" she asked Sean.

"The police? They don't believe I see into my soul through my telescope."

Sara downed her drink. "What kind of things do you see?"

"When I was writing *Love Interrupted*, I often saw the healing woman. I'd train the telescope to the sky and think of her. She would emerge from the center of the sun, draped in golden gauze. Or, if I looked at night, she would dance over the Milky Way covered in stardust and moonbeams. When I spoke to her, she looked directly into the lens of my telescope and answered me. You must read my book to know what she said."

"I'm not interested in her. She throws women back into a

subservient role they've been fighting to get out of for hundreds of years."

Sara watched the color drain from Sean's cheeks. Arielle sped to her father's side and rubbed his shoulders. "Tell us about your trip to Hollywood, Daddy."

Sean sat up straight. "Yes. Yes. While I was at Lumina Studios, I was given a private screening of Carlo DeLuca's new movie, *Saint*. I was blown away. He's the only director I'll allow to touch *Love Interrupted*."

"What about his son?" Arielle grinned. "The dishy Ross, when am I going to meet him?"

"Never!" Sean slapped his hands on his thighs. "Ross DeLuca is a dark prince."

"Ross DeLuca?" Dan looked at Sara. "Isn't he the guy you met a few days ago?"

"I had a business meeting with him, but I didn't mention it to you."

"No you didn't," Dan said in a slighted tone of voice. "Vicki told me when she called to invite me to your partner's birthday party next week. She said you chased after Ross in the park and somehow lured him into giving you guys a chance to win the Lumina account."

Sara shook her head. The Machiavellian Vicki had struck again.

"You chased after Ross in the park?" Sean clapped his hands. "I love it. I knew you were a Hitchcock blonde." He lowered his voice to the hushed tones of a storyteller. "Let me tell you a tale about Sara and Ross and me." He moved to the edge of his chair. "We're caught in a love triangle … one with deadly consequences."

"Ooooh, yes," Arielle chimed in, "and someone must die."

Father and daughter laughed with the familiarity of people used to playing games. "Let me start the story, Daddy."

Sean nodded. "Take it away, my darling girl."

Arielle jumped to her feet. "On a cold January morning, the Hitchcock Blonde chased the Dark Prince into Central Park with business on her mind, but when she looked into his eyes she fell madly in love with him. However, the Dark Prince could not love her back because the devil controlled him. The Dark Prince had exchanged his soul for killer good looks and the seductive prowess that no woman could resist."

Sean applauded vigorously. "Excellent, my darling girl." He stood and kissed Arielle on the forehead. "I'll take it from here."

He tapped his fingers together. "So, the Hitchcock Blonde, having just read *Love Interrupted* and overcome with admiration for me, broke into my house, stole a piece of my soul and implanted it into the Dark Prince by way of a long, passionate kiss. And with that, she became the Dark Prince's healing woman."

Sean dashed to the trestle table, grabbed a copy of *Love Interrupted* and scrawled something on the inside. He walked over to Sara with the book open and held it out to her.

The competitor in Sara rose up. She'd been the butt of Sean's amusement all evening, and it was time to put him in his place. She took the novel and slammed it closed. "As I said, I don't have time to read fiction."

The light of conquest dimmed in Sean's eyes. A tightrope of tension pulsed between her and the author.

"For heaven's sake, Sara." Dan snatched the book from her lap. "Read Sean's inscription."

He opened the novel to that page and shoved it in front of Sara. Guilty because she planned to dump Dan, Sara didn't want to harm his relationship with Sean. She glanced at the inscription.

Elizabeth Sara,
Return me to my soul,
Sean Edward

Sara's conscience over Dan vanished. "Return me to my soul? That must mean you're the one in the love triangle who dies."

"No!" Arielle ran to her father's side. "No one dies. I take that back."

The girl's effervescence faded. She clung to Sean like a child who believed absolutely in the story. Sara felt Sean's gaze boring into her, pleading with her to retract her question, but it was too late. The competitor was off the mark. Sara had to win the moment.

CHAPTER EIGHT

Friday arrived—the day of the Lumina presentation. Sara wore a skirt and jacket by Piazza Sempione, one of her favorite designers, in the color of bitter chocolate. She stepped into high heels, then swept her hair back and wove it into a single braid. She studded large gold loops in her ears, then walked to the foyer and hauled her long overcoat from the closet.

Her attention strayed to Sean's novel on a shelf on the hat stand. She had dumped it there last night after returning from the author's house. She had a big fight with Dan. He accused her of acting up with Sean as a way of flirting with him. This misconception had magnified their lack of compatibility, but Dan had been so needy that she didn't have the heart to deliver the breakup speech she rehearsed on the way home in the cab.

Sara snatched Sean's novel and left the apartment. On the way to the elevator, she swung into the service area, opened the chute to the incinerator and flung the book down the metal tunnel. "Burn with the rest of the trash!"

She spun around. Eggshells crackled. Sara stared at a man holding a bag of garbage in his arms. "Sorry, but you shouldn't be standing so close to me."

"What's the matter with you?" The man scowled. "You just threw away a great book."

Sara elbowed past him and hurried to the elevator.

In the lobby, Pedro tipped his cap. "You look beautiful this morning, Miss Sara. Big meeting?"

"Yes. Keep your fingers crossed for me today."

"I always have my fingers crossed for you."

She met Pedro's dazzling smile, wondering how a man who spent the day opening a door for others stayed so happy. A cab swung to the curb. A young couple got out. Sara jumped in. Her phone rang. "Yes, Vicki."

"Ross's assistant just called. Carlo DeLuca is coming to the presentation with him."

Sara's gut tightened. Carlo was not only Ross's father but a Hollywood legend. He won an Oscar for his first film, then sunk every penny he had into making a movie of a story he'd written when he was twelve, *The Purpose*. It became a mega hit. He then founded Lumina Studios, continued the saga of *The Purpose* in a TV series and produced some of the best films of the last decade. And she and Vicki planned to perform their Thinking Woman skits for him?

"Say something, Sara!"

"Why is Carlo coming? I thought he'd turned the running of the Studio over to Ross."

"I don't know. Call Ross and ask him."

"We don't want to look anxious."

"But we are!"

Sara held the phone away from her while Vicki ranted. The cab sped down Ninth Avenue and screeched to a sudden stop, barely missing a truck barreling through a red light. Sara cursed, gripped the leather strap by the window and eased herself back onto the seat. She pressed the phone to her ear.

"Where the hell are you, Sara? They're going to be here in fifteen minutes."

"I'm pulling up to the office."

"Call Ross now!"

Sara tossed her phone in her bag and fumbled some money into a cup wedged in the partition between her and the driver. She crossed the icy pavement, stretching her arms out for balance. Darned weather—the temperature had dropped back to freezing overnight.

Vicki waited for Sara as she stepped from the elevator. Vicki wore a pants suit, the color of eggplant with a bejeweled pink and purple stole draped over her shoulders.

"Great look." Sara tucked her gloves in her coat pocket.

"What did Ross say?"

"I didn't call him. He's got to be with Carlo on his way here. Anyway, my guess is Carlo's coming because he's in town. He's been on a number of talk shows promoting his new movie. Maybe this is his way of spending time with Ross."

"And maybe, he wants to see what his son is doing with a woman twelve years his senior."

"Don't be silly. Show me the conference room. Is the paint dry?"

"Barely."

Sara followed Vicki to a set of ancient carved-wood doors that looked as if they had once led into a Burmese Temple. Vicki threw them open.

Sara's breath caught in her throat. The room looked spectacular. The table, a long slab of glistening black marble, hung from the ceiling on jewel-encrusted chains. The Victorian, high-backed chairs had been tufted in bottle-green satin. Swirls of light and dark green paint gave the walls the gem-like effect of malachite. "It's fabulous!"

"What do you think of the art? I tried to keep it cool."

Sara studied two huge black canvasses with fine emerald lines running through them. "They're perfect."

Zoey, their receptionist, pranced into the conference room. Her eyes shone bright as spotlights at a movie premiere. "The Lumina limo just pulled up."

"Thanks." Vicki flicked the girl off with a dismissive wave and steered Sara outside. They paced back through the loft, their steps measured like brides walking to the altar.

"There was background info on Carlo in those files I gave you," Vicki said. "I'm sure you read it, so you take care of him. I'll concentrate on Ross and the others."

Typical Vicki. Thrusting Carlo into Sara's care. She would get the blame if anything went wrong. Sara smiled at their coworkers, sitting at their work stations, trying to look busy. Obviously, everyone waited for a glimpse of the glamorous men from Hollywood.

Sara stood beside Vicki in the reception area, facing the elevator. A rush of memories welled up—remembrances from their college days when they had visualized themselves as they were now—ready to claim success. The elevator rumbled in its shaft.

"We should have nabbed tickets to a preview of Carlo's new movie," Vicki said. "Keep the conversation off that."

"That'll be easy. I'm a theater person. Remember?"

Vicki glared at Sara. "If you say that, I'll kill you."

Sara laughed. Vicki could cave in under pressure. Not Sara. The ever-eager competitor pulsed beneath her skin. "Break a leg."

"Yeah, yeah. You too."

The elevator shuddered to a stop. Through the iron-caged door, the men from Lumina resembled a group ad for Armani—their fine-spun wool coats blending in soft, earth-tone colors. Ross and Carlo got off first followed by two other men. Sara noted a familial likeness between Ross and Carlo, but more in the manner of their movements than appearance. Ross stood several inches taller than his father. Carlo had fleshy cheeks rather than his son's finely chiseled features. His eyes shone dark—black as licorice.

Sara met Ross's deep blue gaze, and she could think of nothing except standing naked with him in the shower. She sensed a feast of possibilities pass between them. Her heart surged with happiness. His smile told her, he felt the same. The sound of someone clearing his throat brought Sara back to reality. She spun around and met Carlo's dark glance.

"Sara Jensen." She extended her hand to the famous filmmaker.

"The woman who thinks on her feet." Carlo shook her hand

with a warm grip.

She sensed something hostile in his look.

Ross introduced Sara and Vicki to the other men—Gianni, one of Carlo's brothers, an Executive VP of Lumina and Mike Nelson, their director for in-house advertising.

Zoey collected everyone's coats. Vicki latched onto Ross, Gianni and Mike and led them toward the conference room.

Sara smiled at Carlo. "Shall we?" She took a step forward, feeling awkward like a girl inviting a guy to dance.

"Wait." Carlo held up a hand. "I didn't meet the young lady with our coats."

Zoey dumped the heavy garments on the reception desk and dashed up to Carlo. "I'm Zoey Phillps."

"Great to meet you. Tell me, Zoey, what will you be doing two years from now?"

The girl glowed. "I'll be your Account Executive."

"Terrific answer." Carlo pounded his fist against his palm and strolled into the loft. He walked around, introducing himself to each person, asking them about their work. Sara cringed when Sharon, their newest recruit, asked him if he knew the sex of the baby he and his new wife expected any day. Carlo had dodged that question repeatedly in a recent round of publicity stints to promote his new movie.

Carlo grinned and raised two fingers. "Twins ... boys. That's our secret."

A soft collective "Oooh," swept the room. It proved to be a magical moment. Carlo had taken them into his confidence. He wouldn't do that if Lumina had not already decided their account belonged with HMJ, would he?

Carlo looked slowly around, catching the eye of each person, infecting them with his fame and power. "It takes a team. That's our motto at Lumina."

Eyes glistened. Hope soared. Endless hours at the drawing board would soon pay off.

Sara escorted Carlo into the conference room. Ross stood at the far end of the black marble table, studying graphs in a folder. Vicki sat at the opposite end from Ross. The other men sat across from each other. Sara directed Carlo to the chair at Vicki's right, but he didn't sit right away. He walked around, peering into the paintings and feeling the jeweled chains holding the table.

"What a fantastic place." He finally took his seat. "These are the most creative offices I've ever been in. Who did them?"

"I did." Vicki slapped her hands on the table.

Ohmigod! Not a team answer. Right away, Sara noticed a tightening of the muscles around Carlo's mouth and a slight closing of his energy field. Sara spoke quickly, trying to cover Vicki's mistake. "We're fortunate to be located in Chelsea among so many galleries. Vicki knows a number of artists, and they helped—"

"Right," Vicki butted in. "Santos is a fantastically gifted artist from Columbia, and he crafted the table. I suggested we hang it from the rafters on those chains. You know … this is a loft … the exposed pipes and beams are works of art in themselves. Then to juxtapose the industrial, I chose a jeweled look for the walls. I've always loved malachite, so I—"

"Yes." Sara laughed. "Yes, malachite turned out to be everyone's favorite idea." Sara kicked Vicki under the table. To her credit, Vicki showed no reaction. She opened the meeting as planned, delivering the agency's overall strategy for the Thinking Woman campaign with her customary aplomb. Carlo's brow remained furrowed throughout her speech.

Sara took the floor. "We'll now act out some skits for you." She flashed a bright smile at Carlo, then Gianni and Mike, and briefly at Ross. "We thought it would be fun to show you several ideas for the Thinking Woman."

Carlo leaned back in his chair, twisting his lips in a skeptical smile. Sara winced. They launched into the skits.

Vicki gave the performance of her life. Playing a woman in chaos until she put on her Thinking Woman's shoes, she went from being ridiculously funny to unbearably endearing. Sara stood behind her and acted as the wings on the heels of her shoes. She flapped her arms, took flight and became the Thinking Woman's expanded consciousness, coaxing her to look at her problems from a different prospective. Annie had written the dialogue with cutting-edge humor. At times, the men laughed so loudly Sara and Vicki had to pause and wait for them to stop.

At the end, Ross, Mike and Gianni applauded. Carlo didn't. Sara tried not to dwell on that. Buttoning her jacket, she presented the nuts and bolts of the campaign, then asked if they had questions.

Ross slid papers into his briefcase. "That was great. I was blown away. I suggest we—"

"Yes." Carlo interrupted his son. "That was indeed a terrific show." He tapped his pencil against the pad in front of him. "But we've ordered a study to consider expanding our in-house ad department to handle all our advertising." He smiled at Vicki. "So until that study is completed, we're not in a position to commit our account to your agency or any other."

A stunned silence settled over the group. Ross looked as if he contemplated Carlo from another planet, on a wavelength that might never reach earth. Gianni and Mike shuffled papers. Carlo doodled on a yellow pad. Vicki, probably for the first time ever, sat with her jaw open, speechless.

Sara shoved her chair back, making a loud scraping sound on the stone floor. She stood and stared at Carlo until he looked up from his doodling. He tossed his pencil on the pad and folded his arms like a man resolved to take his punishment. Sara readied herself to give it to him.

"There are twenty-two of us here at HMJ … the people you just made a point of meeting before we began our presentation." She paused, waiting for a sign of discomfort to cross the filmmaker's eyes, shame for having lured their staff into believing the account was already theirs. He looked down at his doodling. Sara continued. "Some of us left high positions and gave up fat paychecks for a chance to work with Vicki. We did that because she is the best at what she does, and she knows how to get the best out of us, her *team*." She emphasized the word. "It's been exciting for us to pool our talent and present you with the Thinking Woman campaign. Our agency will be chosen by some of the most innovative companies in the world to market their products. We hope that one day yours will be among them. So, on behalf of our team, thank you for your consideration of our agency. Unless you have any further questions, this meeting is over."

Carlo kept his head down and his hands folded in his lap. Sara marched to her office and ripped the zigzag sculpture off the wall. She buckled the lightweight metal, flung it on the floor and kicked it across the room.

"Sara." Ross stood in the doorway. In his dark suit, dark shirt and tie, he looked every bit the Dark Prince Sean had labeled him.

"So, Daddy let you out of the playpen."

Ross ambled toward her. "It's just business."

"Just business! Carlo snatched the reins of command from you and laid a pathetic little in-house-ad-department excuse on us and all because Vicki didn't fit his idea of a team leader." She stalked over to her desk. "This isn't a movie set. We're not characters he can manipulate to fit some story made up by him. We're real people. And," she laced her voice with sarcasm, "guess what? We're flawed … all of us, and Vicki is an ego-driven bitch. Most of us don't like her, but she recognizes talent and offers a place for it to flourish and for that, most of us love her. And she damn well did decorate the offices."

"Sara, calm down."

"Calm down? I've had to work *my* way up the career ladder, and I'm not stopping now. Go away. I don't need you." Sara slumped into the chair behind her desk.

"You look pretty needy to me."

"Get out. I'm too old for you." Sara swiveled her chair around and stared at snow falling on the iron bars outside her window.

Ross swiveled her back to face him. "I don't know that you're old enough for me. I think there's a hurt little girl inside you. She's angry with men, but I'm not taking that personally."

"You don't know me at all."

He leaned over her desk until she could feel his hot breath on her cheeks. "We've got a date. Let's go."

"You assume an awful lot from one little e-mail."

"There's a whole lot going on between us. I want to explore it, and so do you."

"You were going to give us your account before Carlo interrupted, weren't you?"

"It doesn't matter. What's between us isn't about business."

"It is for me."

"I can live with that."

"Doesn't it bother you that your father totally crushed you a few moments ago?"

"Did he?" He raised a brow, crinkling his scar.

God, he was different, but maybe he was just a different kind of fighter than her, and she shouldn't give up yet. Sara got up and walked over to him. She felt a strong, brooding layer of sorrow morph off him and wave around her. Unable to resist, she traced her finger over his scar. A sharp pain struck her between her shoulders—a stab just like the one she'd felt when they showered together. Her insides cringed. She ought to back off. Except for when she had been pregnant with Jake, she had never felt so close to another person in her whole life.

Ross strolled to the door. "Well … are you coming?"

CHAPTER NINE

Sara steered her car off Route 27 and onto the road leading to the Easthampton Airport. Ross had agreed to come to her beach house, his being in Hawaii—a distance too far for Sara to travel. A sleek jet combed the night sky, banking sharply for a landing. Moonlight glowed on its tail, revealing a purple zigzag. It had to be Lumina's Gulfstream V. Sara had seen pictures of it in Vicki's files.

She parked curbside at the airport. Light traffic—a perk of winter in The Hamptons. She hoped she wouldn't get shooed off by some overzealous guard. The shadow of a woman formed outside Sara's window, and a strange scattering of memories surfaced. The woman's features developed slowly like a Polaroid photo. Blue eyes, deep like a far northern sea—porcelain skin— shiny, honey-colored hair. Beautiful—hauntingly beautiful.

"I am Elizabeth Sara." The woman opened her arms. "Come. Spend a while with me."

Sara trembled with longing—longing to be her—to know the love shining in her eyes. Suddenly, Sara found herself in Elizabeth's arms, and her world as Sara ceased to exist. She became a woman in love—running through misty rain toward an airstrip, making deals with God.

Keep Nicky safe, and I'll do anything. I'll never see him again, if that's what you want.

She came to a halt and stood breathless. Nicky climbed down from his Spitfire, his handsome face smudged with soot. Their eyes met. He sprinted toward her, wrapped his arms around her and lifted her off the ground. They spun around and around, giddy with love, until thoughts of her lost husband prevailed.

"Is there any news of Ed?" she asked.

Nicky shook his head. "He's still missing."

"Where could he be? He must have been terribly wounded in the crash. How could he get out of the plane, let alone disappear?"

"Elizabeth, everything that can be done to find Ed is being done."

The blue cornflower light of Nicky's eyes shone with sincerity. Elizabeth choked back guilt and initiated a passionate kiss with her lover.

Knock, knock. "Sara."

In an instant, Sara became herself again, sitting in her car, a woman leery of love.

Knock, knock.

Sara looked up. Ross stood outside, clutching a bag of groceries, tapping his knuckles against the window. Sara massaged her aching forehead, pushing back thoughts of Elizabeth and Nicky. She slid her window down and smiled at Ross, hoping she appeared normal.

He opened the car door. "I'll drive."

"Why? Is it a macho thing?"

He laughed. "A few hours ago, you accused me of being a pussy."

"No. I didn't."

"Yeah, you did." He gripped her arm. "Come on."

Sara got out of the car. As a rule, she wouldn't allow this sort of thing, but rules seemed a little beyond her grasp right now. Ross led her around the Audi. She climbed into the passenger seat. He placed the groceries on her lap.

"Better hold onto them. The eggs might break."

He swaggered back to the driver's side, a leather overnight bag swinging from his shoulder. He tossed the bag on the backseat, climbed in and slid the seat back to accommodate his legs.

He eased the Audi onto the road. "My father has a house nearby. I need to drop off a script for someone staying there. It won't take long."

His father. Carlo. Anger flared through Sara. She plunked the groceries on the floor between her legs. "Look, I love what I do. Other than my son and a few friends, my work is my life. I can't open myself up to whatever this thing is between us until I know where our agency stands with you."

He drove in silence. They passed the exclusive estates backing onto the Georgica Pond. He drew up to a pink brick mansion perched on a dune overlooking the ocean. "Trust me, Sara."

"I don't know you."

"I think you do."

"Why do you say that?"

"Must there be a reason?"

"Yes."

"You and I don't fit into reason."

Sara eyed Ross, taking stock of his strong resemblance to Nicky, the man Elizabeth loved. She wondered how long Ross stood outside her car before she noticed him. Had he felt Nicky's presence as she'd felt Elizabeth's? She didn't ask. He might deem her unbalanced. Business first.

Ross reached into his bag and withdrew a script. Sara scanned the title page, *Love Interrupted* by Sean Granger.

Oh, God, no! Not that insufferable man.

Ross ran his finger under Sean's name. "Want to come into the house and meet the author?"

Sara shook her head. "I'll wait in the car."

But she was not to escape the author. Sean bounded out of the house and down the wooden steps scaling the side of the dune, waving wildly.

Ross lowered his window and waved back. "Be right with you, Sean."

"Yes," Sean shouted. "Come and join me for dinner. Your wonderful Rosa is preparing corned beef and cabbage." He stopped abruptly in front of the car. "Well, well, if it isn't the Hitchcock Blonde." Sean clapped his hands. "You must both dine with me."

Ross looked at Sara. "You don't want to do that, do you?"

Sara mouthed an emphatic no. Then did a feeble wave at Sean.

"We can't stay." Ross handed Sean the script. "Read it tonight. We'll get together tomorrow and discuss the changes."

"Oh, come in for just one drink," Sean pleaded.

"Not tonight. I'll call you in the morning." Ross put the car into reverse. They backed away.

Sara gave him directions to her house.

"How do you know Sean? Why does he call you the Hitchcock Blonde?"

"I date Sean's architect. We all had dinner together one night, and Sean made up a story about me, calling me the Hitchcock Blonde."

"Is it serious with the architect?"

"No. How about you? Is there someone special?"

He ran a finger over the scar above his eyebrow, rubbing it back and forth, so lost in thought that he shot past the turn to her house.

"You missed my street."

He screeched to a halt, pulled onto the shoulder of the road and swung the car around.

"It'll be the next road on the right." Sara asked again, "Is there someone special in your life?"

"Hmm?"

"You heard me. Is there a woman? Are you in love?"

He hunched forward, tightening his grip on the steering wheel. "I'm attached to someone, but she's not here anymore."

The woman was dead. Sara sensed it the moment he mentioned her. This must be the sorrow she had intuited from him earlier. Trees swayed above the road, their arms tangling beneath the starry night. She pointed to a gray-shingled cottage nestled beneath three huge oaks. "That's mine, it's not quite a beach house, but it backs onto a pond."

Her gaze swept over the potato fields that wended down to the ocean. "It's glorious here in summer. Actually, in every season, but I especially enjoy the smell of the land after a summer shower. The scents of the earth and the sea traveling on a warm wind … um!"

Ross pulled into her driveway. "It happened a long time ago."

Sara touched his hand.

He got out of the car and came around to her side. Opening her door, he took the groceries and set them on the driveway. He hauled her from her seat, tossed her over his shoulder and strode up to the house.

"You're mad!" She laughed. Her ribs crunched against his bones and hurt, but she loved the ride. Her hair floated around his buns. She recalled how they had looked naked.

He gripped her legs against his chest and jangled her key ring. "Which one?"

"It's not locked."

He opened the door. The squares of her parquet floor passed beneath her, glowing in the soft amber light of the hall. He placed her on a comfy old couch in front of a log fire she'd lit earlier. He sat beside her and ran the back of his hand over her cheek. That exquisite softness floated over his eyes. His lips moved lightly onto hers, teasing in the way of new lovers finding their journey into each other. Desire swamped her. It was cut short by a fierce stabbing sensation between her shoulders.

"Ouch!" She writhed with pain.

"What's the matter?" Ross drew back.

"Something's hurting my back. My son and his friends used to sleep on this sofa, but they also jumped up and down on it a lot." She laughed. "The springs are probably shot. Maybe one's come uncoiled." She felt beneath the cushions but found nothing unusual.

Ross got up. "I'll make dinner."

He disappeared into the hall and out the front door. Sara strolled over to the counter that divided the kitchen from her living room and perched on a barstool. Ross returned with the groceries and unpacked them, lining up items like soldiers ready for battle.

"It felt as if someone was sticking a knife in my back." She flinched. "On the couch, a moment ago."

He spun around, opening and closing cabinets, finding pots and pans, twisting and turning like a dancer in a one-man ballet. He lit the gas beneath a tall pot of water. "Tell me about your ex-husband."

"Let's not start there. He's my least favorite subject."

"All the better to get it over with." He wrapped fennel in a piece of cheesecloth, tied it with string and dropped it in the boiling water.

"I'd like to start with business."

"Nah, that'll work itself out."

Her heart raced. So there was hope. She leaned her elbows on the counter. "The best thing about my ex, Jack McBride, was his mother, Gracie. Gracie saw no wrong in people, not in her irresponsible, adulterous husband nor in her equally afflicted son. And thank God, not in me either. When my son was born, she looked after him during the day so I could finish college. Later, she took care of him so I could go to work. I'll love her forever for that."

Ross scraped onions and anchovies into a skillet of sizzling oil, then whacked the heads off sardines. "And Jack, where was he while all this was going on?"

"What are you making?" Sara was not particularly fond of the ingredients going into the dish and worried about having to eat it.

"*Soffretto.*"

She was none the wiser, but too enamored with the way he rolled the word off his tongue to spoil the effect by asking what it meant.

"So, about Jack?" He turned the oven on.

"I met him at Columbia. He was a graduate student when I arrived. A poet of considerable promise, but Jack's first love was booze. The rest goes without saying."

"Did you love him?"

"Jack could mix whisky and words and seduce the sun from the sky. I was seventeen. Of course, I loved him."

Ross fished the fennel from the boiling water, smashed it with a wooden mallet, then mixed it into the onions, anchovies and sardines. "And your son, tell me about him."

"Jake, he's the best part of my life. He's at Stanford University. Wants to be a lawyer, a champion of the less fortunate. He's sweet like his Grandma Gracie."

"I'm glad you've got him." Ross dropped sultanas, pine nuts and saffron into the boiling water, then swiveled around and opened a cabinet over the dishwasher. "Oh!" The graceful fluidity of his movements came to a halt. "There's food in here." He looked at her with the same horrified expression as when he'd found her coat on the peach silk bench in his hotel suite. "Dishes should be in this cabinet."

"Dishes are in the cabinet by the oven."

He crossed the kitchen, wiping his hands on his faded *Purpose* T-shirt. "I'll switch things around later."

"No, you won't. I like them the way they are."

He tossed the bread in the oven and stacked plates and serving platters beside it, warming them, she supposed. Glancing at Sara, he tapped the front of the dishwasher. "Clean dishes." He pointed to the cabinet above it. "Storage for clean dishes."

Sara shook her head. "Have you ever lived with anyone?"

He dumped lettuce and vegetables on the counter in front of her. "Prepare for salad."

"Well, have you lived with anyone?" Sara pulled a knife from a slotted wooden block.

"If by that, you mean shared who I am, no. A few women have moved in and out of my house."

"Tell me about them."

"I wasn't communicating with them. There's nothing to tell."

He was a cool piece of work. She sliced tomatoes and wondered if he would tell her about his dead lover. He fed pasta into the boiling water. She steered the conversation toward business. She told him how Carlo had ingratiated himself with her employees before he came into the conference room.

"He made us feel as if your account was already ours." Her voice rose on a note of question.

Ross opened a bottle of Pinot Noir, poured two glasses and handed one to her. He tapped his glass to hers. "To trust."

"A-hum."

He drained the pasta through a sieve, then mixed it energetically into the pan of onions, sardines, anchovies and crushed fennel. "We need music."

Sara slid off the barstool. Before leaving the city, she'd searched the shelves of a couple of music stores and found an old recording of *I'll be Seeing You*, sung by Frank Sinatra. She'd already loaded it into the CD player, but as she fingered the PLAY button, she chickened out. Later. Maybe. She set the second disc in motion. Diana Krall sang.

> *There may be trouble ahead*
> *but while there's music and moonlight*
> *and love and romance*
> *let's face the music and dance.*

She caught Ross's glance. They laughed—the promising laughter of lovers—laughter almost forgotten to Sara.

She lit candles that smelled of lemon grass. They sat down to eat at an old refectory table she'd bought from a local antique dealer, a table where monks had once dined. Frost dusted the tall windows overlooking the pond at the rear of her cottage. A thin layer of ice shimmered on the frozen water.

Sara forked a morsel of pasta into her mouth. The sumptuous flavors seeped into her taste buds. "Umm, it's delicious." Her shoulders sank with relief.

"*Mi sento bene con te,*" he said.

"What does that mean?"

"I feel good with you."

She felt very European, the older woman with her younger lover. She pondered the pluses of that relationship. There would be no disappointments because there could be no possibility of them being more than lovers. They'd have a bicoastal affair with stolen trips to romantic places. She would have an inside track to new products in Lumina's line of merchandise. And last, and far from least, he turned her on.

"Tell me about your life in L.A."

Ross talked about movies and TV shows Lumina had in development. He was in his office by eight in the morning and worked late into the night. In his two years as president, he'd formed a distribution company and had a record label in the works. Profits were up. Way up. "What's your favorite movie?"

Sara sucked in a stray strand of pasta. "Movies aren't my first love." She laughed in a playful way. "There's no risk involved in watching a film … nothing can go wrong."

He raised his brow. His scar crinkled deliciously. "How do you like your risk?"

Sara dabbed her mouth with her napkin. "When I was nineteen, I heard a recording of Maria Callas singing, *Tosca*. When she plunged a knife into the wicked Scarpia, which he deserved for torturing her lover, I felt every ounce of her passion and the risk she took in exposing it. I knew then I had to be in the audience when someone sang like that." Sara set her fork down. "With opera you already know the story, so the singers must infuse something into their performance that leaves you with a greater understanding of what it was about … love or revenge or redemption. They draw that extra something from the audience. I risk my feelings too, and the singers absorb them. I love and I kill with them." She gulped wine, expecting an enthusiastic response and imagining the two of them touring the great opera houses of Europe. After all, he was of Italian descent. They came programmed to like opera, didn't they? She glanced at him. "You do like opera, don't you?"

"Sure, but will I survive if I go with you?"

"You might."

He twirled pasta on his fork and slid it into his mouth, licking in the ends with his tongue.

Slick … sensuous … no spoon for him. The antithesis of

Dan—the two-fisted hamburger

man.

"About risk." Ross tore off a hunk of bread. "Did you fall in love with the risk of loving Jack?"

"Jack? Why do you keep asking about him? As I said, I was seventeen. I didn't know what I was doing."

"Sure you did. Falling in love is falling away from yourself and into the allure of another person, but it can be an illumined moment. The falling and the outcome are both in play. The fear that the person will not love you as you love them rides alongside your greatest hope that they will. At the same time, deep inside, you know what will happen."

She stuck her fork into a tomato wedge. "You don't know what will happen when you're falling in love. You know in retrospect, then you go back and color things, often to make yourself look better than you actually were."

"What do you want in a man?"

Sara pushed the tomato around in the salad oil and thought of the usual things: truth, respect, sense of humor. But there was something more. She thought of the vision she had of herself running in the Lumina shoes, chasing after something. She got an uncomfortable feeling that the something might be more about her relationships with men, rather than her goal. "I'm not sure. What do you want from a woman?"

"Acceptance."

No pondering for him, but … "You said you didn't communicate with those women who moved in with you. How can you be accepted, if you're not willing to expose who you are?"

"They each had an agenda, a limited vision, that didn't interest me. If you think there's more, there is. You think it because a part of you already knows what it is." He mopped his plate with a hunk of bread. "When we were in the shower, you searched inside yourself and came up with the idea for the Thinking Woman. You knew it was there. As you told me about her, you became the most beautiful woman I had ever seen."

Sara choked with surprise. A tomato wedge bulged into her cheek. She wished she had cut them into smaller pieces. Pulp oozed over her tongue, creeping dangerously close to the corners of her mouth. If she didn't swallow soon it would dribble onto her chin.

"What are you thinking?" He munched bread.

Sara gulped the tomato down. *I'm thinking when I'm fifty, you'll be thirty-eight. One year older than I am now.* "Oh, nothing."

He got up. Assuming he was going to the bathroom, Sara swigged the rest of her wine, hoping to calm her fast beating heart. Next thing she knew, the lush orchestral strains of *I'll be Seeing You* filled the room.

"Let's dance." Ross grasped her hand and pulled her to her feet.

"No, I don't think—"

He gathered her in his arms. In a flash, Sara vanished. She was Elizabeth, dancing with Nicky. They swayed gently, pressing their cheeks together. The lyrical voice of Frank Sinatra floated on the air.

I'll be seeing you, in all the old familiar places
That this heart of mine embraces, all day through
In that small café, the park across the way
The children's carousel, the chestnut trees, the wishing well

Elizabeth led her lover upstairs to her bedroom in the eaves of the house. Nicky laid her on the bed and touched her in all the old familiar places. His magnetic warmth fused through her whole body. The hot, electric rush of his tongue surged between her legs. His animal scent filled the cavities of her soul. The shiver and blink of moonlight bounced off the frosted windows. She flung back her head. The sounds of their ecstasy floated through the windows and over the ocean.

In the silence of aftermath, they lay still, holding hands the whole night through.

Sara opened the bathroom cabinet and stared at the box of condoms on the top shelf. Safe sex had not been an issue for the love-struck Elizabeth who captivated her last night. Sara towel-dried her hair and searched her face in the mirror. Did she have a multiple personality disorder? Did madness lurk in her eyes?

She donned her bathrobe and trudged downstairs. The aromas of coffee and bacon greeted her. Ross sprawled on the couch, scribbling on a script, blindly forking scrambled eggs into his mouth. She stood behind him. Winter sunlight splashed across his face.

I'll find you in the morning sun
And when the night is new
I'll be looking at the moon
But I'll be seeing you.

Ross stood. "Are you all right?" He engulfed her in his arms.

His skin was clean-shaven and soft. He smelled of lemon soap. The gentle push of his breath caressed her cheek. She eased herself from his embrace.

He reeled her back into his arms. "What's wrong?"

"Last night when we danced to *I'll Be Seeing You*, something overtook us. What was it?"

"Passion. We made beautiful, incredible love. That's got to be our song, strange as it is."

Sara looked at him, expecting him to say he'd felt himself become someone else, a man called Nicky. He didn't. He just kept smiling at her.

He's not going to give his account to a crazy person.

She strolled into the kitchen. His purple running shoes lay next to the laundry room. The dryer rumbled. He must have already gone for his morning run and washed his clothes. He came up behind her and pressed his cheek to hers.

"I didn't think I should wake you. You stirred as I took my hand out of yours, but then you fell asleep again." He lowered his voice. "Did you ever hold anyone's hand all night like that?"

"No. Ross ... I ... we ... we were careless last night. You didn't use a condom."

He stroked her hair off her face. "I've never been overwhelmed like that before. I'm careful. You won't catch anything from me."

"You weren't careful last night. I'm not on the pill."

He strolled into the living room and gazed into the fire. "Can you keep a secret?"

Sara shoved her hands into the pockets of her robe. "I don't like secrets, they're a terrible burden."

"That's because you can keep them." He spun around and took her hands in his.

"You won't get pregnant by me. I ... if this got back to my father, well, he wouldn't understand, and it would hurt him. I've had a vasectomy."

Sara rocked on her feet in shock. "Why? You're only twenty-five?"

"I'm not a statistic in an age group."

"But you'll fall in love one day, and you'll want kids."

"Do you want more children?"

"Heavens no! But you'll find someone—"

"I'm with the woman I'm with. End of subject."

He wedged his arms beneath hers and hoisted her off the ground. His energy shot through her like liquid fire. She wrapped her legs around his waist and swayed on the motion of his stride as he carried her to the refectory table. He laid her on it and fanned her hair about her with ceremonial flare. Outside, snowflakes dropped from a dove-colored sky. Crows cawed.

Ross stripped and strutted naked around the table, glancing at her over his shoulder haughty as a matador. She chuckled, enjoying the drama of him. He stood at her feet. "Want to have sex or make love?"

"If last night was making love, show me sex."

He parted her legs and climbed between them. His eyes locked onto hers and lit up with the hard purpose of lust. They exchanged no kisses and spoke no words. He fucked her with a force that almost hurt. Her world hurtled and plummeted until her whole body trembled in a cymbal spill of pleasure. He sunk his head against her neck and caressed her cheek, his gentleness all the sweeter after the brute strength of him.

She stroked his scar. Knife-like stabs struck her in the back. "Ouch! My back is hurting again."

"Sorry." Ross hauled her up from the table and rocked her gently. "It's her, the girl I love. She's jealous of you."

"The girl you love? I rather thought she was dead."

Ross hauled on his jeans and loped to the kitchen.

Sara strode after him and tapped her fingers on the countertop. "So … is she dead or alive?"

CHAPTER TEN

"Lily was her name." Ross poured milk into a saucepan. "I've never told anyone the story of Lily and me, but I want to tell you."

Sara sat on a barstool facing the kitchen. Her feet tingled, warning her that this would be an intimacy from which there could be no return. "I'm not very good at affairs of the heart."

"You're strong, Sara. You're the right woman for me." He lit the gas beneath the saucepan. "Coffee?"

She rubbed her feet back and forth over the wooden brace at the base of her barstool, wondering what made her the right woman for him.

The milk bubbled. He aimed the saucepan and the coffee pot over a mug. "Black or white? If white, how white?"

"A third milk."

He slid the mug of coffee toward her and ambled around to her side of the counter. "A lot of me is locked up in the secret of my love affair with Lily." He eased himself onto the barstool next to hers. "And, as you pointed out, if I want to be accepted for who I am, I must share myself."

Exit speeches ran through her mind. She tried to snatch one and say it, but the memory of waking up with his fingers laced through hers held her captive. She smiled, inviting him to continue.

"Did you read Sean's first novel, *David and Danielle*?" he asked.

"I glanced at it a long time ago but found it too depressing."

"It's the story of a boy and girl who fall in love. They both come from very dysfunctional homes. As they watch their parents' love turn to hate, they make plans to protect theirs from the same fate. They decide on suicide as the ultimate protection."

Horror sledged over Sara. "Don't tell me you tried to ...."

He stared into the distance. "Lily lived a couple of houses down the street from me. We met in kindergarten and grew up together. Lily was an only child, a bright little girl with an upturned nose and chestnut hair. Her father was a surgeon. Lily intended to follow in his footsteps."

Ross lowered his eyes. "Lily was often willful, but sometimes she was so soft and loving that I thought she'd come under the influence of an angelic force." He smiled. "When she was like that

I couldn't refuse her a thing."

"What about her mother?" Sara asked, forming an instant mistrust of the sometimes angelic Lily.

"Her mother was a wedding planner. A business she ran from an apartment over their garage. She had an affair and left Lily's father at the same time my father fell in love with Ilana and left my mother." He paused. "You have to know about my father and Ilana. The tabloids didn't miss a beat in their love affair. Dad had just directed Ilana in *Goddess,* which made her a megastar. All the publicity was hard on my mother."

"I bet." Sara remembered the media blitz, and the exquisitely beautiful Ilana, who later died in a car crash at age twenty-six. "It must have been awful for you."

"Lily and I were ten at the time. Like kids will do, we assumed we had been the cause of our parents' breakup." He tapped a finger on the rim of his mug as if drumming up thoughts from long ago. "In many ways, my dad was a magical father. We wrote stories together and made movies of them. Of course, he was away a lot, so when he was home we were seven kids vying for his attention. Being the eldest, I figured out how to get most of it."

A soft light shimmered in his eyes, the light of fond memories, Sara thought. "How did you do that?"

"Dad was a voracious reader. He had stacks of books in his study. In one pile were novels he thought would translate in movies. He made notes on them, giving his reasons and any changes he would make. I studied those notes, then when he was off on location. I'd choose a book from those he had yet to read and write my own." He laughed. "The moment Dad walked into the house I accosted him with my opinions. He loved it. I owned him."

He talked on about how he'd studied the production side of movie making because his father didn't like being bothered about money. How before Carlo founded Lumina Studios, he'd learned to be a voice of reason between his father and the executives of other studios. Sara sipped her coffee, impressed by the way he'd recognized his father's genius and made things easier for him.

He fell quiet. Sara touched her hand to his. "Ross, I was angry after our presentation. I was out of line when I insinuated you'd not earned the position of President of Lumina. I'm sorry."

"Nah, I'm used to that, but apology accepted."

She sensed an opening for her to ask him what had happened, if anything, between him and Carlo after their presentation. She took a breath, readying herself, but a pained expression crossed his eyes. "What happened next with Lily?"

"Among the books my father had not yet read, I found Sean's novel, *David and Danielle*. My heart raced as I scanned the blurb on the back cover. Here were these two kids whose lives paralleled mine and Lily's. I took the book to Lily's house that night. She tore into the story as if she'd been waiting for it all her life. She read the opening chapter, then said, 'This is our story, we'll always read this book together.' And so we did, huddled in the garage apartment where Lily's mother had once organized elaborate weddings. Sean's writing was hypnotic. We soon realized that just like David and Danielle, we weren't the cause of our parents' pain—they were the cause of ours. We had the power to punish them, and at the same time end our suffering."

Sara's back stiffened. "Didn't someone in your family notice you spending all that time with Lily, slipping into another world?"

He laughed. "Living in a fictive world was the norm in my family." He leaned closer to her. "At thirteen Lily and I became lovers. To protect ourselves from the horrors of our parents' mistakes, we wrote the same suicide pact as David and Danielle. If one of us hurt the other to the extent that they could not recover, the one who had been hurt would carve a scar onto the face of the other. It would be a death mark … a ritual to seal our pact. Then we would kill ourselves, knowing our love was stronger than death, knowing we would be together always. Happy. Free."

"Oh, no!" Sara wanted to reach back in time and yank Ross away from Lily. "Didn't you have other friends, boys?"

"Sure, but I spent my nights with Lily in the garage apartment. Her father worked long hours at the hospital, and their housekeeper spent long hours in front of the TV. My mother drowned her misery with booze. She was passed out by early evening. For three years, I spent almost every night with Lily, except for when my father was home," he said, his voice breaking with emotion. "When our friends began dating, we came out in the open about our affair and joined them."

He sipped his coffee. "One night, the guys pressured me to go partying with them. We smoked dope, drank beer and picked up some girls. They were all making out." His soulful gaze locked onto Sara. "I joined in. I just wanted to be one of the guys."

"You were a kid, Ross. That was natural."

"Yeah." He stretched his arms above his head as if pulling himself into something beyond the awful story. "Lily found out about it. She told me her heart was broken beyond repair. The only way I could prove my love for her was to keep our suicide pact."

"But you refused," Sara said, sounding like a child trying to change the story.

"No. The next night I grabbed a bottle of vodka from the freezer … Stolichnaya … hundred proof … and went to Lily's house. She was on the back deck of the garage apartment dressed in a black silk kimono. It was a steamy summer night, loud with crickets. A quarter moon glowed. A scalpel lay on a wooden table beside lethal amounts of Seconal and Tuinal, drugs Lily had pilfered from her father's supplies. Reality struck. I was suddenly scared. I slugged vodka and said maybe we should think about things some more. Lily stared at me, an incredulous look on her face. 'I can't live,' she said. 'My heart is broken.' She flung open her kimono. Her thighs were covered with bloody scars, little curves cut like the rind of the moon. She said she had been practicing on herself without any anesthetic. She didn't need it because the pain I caused her could not be surpassed."

His voice trembled. His eyelids fluttered. Sara rested a hand on his knee.

"I gulped more vodka. The ice-cold liquid burned in my stomach. My senses dimmed. I hauled a chair out from the table and sat on it, ready to receive my death mark. Lily slit the skin above my brow. Blood gushed into my eye. We started popping pills, swigging them down with booze. The deck waved beneath me like a swelling sea. Time spun out. There was no beginning and no end. A blazing white light flashed in my head, and I felt nothing but love—unfathomable love. We knelt, held hands and recited the words of our suicide pact. I began floating out of my body. 'Wait for me,' Lily said. She grabbed a fistful of barbiturates and downed them with the last of the liquor. She crashed onto her side and rolled onto her back. I eased my arms around her. She said, 'Die with me. You promised.' An agonizing look crossed her eyes. I will, I said. Her body went limp in my arms. I palmed pills from the table, but before I could take them Lily's father exploded onto the deck. I passed out. Lily died."

"Oh, how awful." Sara gulped coffee to steady her nerves. "How come Lily's father was home that night?"

"He'd lost a patient on the operating table and left the hospital early. He'd planned to take a sleeping pill and go to bed. When he found them all gone, he charged through the house looking for Lily. Weeks later, he told me he'd thought she'd been acting strangely."

"But what, he was too busy to help her?"

Ross got up, stacked fresh logs on the fire and poked the embers back to life. "Losing Lily almost destroyed him, Sara. A few months later, he left town and joined Doctors Without Borders. I've not heard from him since."

He balanced the poker against the fireplace. "After he found us, he pumped my stomach, stitched my wound and called my mother. It was a terrible time." He sighed. "In the end, Lily's father suggested that because of my father's fame, they should pretend I was never there, or the media would ruin all our lives. My mother agreed. They burned our suicide pact. Lily's father reported her death to the police. No one ever knew I was with her."

"Not even your father?"

"No." Ross brushed wood chips from his hands and sat back down on the stool next to her. "Carlo was on location in Rome shooting a picture with Ilana at the time. My mother was fighting him for custody of us. She was terrified that if Carlo found out about me, he would take us from her. My mother ... well ... all she ever wanted was a family. Without us ..." He grimaced. "I wasn't sure she'd make it. So I told her that if she got sober, I would never tell Dad. She stopped drinking that very day. Later, when Dad came home, I told him I got the scar from a broken glass in a brawl with another guy."

He stroked Sara's cheek. "I was glad about that, because I knew then that he hadn't left me. He had fallen in love with Ilana, and I understood."

Ross's love for Lily hovered outside the bounds of acceptability for Sara. *It's her, the girl I love.* He'd spoken of her as if she were still alive, and in a way she was. Her ghost presence had touched Sara.

Ross nuzzled her cheek. "Now you know my secrets."

"Yes, but ..." Sara drew away from him. "How do you feel about all this now? I mean suicide. Did you ever try it again? Would you?"

He swept her hair off her face. "Right now, I can't think of anything except how much I want to make love to you." He caressed her breasts and kissed her on the throat, on the place where she kept love locked up behind reason. Sara reminded herself that they would be lovers only, lovers with no expectations of anything more.

His lips brushed hers. They melted into a long, passionate kiss.

The doorbell rang—an impatient ding de ding ding. Still they kissed. The bell rang again and again. Finally, they pulled away from each other. Ross leaned his forehead against hers. Her skin quivered over her bones. She tugged on the reins of their story, trying to haul it back and fit it into reason.

"Did we lock the door?" Ross asked.

Sara shook her head. The door creaked open. Footfalls clomped over the old wooden floors in the hall.

CHAPTER ELEVEN

"I hope I've not arrived at an awkward moment." Sean stood beneath the arch leading into the living room, a cocky smile on his lips.

"You have." Ross swung around and faced Sean.

"Ah, well, you should lock your door."

Ross swiped his sweater off the floor and pulled it on. "You should call before barging in on people."

"I tried, but Sara's not listed. I left three messages for you on your cell phone last night, but obviously you've been too busy to pick them up."

The sandy-haired author glanced at Sara. "My goodness, you look radiant ... like a bride on her honeymoon."

Sara folded her robe closer over her breasts. "Why are you

here?"

"I have great news." Sean sniffed the air. "Coffee smells good."

"Give me an hour," Ross said, "then I'll come to the house, and we'll tackle the script."

"I hate scripts. The flow of my writing is lost, and your father's house is so big, and I'm so alone."

"What's the news?" Sara asked, ignoring the author's petulant outburst.

"Yes, yes, yes." Sean strode into the room as if her question had been an invitation to join them. "What a cozy place. I love it." He claimed a chair by the fire. "Your father has been trying to reach you, Ross. He thought you were staying at his house with me."

Ross ambled into the kitchen. "How do you like your coffee?"

"Black … with a double shot of whiskey." The author beamed at Sara and whispered, "The Dark Prince can be a nice fellow, eh?"

"How did you find my house?"

"Aaah," Sean sang the little word. "I called Dan, didn't I? Poor old Dan."

"Who's Dan?" Ross handed Sean a mug of coffee.

Sara sat on the sofa. "He's the architect I told you about."

The author grinned. "So, we've already told each other about the other people in our lives."

"What does my father want?" Ross asked.

Sean swigged his coffee and smacked his lips. "He's the proud new papa of twin boys. They were born last night a little after nine o'clock. He wants to tell you all about them."

"Okay, I'll call him." Ross sat next to Sara. "That's all?"

"That's quite an event." Sean crossed his legs. "That makes Carlo the father of ten children … two sets of twins. What a virile devil, eh?" He reached over and slapped Ross on the knee. "You'll have to get busy if you want to catch up with him."

"Drink your coffee, Sean. We need to leave."

Sean smiled at Sara. "I'm wildly in love with Carlo's wife. Have you met Anna?"

"No."

"Then you're in for a wonderful surprise. Anna was born in England. Her mother died when she was three. Ten years later, her father died. So at age thirteen, Anna ran off and joined a silent order formed by a mystic back in the fifteenth century. The monastery stands in the Isles of Scilly … remote islands off the far western tip of England. There, Anna contemplated the Universe for twenty years. Imagine what she knows."

"Enough to marry Carlo." Sara folded her arms across her chest.

"Witty, aren't we? Actually, Anna is Carlo's healing woman."

Ross stood. "I'll call my father, and then we'll go to work."

Sara watched him leave the room, his stride even less hurried than usual.

"Alone at last." Sean squinted at Sara through his black-framed glasses. "Any little confession you'd like to make, like why you still haven't read my book?"

Sara recalled the satisfying sound of his novel hurtling down the chute to the incinerator in the basement of her building. "As I said, I don't have time for that kind of reading."

"I asked you to return me to my soul. Once I've inscribed a book with a personal message, it must come true."

"You place me among the angels?"

The author lowered his glasses. "I do." He slid the glasses back and glanced behind him. "I like that old table. My, my, are those Ross's undershorts beneath it?" He looked back at Sara. "On the table, eh?"

"Is your own life so dull, Sean?"

"Ross is crazy about his stepmother. Carlo told me Anna is his confidant. Imagine a beautiful wife and a beautiful son all alone exchanging secrets."

"What about it?" Ross lolled against the doorframe.

"Everything." Sean leaned forward, not in the least disturbed by Ross having heard his tacky innuendo. "I used to dream of fucking my stepmother, and she looked like a gorilla. Thy father's wife … forbidden fruit." He licked his lips.

Sara ignored Sean and glanced at Ross. "Is everything all right with the babies?"

"Everyone is fine." Ross strode over to Sean. "Come on. Let's go." He yanked on his arm.

"No. Please. I'll be good. I like it here, and we need Sara's input on the healing woman. She doesn't come across well in Carlo's script."

"I can't help." Sara thought again of those women on TV, raving over their do-good deeds for broken-hearted men. "I don't believe anyone should martyr themselves for another."

"The healing woman is not a martyr," Sean objected. "She knows that when she gives love to another without asking for anything in return, she obligates the universe to reward her."

Sara laughed. "With what?"

"With whatever blessings it deems right for her."

"What about that doesn't come across in the script?" Ross

asked.

The author drank the last of his coffee. "In the scene where the healing woman walks into Ed's life …" Sean paused and turned to Sara. "You should know that Ed is the main character in the story. His plane crashed over Germany during World War II. He's been missing for over a year. When Ed returns to England, he finds his wife living with his best friend." Sean looked back at Ross. "Jesus Christ, Ross! Ed would not have survived this tragedy without the help of the healing woman. Then Carlo goes and removes the scene where she tells Ed there is nothing he can ask of her that she will not do for him."

"The healing woman is more mysterious if she doesn't say that, Sean. It creates suspense … the audience isn't quite sure about her."

"But everybody's read the book! Well …" Sean glared at Sara. "Almost everybody."

Sara got up. "I've got to take a shower and get back to the city."

"Wait." Sean gripped her arm. "Tell me, can you imagine yourself saying to a man there is nothing he could ask of you that you would not do for him?"

Sara stuck her hands on her hips. "Tell me this, Sean, why isn't there any man saying that

to me?"

Sara dressed for the drive back to the city, then sat on the edge of her bed. Her fingers strayed to a dent in the pillow where Ross's head had rested last night. She recalled the sound of his dream breath and the touch of his fingers.

Her phone rang. She answered, half lost in memories.

"What's going on with Lumina?" Vicki demanded. "Are we back in the game?"

Sara held the phone away from her ear as Vicki ranted, blaming Sara for what happened with Carlo. Sara had heard it all before. Vicki stormed into her office after the presentation, brushing shoulders with Ross as he left. She claimed Carlo had been pissed off by a gooey-eyed look that passed between Sara and Ross before the meeting. Sara let it pass. Vicki might have blown an artery if Sara had put the blame where it belonged.

"Well, what's happening?" Vicki's voice boomed through the phone.

Ross strolled into the room. "I'll call you back." Sara closed the phone.

Ross sat on the bed beside her. "Want to fly back to the city with me?"

"Can't. I need my car. Ross, about business—"

"Sara." He laid his hand over hers. "There are healing men, you know."

"And what, you're mine?"

"If you like."

"So, there's nothing I can ask of you that you won't do for me?"

"Imagine."

"Yeah. What's the catch?"

"None that I know of."

He dangled the Lumina account before her like steak to a starving person, but this healing man-healing woman thing bothered Sara. Anything associated with Sean Granger bothered her. Taking Sean's writing as gospel had almost killed Ross when he was a teenager, why would he even consider experimenting with that again? But that was his business, the agency was hers.

"Okay. I want—"

"Sush." Ross touched a finger to her lips, then reached in his jacket pocket and pulled out a gold chain-link bracelet. "I want you to have this."

A prism of blue-white light flashed off a small diamond embedded in the clasp. That fluttering sensation swept across Sara's chest. "Why?"

"So you won't forget your healing man."

He clasped the bracelet on her wrist. From having once worked on the DeBeers account, Sara guessed the diamond to be a one carat, D flawless gem. A sound rustled in the air—a sound like silk skirts swirling in the wind. She broke out in goose bumps. "What's that?"

"What?"

"That rustling sound."

A branch of the old oak tree tapped against the window.

"It's just the wind." Ross brushed his hand against her cheek.

Sara stared at the bracelet. Why wasn't it in a gift box? Had he given it to someone before? To Lily?

"What are you thinking?" he asked.

"About what I want from you as my healing man."

"Don't ask yet, Sara. Things aren't in place."

"What do you mean?"

"Trust me."

"I've got a lot hanging in the balance, Ross. I need to know if you're still considering HMJ to handle your advertising."

He strolled to the door. "Risk." He smiled back at her. "Trust and risk, they go hand in hand."

CHAPTER TWELVE

Vicki had organized Jonathon's fortieth birthday party—an extravagant affair. Models swarmed Jonathon's SoHo loft, strutting their stuff in slinky gowns, alongside trust-fund babies decked out in anything from jeans to the sequined creations of Christian Lacroix. Likewise, some men looked as if they belonged on the beach while others wore tuxedos. Drums throbbed beneath the buzz of the crowd. Sara passed tables unruly with food. Caviar mounded in crystal bowls resided with glazed and elaborately decorated whole poached salmons. Filets of beef stacked on smoked wooden planks. A pasta bar accompanied by a singing chef.

Sara spotted Dan pushing through the crowd, waving at her. He arrived at her side. "Why did Sean call me for your address in Wainscott?"

"Hi to you, too."

"Geez, Sara, you don't return my calls. I'm beginning to think Vicki's right."

"Vicki?" Sara cocked a brow.

Dan slugged on his drink. "It was just dinner. You know, I'm lonely without you."

"And what was Vicki right about over *just dinner*?"

"She thinks you're screwing that young guy, Ross."

"And that made it all right for you to screw Vicki?"

"Oh, shit! She told you."

Sara kept her smile in check as Dan's eyes widened with fear. She patted his arm. "Don't sweat it, Dan."

"Geez, Sara, it didn't mean anything. She just ... well, geez ... you know, she attacked me in the cab. She ripped my fly open."

"Poor defenseless little you." Sara felt a twinge of guilt for making Dan squirm, but it soon passed. She eyed Vicki across the room, draped in crimson silk and hanging on Jonathon's arm. "Excuse me, Dan."

Dan nabbed her by the elbow. "Please. It was nothing. Don't let this break us up."

She shook her arm free. "Vicki was right. I am sleeping with Ross. Sorry." She barged through the crowd, heading for Jonathon.

"Hi." She sidled up to him.

Jonathon air-kissed her on both cheeks. "Sara darling, you look fabulous."

The pungent aroma of sandalwood wafted off him and irritated Sara's sinuses. She stifled a sneeze. "Thanks, I like your new haircut."

Jonathon swept a hand through his cropped blond hair. "Vicki tells me you've sorted things out with Lumina, and the account will be ours. Is that right?"

"Ought to be." Vicki fingered her earrings—diamonds dripping from her lobes. "Sara's been working on Ross day and night."

"Dan's looking for you, Vicki. He wants to hear more about the proposition you made to him in the taxi." Sara smiled at Jonathon. "Another possible client."

"Go to it, Vicki." Jonathon nudged her away from him. "I like the way you two operate … all business all the time."

Sara oozed a smile at the man who might still hold the purse strings to their future, then glared at Vicki, waiting for her to leave.

Vicki spun off, jaw clenched, elbowing her way through the crowd.

"Jonathon, I'm glad to hear your father's recovering. How do you stand with him? I mean in regard too—"

"I've every confidence in you, Sara." Jonathon waved at someone behind her.

The heir to the Hoffman real estate empire was the only son of German immigrants, children of the Holocaust, straight arrows—so straight they seemed blind to their son's homosexuality. Jonathon was locked in the closet. Vicki often planted items about Jonathon and some suitable young lady in the gossip columns. Vicki even denied Jonathon was gay, claiming she'd slept with him, and he was a stud. Vicki could be loyal, if the stakes favored her.

Sara flashed Jonathon a come-on smile. "Pretty hanky." She adjusted the floral silk square flowing from his breast pocket.

Jonathon twisted his neck inside the collar of his shirt. "How come a beautiful woman like you isn't married?"

"All the best men are already married … or gay."

A muscle twitched at Jonathon's temple. Sara regretted making him nervous, but she needed to knock him off kilter for her next move. "Look, I'm upset because you and Vicki hid your unstable financial situation from me."

Jonathon blinked and sipped on his drink. Sara plowed on. "On top of that deception, Vicki insisted her name precede mine on the masthead, claiming that was her due for finding you, a solid backer, not to mention the extra hundred shares she finagled."

Jonathon's cheeks flushed. He withdrew a white linen

handkerchief from his jacket pocket and blotted sweat from his top lip. "I'm sorry, Sara, but after my father met you, he said you were solid gold. We had to have you on board. I would have been up front with you, but Vicki said you wouldn't agree to the partnership if you knew my father said he'd disinherit me if this venture failed."

"No, I would not have gambled the security of my family on the whim of your father."

"Sara, please ... is there anything I can do?"

"Actually, there is, Jonathon. Bringing Lumina to HMJ is like bringing in Nike. "When I do that, I want to up my shares to thirty thousand."

"But Vicki only has twenty-six thousand."

Jonathon looked frightened, as if the ground beneath him had shifted. "I'll help you gain your father's respect," Sara said.

"You will?" Jonathon cleared his throat.

Sara laid a reassuring hand on his shoulder. "Come and work at the agency. I'll help you. I'll teach—"

"Sara, I like to travel and shop and party. I'm a shallow guy."

"Hey, who wouldn't kill for a life like that?"

"You wouldn't. You'll achieve what you want ... you won't let anything stop you."

"I want the extra shares, Jonathon."

"If I agree, will we survive Vicki's rage?"

"If it looks like we won't, we can run off to the South of France together."

Jonathon's face lit up. "Now that would improve my relationship with my father."

"There you are … it's a win-win situation."

Jonathon raised his glass. "Thirty thousand, it is."

Sara raised her glass. "Happy Birthday."

In her office, Sara fondled the bracelet Ross had given her and pondered the healing man arrangement. Would Ross give her anything she asked for? Other than his account, which their agency deserved on merit, what did she want from him? Her mind went blank. How strange. It was also strange that she'd not heard from Ross since they parted in The Hamptons a couple of days ago. She stared at her e-mail screen. Was he suffering from that man disease—come-on-strong-then-flee? Or was this a test of her trust in him?

Zoey, newly promoted to Sara's assistant, stalked into the office, blowing a pink bubble between her lips. "Vicki wants to see you."

Sara poked the bubble with her pen. "Not account executive behavior." She swung into Vicki's office. Sara had asked Jonathon to let her be the one to tell Vicki about her extra shares. She hoped he had kept his word.

Vicki glanced up from her desk. Sara relaxed, seeing no trace of outrage in her eyes. "What's up?"

"Carlo DeLuca's assistant just called. Carlo wants us to come to his apartment today at two o'clock."

"Why?"

"His assistant didn't know, so why don't you get on the phone with boy-head-of-the-studio and find out?"

Sara remembered Ross talking about his childhood—of how he'd learned to manipulate Carlo and get his way. Had he done that now? Had he insisted HMJ have the account? Why else would Carlo want to see them? Sara kept the prospect of good news to herself. Revealing anything about Ross to Vicki would open a minefield of inquiry. "It's already one thirty, we'll know soon enough."

Sara swung back into her office. "Reschedule my meetings, Zoey. I'll be out for the rest of the day." Sara grabbed her coat.

On the long cab ride uptown, Vicki obsessed over why Carlo wanted to see them, insisting it must be about Sara's involvement with Ross.

"That's ridiculous." Sara lost her patience. "If this was about me personally, Carlo would speak to me alone. We're going to a business meeting. Keep your mind on that. We'll need our wits about us."

The cab pulled up to Carlo's building. The doors to the elegant Fifth Avenue façade swung open. The DeLuca name was given. A white-gloved man led them through a gilded lobby. They stepped into a gleaming mahogany elevator. Another gloved man slid his hand over a brass plaque and pushed the penthouse button.

They rode up in silence. The elevator opened into the entrance gallery of Carlo's New York home. A maid with a heavy Spanish accent greeted them.

"*Señor* will be with you shortly." The woman ushered Vicki and Sara inside and gestured to a seating arrangement. "May I bring you coffee, tea?"

They both declined. The maid scurried down a hall where video art splashed the walls, forming abstract patterns in neon-bright colors.

Sara gazed at an ornate limestone staircase, winding upward and ending in a jungle of foliage. A glass-domed ceiling rose above the trees. For all Carlo's success, he was most famous for having discovered Ilana and molding her into the biggest star since Marilyn Monroe. Their fiery affair came to a tragic end when Ilana died in a car crash. Carlo had never spoken publicly about what happened between him and the movie goddess before she jumped into her Ferrari, sped down the winding road of his Hollywood estate at eighty miles per hour and smashed into a truck on the highway.

The movie mogul appeared and bounded down the stairs, carrying a little girl in his arms. "Thanks for coming. This is Claire Michaela." He beamed at the child nestled in the crook of his arm. "Say hello to Vicki and Sara." He proffered her tiny hand.

The child gurgled with delight. Vicki, whose interest in babies wavered between zero and zero minus ten, cooed and tickled the baby's chin.

"Only a year old and already so clever and so beautiful. Look at those gorgeous eyes and those cute curls."

Vicki carried on and on. Sara worried she would go over the top, but there was no top.

Carlo beamed at the baby and nodded his agreement with Vicki's every word. "Come and sit down."

They followed him into a large room with tall windows overlooking Central Park. The furnishings consisted of a combination of antiques and sleek contemporary pieces. A painting of multi-colored dots hung above a fireplace that looked as if it had been salvaged from a Venetian palace. Sara's eyes settled on a black marble sculpture, a tall, elongated figure of a man with a baby pressed to his heart. It evoked a feeling of tenderness.

"My wife, Anna, did that." Carlo gestured for them to sit. "She's a sculptor."

"It's elegant." Sara smiled. "And congratulations on your twins." She sank onto a sofa beside Vicki, trying to present a united front with the woman whose fling with Dan had further weakened their friendship.

"Thanks, they're fantastic." Carlo smooched with Claire Michaela, assuring her that she would always be her papa's most precious little girl. He glanced at them both. "I want you to meet Anna." He picked up a phone, wrestled with the child for sole use of it and asked Anna to join them.

Sara's glance wandered to a cluster of framed photographs on a table behind Carlo.

Carlo swung around, picked one up and handed it to Sara. "That's Ross when he was a little boy. Beautiful wasn't he?"

Sara gazed into his young eyes—eyes not yet afflicted with secrets.

"He's cuter now," Vicki said.

Carlo let out a hearty laugh. "That's what all the girls tell me." He selected another photo. "Here's Ross with Claire Michaela." He set the silver-framed picture on the table between them.

Ross held the little girl above his head and smiled adoringly at her.

"Ross is Claire Michaela's godfather, and she's crazy about him, aren't you?" Carlo bounced the child on his knee. "Say yes, and say I flirt with him shamelessly and I can get anything I want from him because he's crazy about me too."

Sara felt a wave of pity for Carlo. What if he found out Ross had attempted suicide with Lily, and that he had a vasectomy? She shivered under the weight of Ross's secrets. A jab in the ribs from Vicki jostled Sara back to the moment. She glanced up. Carlo stood on the other side of the room greeting a woman.

"I hope you're reading Carlo loud and clear," Vicki whispered.

"About what?" Sara asked, but Carlo returned before Vicki could answer.

"This is Anna." Carlo guided his wife to a chair.

The woman had creamy skin, pearl-gray eyes and hair that hung to her shoulders like sheets of black satin. She was beautiful in the style of her sculpture—long and elegant and surprisingly slender for having recently delivered twins. She sat and looked straight at Sara. "I've heard a lot about you."

Anna smiled like a person delighting in some secret knowledge. Sara knew at once that Ross had told her about them.

The baby pawed at her mother. Sara expected Anna to take the child and leave Carlo free to get down to business. Instead, Carlo raised Anna's feet onto an ottoman and arranged pillows behind her, all the while cradling the boisterous baby with one arm. Anna smiled at Sara, a mischievous, conspiratorial smile that endeared Anna to her.

"Ross told me about your presentation," Anna said. "I would have loved to have seen Vicki as the Thinking Woman in chaos, and to have heard you, Sara, deliver your ice-maiden speech to Carlo."

"Yeah, that's what I want to talk to you about." Carlo handed the baby to Anna and stroked his chin. "When Ross took over as president of the Studio, I had every confidence in his leadership abilities. They differ from mine. He's tolerant where I'm not, and vice-versa, but there can only be one leader. It was wrong of me to impose my opinion over whatever decision Ross was about to make after your presentation." He got up and stood behind Anna, resting his hands on her shoulders like a man posing for a family portrait.

"I've apologized to Ross, and I've invited you here to apologize to you. I'm sorry for any disruption I might have caused in your lives and within your firm. I hope you'll accept that."

"Of course." Vicki leaped to her feet. "That's most generous of you, but where does that leave us in regard to your account?"

Carlo folded his arms. "That's between you and Ross."

CHAPTER THIRTEEN

Vicki marched Sara into Bemelman's Bar at the Carlyle Hotel. "Over there."

Vicki pointed to the burgundy leather banquette beneath the famous whimsical murals of Central Park. The room buzzed with chatter. Elegant women sipped after-lunch drinks while executives scoffed espresso and sealed deals. Sara slid into a corner booth beside Vicki. A waiter swished to their table.

"And what would the ladies like?"

The waiter sniffed the air in a condescending manner—an attitude bound to annoy Vicki.

Vicki scowled at him. "Two vodka martinis … Grey Goose … straight up … chilled stem glass … olives. And the lesser the attitude, the bigger the tip."

Sara stifled a laugh, watching the man hurry off, his shoulder up as if in a huff.

Vicki dug into a dish of nuts. "Now, before you get on the phone with Ross and officially bring in Lumina, tell me what that scene with Carlo was about."

"He wanted to apologize to us."

"The fuck he did. He was showing us his values, family, children, the things he wants for Ross. He was saying you can have the account but not his son. So tell me this thing between you and the young scion is just a fling."

"I don't know what it is, but it's none of Carlo's business."

"What the hell are you thinking?"

The waiter sallied back and set their drinks on the table.

Vicki turned to Sara. "Fill me in on the whole scenario."

Sara twisted the stem of her glass. "There's nothing to tell."

Vicki swigged on her drink. "So he's young. He's fantastic in bed and Jesus Christ, after Dan you certainly deserve a good fuck, but Lumina is vital to our future. With their name on our roster, other companies will come begging." She slid closer to Sara. "In a couple of years, we'll start acquiring companies. We'll be on our way to building our media conglomerate. In a few more years, we'll take HMJ public. We'll be filthy rich. Then you can screw all the beautiful young men you like."

Sara swallowed a gulp of her drink, wondering what it was like to be Vicki and see men solely as objects of sexual pleasure. "You're placing too much on this thing between Ross and me. I can't believe Carlo is worried about it."

"Don't make an enemy of Carlo. He's a fucking barracuda. He's telling you there's no future for the thirty-seven year old Sara Jensen and his twenty-five year old son."

"There's friendship. Ross and I are friends."

"Don't fuck with me." Vicki beckoned to their waiter and ordered another round of drinks. "If this attitude is to punish me for Dan, let me tell you a real friend would have told me what a terrible fuck he is."

Sara gaped at the woman. Vicki's twisted morals rendered her speechless.

"Don't go all righteous on me. You were through with Dan. You were already shacked up with Ross."

"And my husband?" Sara's pent up rage spilled into her words.

"Christ, that was forever ago, and at a time when you were so mad at him you could barely function."

"All the more reason for my best friend not to screw him."

"Okay, I'm sorry about Jack."

Their fresh drinks arrived. Sara sucked down the dregs of the last one and dumped the glass on the waiter's tray. He waltzed off. Sara's fury eased a little. "It's not just the things you've done, Vicki. It's the way I've reacted to them. I've turned into someone I don't like."

"Jesus! What's this about?" Vicki called after the waiter and told him to bring another round right away.

Sara munched on an olive. "I went behind your back and got Jonathon to up my shares to thirty thousand."

"I know."

"You know and you're not mad?"

"I was fucking furious, so furious that I threatened to out Jonathon if he didn't up mine to the same."

Sara shook her head, feeling sad for Jonathon. "We should help Jonathon, Vicki. He needs a true friend."

"Hey, he's lucky to be our partner. We're gonna save his ass with his father."

"But his father doesn't seem to care about his feelings."

"Jonathon gets all the care he needs from that cute ass he chases on the Côte d'Azur. That's who he is, Sara. Let him be. We don't want him at the office. Right now, we've got control of the company between us, which is the way it ought to be."

The waiter glided up to the table and placed their drinks in front of them. "And would the ladies like to order another round *now*?" he asked.

"That would be great." Sara waved him off before Vicki could cut him down to size.

The third martini slid down Sara's throat, weaving its silvery magic, softening her anger over Vicki's deception in business. "Friends don't lie to each other, Vicki. You concealed vital financial information from me about Jonathon, and that's not all right."

"I gambled and won. That's what matters."

"No, it's not. You lied—"

"Sara, if you hadn't thought our financing was rock solid, you wouldn't have been able to convince Peter and Annie to come and work for us. We had to have a first class team. We couldn't have kicked down the doors to a client like Lumina without that."

Sara shook head, trying to clear her vodka-soaked thoughts. "How do you sleep at night?"

"Opening our own agency was a huge gamble. You knew that. Peter and Annie knew it when they came on board. Now we're riding high, so tell me you're not going to blow everyone's future over your affair with Ross?"

"Get off my back about Ross. It was you who turned Carlo off at the presentation. You, when you took credit for decorating the offices. Why do you think I kicked you under the table?"

Vicki's eyes widened. "I thought I might have carried on too long on the subject, but I didn't lie. I did decorate the place. I oversaw everything."

"It takes a team." Sara repeated Lumina's motto. "Taking the glory for yourself is not Carlo's idea of what a good leader would do."

"Who the hell does he think he is?"

"The client."

"Jesus Christ!" Vicki slammed her fist on the table. "Carlo's got a past that would shame the ass off a rhinoceros. Does he think because he married some broad from a monastic order, that makes him a fucking saint?"

"Look, Vicki, we deserve the Lumina account because we created a fantastic campaign. I'll call Ross and talk to him about that, but right now I'm getting drunk, so back off. Meanwhile, to hell with Carlo, it's none of his business who I sleep with or if you act like the egotistical bitch that you are."

Vicki swung her jaw to one side. Sara sensed her mind tracing back and forth over the fault lines of their friendship, assessing its worth. Vicki grunted as if coming down on the plus side of things.

The waiter arrived, set their fourth martinis on the table and swept off without a word. They drank in silence. The liquor blurred all of Sara's grievances, and happy memories surfaced. "Remember when Jake was born?" Her words slurred together. "Jack wasn't there. Well, of course Jack wasn't there. He was in some bar drinking, and you had to be my coach."

"Shit!" Vicki screwed her face. "All that pushing and breathing, then ugh ... that blood-soaked, scrawny kid arrived. And the cord! That's got to be the ugliest thing I ever saw."

"And you swayed on your feet, saying how could you do this to me?" Sara clutched her ribs, snorting a laugh. "Then they cut the cord, and wham ... you fainted. You crashed to the floor, banging into a tray of instruments, taking the whole lot down with you. God, what a racket."

Sara heard Vicki's laughter coming in spurts and fits, sounding like the engine of an old car.

"Gotta say, Jake grew into a nice kid. You did a good job there."

Tears welled in Sara eyes. "Thanks. He always adored his Aunty Wicki."

"Yeah, his wicked Aunty Wicki. I still don't believe you didn't teach him to call me that."

"I didn't, honestly. I was reading him a story about a wicked witch—"

"I know, you've told me dozens of times about how he clapped his hands and said, oh, a wicked witch, just like my Aunty Wicki."

"That's right, and—"

"Enough cute kid stories. You've got to sober up and call Ross."

Sara drank an Alka Seltzer and slept for a couple of hours. Still groggy, she ambled into the kitchen and brewed a pot of strong coffee. She drank three cups, showered and called Ross.

"Hi, Sara," Ross answered in a low, seductive voice.

"Hi. How are you?"

"Missing you."

"I wouldn't know it."

"You ought to. I'm your healing man. Can't you feel me thinking of you?"

"I guess I'm not attuned to that yet."

"But you know there's nothing you can ask of me that I won't give you, don't you?"

Ross obviously baited her, and she got the feeling he had always known he'd get his way with Carlo. She felt manipulated, but there was too much at stake to confront him. "Vicki and I just met with your father. He apologized for his behavior at our presentation and said it was up to you to award us the account."

"So?"

"Come on, Ross, you know we'll do a great job for you."

"You have to specifically ask your healing man for what you want. That way I can answer with an unqualified yes."

"Why?"

"That sets the Universal Mind in motion."

"To do what?"

"To shower me with the blessings I need to meet your request."

Sara fidgeted on her chair. "The Universal Mind, exactly what is that?"

"You know what it is."

Did she? Sara didn't doubt there was an order to the universe. She'd read numerous books about the laws of success, and in one way or another, they'd all referred to it. She dithered. Yes might be her favorite word, but saying yes to something without knowing what it might bring was a frightening prospect. "This is pretty far out, Ross. Do you really believe the Universal Mind will hear you?"

"There's only one way to know." He dropped his voice to a

whisper. "Risk."

Sara twisted the bracelet—the gift that sealed his healing-man relationship with her. At once, that fluttering sensation waved across her chest. Perhaps it warned her not to do this. "Let's do this healing-man experiment with something other than business. I mean, you'd be giving us your account anyway, wouldn't you?"

He was silent, horribly silent. She envisioned her mother dying in a seedy state-run nursing home, and her son dropping out of Stanford for a lesser university. "Okay." She took a deep breath. "I'm ready to ask for what I want."

"Shoot."

Sara phrased her question according to Ross's request. "Will you please award the new Lumina running shoe account to our agency?"

"Yes."

Yes. Sara tightened her fist. Doubt vanished. Never had the little word sounded so all-empowering. If she stepped off a cliff, she'd sprout wings and fly. *Yes, yes, yes. I love you, yes.*

"Is there anything else you want?" Ross said in an inviting tone.

"When are you coming back to New York?"

"When do you want to make love?"

"What happened to the or-have-sex option?"

"That's not on the table right now."

She laughed.

He laughed.

She said, "How soon can you get here?"

CHAPTER FOURTEEN

The atmosphere at the agency was jubilant. News that HMJ had landed the Lumina account took the industry by storm. Trade papers called for interviews. Of course, Vicki could be found front and center, claiming the glory. First thing this morning, they received a phone call from one of the four global holding companies that owned most of the largest agencies in the world, wanting to discuss a buyout. Sara and Vicki declined without a shred of dissension between them.

Sara jammed a proposal for Xenon Oil in her briefcase. She'd been close to landing that account before she became so involved with Lumina. She would brief herself again on the company tonight. Then, waving the Lumina banner of success, she'd cinch the deal in the next few days. Her cell phone rang.

"This is Anna DeLuca," Anna said in a soft British accent. "Am I calling at an inconvenient time?"

"No." Sara sat on the edge of her desk, wondering why Carlo's wife called.

"Thank you for the lovely mobiles you sent for our babies. They're hanging above their cribs. They gaze at them endlessly." She paused. "Ross told me about you. Do you mind?"

"I don't know. What did he say?"

"That he'd met a beautiful woman, one who could think on his wavelength."

"I don't know about that."

"Maybe I can help you understand him. Could we meet? Carlo has gone to Los Angeles and won't be back until Friday."

Sara liked this woman with the mischievous sense of humor. Maybe she'd turn out to be an ally. She could do with one of those in Carlo's court. "I'm just leaving the office. I could meet you now, if you like."

"That's perfect. Do you mind coming here?"

"Go on up." The DeLuca's housekeeper pointed to the limestone staircase. Anna stood at the top barefoot beneath the glass-domed ceiling. Her satin-black hair had been tied back, and she looked ethereal in a white tunic over white pants.

"I'm so happy to see you." Anna took Sara's hands and held them between hers. "You're cold. Come and sit by the fire."

Remembering the thrill of showing off a newborn, Sara asked, "How are the babies?"

Anna smiled. "Would you like to see them?"

"I'd love to."

Sara followed Anna into the nursery. The ceiling looked like the night sky—midnight blue with silver-painted stars and planets. A plump woman in a navy uniform got up from a chair between two cribs draped with white silk. Anna introduced her to Sara as their nanny for the twins. The little boys slept, swaddled in powder blue blankets, their tiny mouths pouting like baby blowfish.

"This is Trevelyan Paul." Anna gathered a baby in her arms. "I named him for my father. Would you like to hold him?"

Sara lifted the baby from Anna's arms. He opened his eyes and wiggled his little fingers. The cooing words of baby talk came rushing back.

"And this is Roberto Liam." Anna held the other twin.

Sara listened dutifully as Anna recounted their differences of character. Then the nanny placed the twins back into their cribs. Anna led Sara into an atrium-style room made of stone and glass.

In a far corner, plants and trees thrived in a warm, humid

atmosphere created by a fine mist that occasionally sprayed up in their midst. Outside, pine trees flanked a wide wrap-around terrace. Snow flurried at the windows. They sat on a low-slung sectional in front of a blazing fire.

"Have you fallen in love with Ross?" Anna asked.

Sara blinked, aghast at Anna's immediate launch into such a personal matter. She wondered if Anna's lack of small talk derived from a life of silence for twenty years. "Love?" Sara laughed. "Ross is twelve years younger than me."

"How wonderful. You have so much to teach him."

"Is that what Carlo thinks?"

"Carlo doesn't know what we know. It's out of love for his father that Ross keeps his suicide attempt with Lily from him. If Carlo knew about it, he would suffer terribly for not having been there, and it wouldn't change a thing, would it?"

"I guess not." Sara became annoyed that Ross lied to her about never having told anyone else about Lily. "When did Ross tell you about Lily?"

"He didn't. I saw the story in his aura."

"Huh?" Sara raised a brow.

"Your aura … the sphere of light that surrounds your body."

"Oh, that." Sara smiled. "You can see them, can you?"

"Yes. When I was fourteen, I had a vision of IsMara, the fifteenth century mystic who founded our Order. She opened my spirit vision."

"I see." Sara didn't see at all, but she instinctively believed Anna.

"We won't have Ross with us for very long unless he has someone to live for." Anna drew a tray with an iron teapot and cups closer to her.

"What do you mean?"

"Lily is an unquiet spirit. She wants Ross to keep the promise of their suicide pact, and you threaten her power to succeed. That's why I asked if you were in love with Ross."

"But Lily is dead. I mean ... well ... dead."

"Yes, but she died in a state of extreme attachment to Ross and their promise to die together. She can't let go of that. It keeps her spirit close to the Earth." Anna raised the teapot over a cup. "Tea? It's jasmine."

Sara shook her head. "You mean she's a ghost?"

"Yes, a spirit trapped in the dark planes."

"Okay." Sara tried to process that. "What can I do to help Ross?"

"You could have a baby with him. Ross would never leave his

child."

Sara wrung her hands, trying to recover her wits. Obviously, Anna had no perception of how relationships worked. Also Ross could not have confided to her that he had a vasectomy. "That's out of the question, Anna. I'm thirty-seven. I've got a son in college. I'm through with having children."

"I'm thirty-six and just getting started."

"You're married. Carlo is a devoted husband and father. Ross isn't ready for that."

"Love changes everything, Sara. I'm seeing into your spirit nature. You're a warrior angel. You can do this."

"I'm an advertising executive. My goals are far from angelic."

"I see your love for Ross. Surely you want to save him from Lily?"

Sara dug her fingers into the sofa. "You said it was out of love for his father that Ross didn't tell Carlo about his suicide attempt with Lily, so for the same reason Ross won't … well … die before his time."

Anna folded her legs beneath her yogi style. "Have you noticed that at times Ross seems to blank out to this world and go elsewhere?"

Sara recalled seeing him like that at their presentation, vague—

looking as if he were on another wavelength. She nodded grudgingly.

"Ross has excellent powers of concentration. When he appears blank like that, he's actually listening at a very deep level. That's when Lily talks to him."

Anna poured herself more tea, then raised the pot over another cup and glanced at Sara. "Are you sure you won't have some?"

"No thanks." A shot of booze would be more like it—any kind.

"Did you know Ross does competitive aerobatic flying?" Anna asked.

"No."

Anna sipped her tea. "Ross is very passionate about it. It also takes deep concentration, and that draws him close to Lily. She could easily distract him during a dangerous stunt and pull him over to join her."

The air seeped out of Sara's lungs, leaving her deflated and vulnerable to this woman. "Are you implying Ross would be a willing victim to Lily's scheme?"

Anna answered with a long, affirmative gaze.

Sara thought of the night she had shared with Ross in her beach house. The feel of his fingers laced through hers—holding hands the whole night. Her competitive spirit stirred. She would not allow a ghost to intimidate her—let alone take Ross's life. "I'll come up with something, Anna."

"If Ross had his own child—"

"Anna, *please*." Sara struggled not to show her annoyance with the woman. "I've raised one child by myself, and it was hard to do that and meet the demands of a career like mine."

"You wouldn't be alone."

"Ross does not want children. Believe me."

"I believe you, but you're the one person who could change that. You've accepted him as your healing man. If you ask him, he can't refuse you."

Sara laughed—a nervous laugh. "This healing man thing ... well ... it's kind of fun, but it's something Sean Granger dreamed up for a novel."

Anna's eyes shone with sincerity. "Healing woman, healing man ... just names Sean gave to something that we've understood for ages. It's about unconditional love ... the strongest force on the planet ... the love that passes between you and your soul. Trust in that, and nothing is impossible."

Anna's gaze cut right through Sara, blotting out a myriad of questions floating in her mind.

Anna spoke softly, her eyes wide and calm. "When I look into your aura, Sara, I gaze upon the radiant light of your soul, or your super conscious if you prefer that term. What I see is revealed to me through that light. That is how I know I am to tell you these things about Ross."

In some part of herself, Sara understood what Anna said. In another, she wanted to rip it apart and prove it to be nonsense. Meanwhile, a slow itch crawled over the soles of her feet.

Sara tapped her watch. "I've got to go."

CHAPTER FIFTEEN

Sara let herself into her mother's apartment. The atmosphere hit her like hot air when she opened a clothes dryer. She stood for a moment at the door, savoring the cold wind of winter.

"Who is it?" Olivia asked.

Her mother's voice trembled and rasped from the effect of morphine.

"It's me, Sara."

"Elizabeth Sara," Olivia whispered.

Sara ignored the switch in the order of her names and sat on the edge of her mother's bed. Olivia's watery eyes roamed over Sara's face, resting here and there, sparking with recognition.

"It's happening to you."

Her mother sighed pleasurably, and Sara felt as if Olivia had shifted the weight of something painful onto her. "What?"

"You're falling in love. What will love do to you, Elizabeth Sara? Will it eat into your bones and kill you in a slow death like mine? Or will you be murdered like your namesake? Your father feared that for you. Your father … your father …" Her voice faded. Her eyes closed.

Sara sat staring at Olivia, numbed by her fateful words.

"Ross is here." Zoey bounced on the balls of her feet like a girl about to meet the rock star of her dreams. "Oh-my-god, he's so good looking, and I just read that his affair with that actress, Asia Snow, is off … *again*." The breathless girl steadied herself against Sara's desk. "I'll do anything if you'll work it so I can have a moment alone with him. I'll dump a lethal dose of arsenic in Vicki's coffee, if you like."

Sara slipped the Lumina file beneath her arm and headed for the door. Zoey raced ahead of her and slammed her hand against the door frame, barring Sara from leaving.

"You know how to get what you want, Sara. I want to learn that. That's why I asked to work for you. Give me a break."

"Okay. Rule number one, never ask for a break. Create your own. If you get fired for doing it, don't speak negatively about the person who fired you or anyone involved in that decision."

"What if it was unjust to fire me?"

"Do you want to be right, or do you want what you want?"

"What's your point?"

"Negative thoughts work against you. Let them go. Move on."

"Will you help me with Ross?"

"Refer to rule number one." Sara knocked Zoey's arm off the doorframe and headed for Vicki's office.

Ross lounged in an oversized velvet chair, studying sheets of figures. Sara buttoned her jacket and sat next to Vicki.

"We're going over the budget for the campaign launch," Vicki said.

Ross looked up. "Nice to see you again."

Sara nodded, avoiding direct eye contact with him.

He resumed studying numbers, flipping through dozens of pages, sometimes questioning their choice of media for certain markets, occasionally suggesting changes. "I've marked my comments in the margins."

"Good," Vicki smiled. "I'll review them, and we can resolve things next week when I'm in L.A."

Ross initialed the budget and tossed it on the table. "You won't meet with me in L.A. We won't meet again until after I've viewed a rough cut of the first commercial. Mike Nelson will be your contact."

Vicki tilted her head in a coquettish way and trailed her fingers through her hair. "But I'm counting on you showing me the town."

"I don't show people the town."

Ross's dismissive tone pleased Sara to no end. She watched Vicki clench her jaw in an obvious attempt to stop from lashing back at him. The veins in her forehead swelled under the strain of her effort.

Ross looked at Sara. "What about production?"

She handed him a file. "The schedule for the first sixty-second spot is in the blue section. Behind that, you'll find a list of actresses we're proposing for the first Thinking Woman. I've spoken to their agents. All would love to play her."

He flipped to that page and made some tick marks. "Test these three. Who's going to direct?"

"Brad Reese." Sara smiled at Ross, determined to win this job for her friend. "His bio is on the green sheet. Brad's the best. He's won every award in the industry, and—"

"I know his work." Ross scanned Brad's bio. "He had some trouble on a Ford shoot, didn't he? It doesn't say he's worked since then."

Vicki chuckled. "No, he hasn't."

Vicki sat on the edge of her chair, obviously delighted to see Sara on the hot seat with Ross.

Sara kept her thoughts on Brad. They had become friends at the beginning of Sara's career when she worked as a lowly production assistant. Brad had listened to her vision for a shampoo commercial he was directing. When the spot scooped a major award, Brad gave her credit. Sara's career skyrocketed. Brad had also been her major support during her divorce from Jack, but most importantly, he'd always been a dependable friend to Jake. Now he needed her help, and get it he would. She looked at Ross straight on. "Brad took the year off to nurse his lover through the final stages of AIDS."

"So, friendship influenced your choice."

Vicki snorted a laugh. Sara bit back anger. As the client, Ross had every right to ask her such questions, but as her lover, he did not. "Brad is simply the best person for the job."

Ross grinned as if saying, you're cute when you're mad, which further irritated Sara. She directed him to the orange-colored pages in the file. "I'll be Executive Producer." She'd written a glowing report listing her successes in that capacity and watched him smile as he read it.

He glanced up at her. "Are you taking that on to look after Brad?"

As Sara wrestled against giving him a piece of her mind, Vicki got up and walked toward her desk. She stopped behind Ross, where he obviously couldn't see her and mouthed, *Never fuck the client.*

Sara looked quickly away from Vicki and mustered an even tone of voice. "I'm doing it because I will make sure, down to the tiniest detail, that the Thinking Woman commercial meets the Lumina standard of excellence."

Ross arched a brow. "Nice."

Sara smiled, her flirty little golden-girl smile. "I'm glad you like it."

"Hello!" Vicki waved her arms. "I'm in the room, in case you've forgotten."

"Thanks for reminding us." Ross checked his watch.

"Yeah, right." Vicki returned to her chair next to Ross. "Have we covered everything?"

Ross stood. "I've got some ideas for the music. I'll get back to you on that. Otherwise, we're all set."

Vicki leaped to his side. Taking on her presidential manner, she guided him to the door. As she opened it, Zoey stumbled into the room, obviously caught leaning against it.

"Oh!" The girl swayed on her platform shoes. "I've got everyone together, Mr. DeLuca. Could you just say hello to them? Your father did when he was here. You know." She batted her eyes. "The team wants to know you."

"Sure."

Zoey linked her arm through Ross's, darted Sara a triumphant smile and strode forth.

So much for advising her!

"You ought to fire that little bitch," Vicki said. "She was listening in on our meeting. That's way out of line. We've got job applicants galore. We can do better."

"Zoey's a good kid. She's going to Hunter College at night working on a degree in marketing." Sara picked up the production folder. "I don't think she was eavesdropping on us. She's got a crush on Ross."

"That makes two of you."

"Are you sure that's not three?" Sara trailed her hand through her hair, mimicking Vicki's come-on style.

Sara clutched her coat against the wind and rounded the corner to Tenth Avenue. A limo with dark-tinted windows parked a block up. She trudged to it and opened the door. Ross sprawled on the backseat, talking on his cell phone. Upon sight of her, he slipped the phone in his pocket, and his face broke into a wide-open smile—the spontaneous kind that could only come from the heart. Her whole nervous system convulsed. He grasped her in his arms and kissed her on the throat. Reason flew out the door.

He stroked her hair off her face. "Show me some excellence."

"How do you like it?"

"In bed."

"Ah well, giving me a hard time about Brad isn't exactly the fast track to my boudoir."

"A hard time? Are you kidding? I barely touched you."

He eased his fingers into her shoulders and massaged the tense muscles at the base of her neck. "I just wanted you to know, I'm aware no one will hire Brad right now. He's considered unstable."

"Then why did you?"

"Because I believe in you, and I believe in second chances."

His words sunk deep into Sara's mind, so deep they produced a feeling of déjà vu. Somewhere in the future, he would ask her for a second chance. A chill crept over her. Between then and now, he would do something awful to her.

He held her hand. The limo purred uptown. He whispered of how much he missed her. Sara's uncomfortable premonition sank into oblivion. As they entered her apartment, Ross tugged her coat off her shoulders, draped it over a hook on the hat stand and hung his next to it. She wondered if it would be there in the morning and what that would feel like.

She lit vanilla candles in her bedroom. Their soft light flickered on the golden grass-cloth covering the walls. They undressed and lay on her low Japanese-style bed set on angle in the middle of the room. She ran her tongue over his body, tasting him and exploring his erogenous areas. He entered her. She floated in the deep blue ocean of his eyes—losing the last of her resistance to him. He rolled off her. She lolled against the pillows, gathering herself back. She needed to know where she stood with him.

"Asia Snow told *People Magazine* that she's still in love with you."

"Hum?"

"You heard me."

He propped his head on his elbow and looked down at her. "She's a star in *The Purpose*. It's just publicity."

"Reportedly, you've been going together for several years."

"Asia wants marriage and children. Right from the start, I told her that was not in the cards with me." He stroked her cheek. "I'm not with her. I'm with you. What do you want us to be? Ask, and it's yours."

"What?" Sara glared at him. "Is this just about you being my healing man? Do you see me as a woman in need of that? Because if you do, you're wrong."

"Sara." Ross cupped her face in his hands. "I need you. I need everything you're willing to give me and probably more."

Sara had a nasty feeling he referred to his love for Lily and his wish to die and be with her. "Rossano Giancarlo, such a long and musical name … long like the life you should live."

His gaze went straight through her. It felt as if he'd gone into another world and was looking back at her from a different dimension. Sara shook him by the shoulders. "Ross!"

A flash of blue-white light shone off the diamond in the clasp of her bracelet and knife-like stabs pelted into her back. "Ross!" She ignored the pain and kept on shaking him, "Ross, come back."

He blinked rapidly. That unbearable sweetness filled his eyes. Sara gripped his arms. "You blanked out. You were thinking of Lily, weren't you?"

"Sorry."

Anna had been right. If Lily reached Ross while he flew…. Oh, God! "You asked me what I wanted from this relationship."

Ross ran his tongue along her shoulder. "What is it?"

"I want you to live a long and normal life. As my healing man, I'm asking you to take no chances that would interrupt that."

He kissed her cheek. "I love you too."

He buried his head in her breasts. Her heart hammered.

What will love do to you, Elizabeth Sara?

Sara dismissed her mother's drug-induced words. Did Ross really love her? If so, was it enough to forget about dying for Lily? She was about to press him for an unqualified yes to her request, when he reached over to a night table where her CD player stood. Moments later, the lilting voice of Frank Sinatra glided onto the air singing, *I'll be Seeing You.*

"Darling Nicky, please." She kissed her lover's forehead. "We may not have another chance."

"What if Ed is alive?"

"He can't be. You know Ed. If he was, he'd get word to his squadron."

Nicky's eyes clouded. She read in them the guilt he felt over loving his best friend's wife. She shuddered, thinking of the terrible pain they would cause Ed if he was alive. "Ed would want us to be happy." Elizabeth looked past Nicky, trying to convince herself of that.

A tear leaked from Nicky's eye. She licked it off his cheek, guided him inside her and melted in the heavenly heat of him.

Sara awoke to the pungent aromas of Chinese food. She peered at Ross out of half-open eyes, feeling fuzzy-headed as if she'd binged for days on booze. "What time is it?"

Ross set a tray of food on the bed. "Nearly midnight. Are you hungry?"

"Starving. What did you order?" She eyed cartons of food.

"Lobster Cantonese, beef and snow peas, lemon chicken, pork fried rice, Chrysanthemum tea and ginger ice cream."

Ross leaned behind her, puffed up pillows, then wended chopsticks into a box and slid a chunk of lobster in her mouth.

Sara munched on the succulent meat. "I'm in a fog. Did we drink a lot?"

"No. I played our song, and we made love … some kind of love. Then we fell asleep."

Sara rubbed her temples. A vague memory of Elizabeth and Nicky drifted into her thoughts, but then slipped away like an elusive dream. "I have no memory of making love. What happened?"

He chomped on the lemon chicken. "Umm, this is good."

"What happened?"

He scooped more chicken into his mouth and dangled a piece before hers. She bit it off. He dug his chopsticks in and out of boxes, seeming overly focused on the food.

"Did you feel like someone else when we were making love?" Sara asked.

He smiled. "I find more of me every time we make love."

Pretty words or pretty cover up? "You should have asked me before playing that song. It has a strange effect on us. Please don't do it again."

"Okay." He set his chopsticks on the tray and climbed into his clothes. "I've got to go. I'm off to Japan tomorrow. I'll be gone for ten days. You could meet me at my house in Hawaii on the way back." He cocked a brow. "Want to?"

"Yes." The little word rolled off her tongue. Its soft echo hissed in the atmosphere, promising long, lazy days in paradise. She risked the big question. "How much do you love me?"

The words hung between them, heavy, seemingly loaded with disaster. He ambled toward the door, his body lilting with his long, lanky stride. He paused and looked back at her. "Until death do us part, if you like."

Then he was gone.

"Ross!" She fled after him. "You can't say something like that and leave." She belted across the living room but stubbed her foot against a magazine rack and crashed to the floor. "Shit!" She heard the front door slam. "Ross!" She climbed to her feet, hating his slippery way of disappearing. What did he mean, until death do we part? Did he want to be with her forever or just until he left her for Lily?

A white-hot pain sliced into her heart. Sara doubled over in agony. Dagger-like thrusts plunged into her back.

"God damn you, Lily." She waved a fist. "You'll never get him. Never!"

CHAPTER SIXTEEN

It had been a great week at the office. While Vicki visited L.A., familiarizing herself with Lumina's methods of operation, Sara finalized global marketing plans for The Thinking Woman campaign. In the evenings, she went out for drinks with her coworkers, inviting their opinions on the companies now seeking their services. Pierre Montague, the fabulous French designer, had been everyone's first choice. He had developed a new perfume—Monty. Sara scanned the brief for the fragrance.

The scent of a thunder cloud floating in a summer sky above the Pyrenees.

Sara glanced at a list of synthetics the chemists had mixed to produce that smell. Her job would be to make it sound as if the fragrance had flowed from a magical spring high in the Pyrenees straight into its elegant crystal bottle. She tucked the materials into her briefcase. She would meet that challenge over a quiet weekend in Wainscott.

Zoey appeared in the doorway. "I'm leaving, unless you need me."

"I'm fine. Have a great weekend."

The girl lingered. "When's Ross coming back to New York?"

Sara avoided the girl's eyes. "Ross is in Japan. How's it going with that guy you were dating, the computer geek you were crazy about?"

"Over." Zoey screwed her face in disgust. "I slipped a note in Ross's pocket with my phone number. I said I'd like to cook dinner for him next time he's in town. I think really handsome guys have the same problem as really beautiful women—people are scared to approach them, and they're alone a lot." She flipped her pony tail. "Don't you agree?"

Sara sighed. Affairs never stayed secret for long. She'd better pave the way for the day when Zoey learned of hers with Ross. "I've had dinner with Ross a couple of times. I noticed several women come on to him. I don't think he's turned on by that."

"*You've* been out with Ross?"

Zoey's voice rose with shock, and an incredulous expression settled on her face—a look Sara interpreted as, *you, you old bag*? Sara wanted to smack it off her or fire her or both. "We discussed business, Zoey. However, after a few drinks we talked about other things. Ross is complicated. Forget about him."

"After a few drinks?"

Sara almost felt sorry for the young woman. She appeared as hurt as if Sara had gone behind her back and stolen her guy.

Zoey stepped closer to the desk. "What happened after a few drinks?"

Sara locked her briefcase. "Zoey—"

"No." Zoey slapped her hands over her ears and sped off.

Sara's cell phone rang. It was Anna. Sara's breath quivered in her throat. Had Lily taken Ross?

"We're in Easthampton," Anna's cheery voice announced. "Carlo is working with Sean Granger on a script. Sean said you have a house nearby and come out here on weekends. If you're coming this weekend, we'd like it very much if you'd have dinner with us tomorrow. Carlo would especially like to hear how the campaign is going."

The thought of having to endure Sean and Carlo together seemed excruciating. Sara considered changing her plans and staying in town. However, the infamous Carlo was the magnet attracting clients like Pierre Montague. Even the elegant Frenchman had shelved his aristocratic posture and stooped to ask her what Carlo was really like. "*Il es très charmant*," Sara had replied. It was easier to lie in a foreign language.

"That would be nice, Anna. I'll see you tomorrow."

The DeLuca mansion loomed majestic on the great sand dune facing the ocean. Sara parked and sat for a moment listening to the Atlantic heave and crash onto the beach. She cautioned herself to ignore Sean's sarcasm for the evening and not to do anything to deepen Carlo's disapproval of her relationship with Ross. And much as she liked Anna, she wanted to avoid any more talk with her about Ross.

Sara leaned her forehead against the steering wheel. Would she, if Ross hadn't had a vasectomy, go so far as to ask him for a baby to save him from Lily? Surely not. Having a child to solve a problem would be a terrible mistake. Even if Ross lived for the baby's sake, he would still long to be with Lily, and the child would know and suffer. Children could be intuitive.

She opened the car door. Her foot slid on the icy terrain. She tried to regain her balance, but her legs shot out from beneath her. She walloped onto the ground, bottom first. "Damn!"

Footsteps crunched on the frozen snow. A dark clad figure bent over her. Bright hazel eyes shone through his black-rimmed glasses.

"So, the Hitchcock Blonde crumbles at the sight of her lover's house."

Sara ignored the author's outstretched hand, hoisted herself onto her feet but then wobbled and slipped again. Sean laughed. She glared at him. He offered his hand again. "Fuck off, Sean."

"Yes, please."

182

Sara got up slowly and dusted snow off her coat. She marched ahead of the caustic author and mounted the wooden stairs leading to the house.

Sean pounded up behind her. "Here we are a couple about to dine together. I hope Ross isn't the jealous type?"

"Look Sean," Sara said, softening her tone. "Carlo is my client, and I'd appreciate it if you would refrain from talking about my personal relationship with Ross in front of him."

Sean slid his glasses down his nose and peered at her over the tops of them. "You stole into my house in Telluride and looked through my telescope, didn't you?"

"Don't be ridiculous."

He gripped her arm. "Tell me what you saw."

Sara knocked her fist against the door. Sean leaned in front of her and twisted the knob. "It's open." He guided her into a square-shaped foyer with flagstone floors. Overhead, a flamboyant chandelier of peach and white glass swirled in and out of itself like a maze of sea serpents. She glanced down a long white hall to a double-storied window at the end. The restless body of the ocean glistened under the pale light of a quarter moon.

"Hello!" Sean craned his neck and looked up a wide staircase. "Lock up your souls. I'm here with the woman who stole a piece of mine."

Sara sighed. The torturous evening was under way.

A man's voice singing in Italian drifted into the hall. "That's Carlo." Sean smirked. "He sings to his baby daughter before she goes to bed. Such a multitalented man. What big footsteps Ross must fill."

"Ross doesn't measure himself against Carlo. He's his own person."

"Spoken like a woman in love." Sean flung their coats over the banister.

"Why are you so antagonistic toward me, Sean? What do you want?"

A sardonic smile crossed the author's lips. "I rather think it's a matter of what you want from me."

"In your dreams."

"Yes, it will begin there."

Sara was about to ask what he meant, but Anna drifted down the stairs, welcoming them. She'd lost almost all the weight of her recent pregnancy and looked svelte in a long silver-gray skirt and sweater. She wore no jewelry except for a large, emerald-cut diamond ring on her wedding finger. Sara felt appropriately dressed in Jill Sandor jeans and an ice-blue satin blouse, a color that deepened the hue of her eyes.

Anna took Sara's hands in hers. "You look absolutely radiant."

"I have that effect on her," Sean said.

"On everyone, you sweet man." Anna kissed Sean on both cheeks.

Sara watched his face light up like a child suddenly secure in his mother's love. She followed Anna into a room facing the ocean. Carlo sat at a grand piano with his little girl held on his lap in a sling seat. He finished singing to her, and the child banged her tiny hands together.

"Best audience in the world," Carlo said.

He stood and looked from Sara to Sean, beaming like a man well pleased by seeing them together—anything other than Sara with Ross, no doubt.

Anna lifted the child from Carlo. "I'll put her to bed and be back shortly."

A log fire crackled in a big stone fireplace. They sat in comfortable chairs slip covered in colors of sand and sable. Carlo took their drink orders, and while he fixed them at an antique sideboard, Sara perused a large oil painting. It had been thickly textured in white-on-white oils with a single black dot placed slightly off center. The hypnotic dot made Sara feel slightly off center with some truth at the core of herself.

"Anna's father painted that," Sean said. "Magnificent isn't it?"

"Yes."

Carlo handed Sara a glass of red wine, then eased himself into a chair. "You like art."

Sara didn't miss the tone of Carlo's question—someone expecting an educated response. Sara wished she had one. She would like to meet Carlo on any ground that didn't relate to Ross. "I know little about it."

Sean raised his glass as if in a toast to the painting. "It's much more fun not to know about art. Too much intellectual interpretation pulls me into arguing instead of simply experiencing my own reaction to the work. Critics do that with my novels. One said the story of *David and Danielle* was a metaphor for the permanent eclipse of the sun and the moon. Such nonsense never crossed my mind."

"Actually," Carlo said. "That's an astute observation. A couple of sixteen-year-olds committing suicide would black out their parents world, permanently." Carlo slugged on his drink. "You mentioned the passing of the sun over the moon sixteen times in that book. David and Danielle were sixteen—an eclipse for each year of their lives."

"Really?"

Sean sounded surprised—surprise Sara didn't buy for one moment.

Sean glanced at Carlo. "Well, well, I don't suppose you could reach into that infamous photographic memory of yours and quote them, could you?"

"Sure." Carlo relaxed in his chair.

He began reciting passages from the novel. He paused between each, adding mythological comment on the male and female aspects of the sun and the moon, relating them to David and Danielle. Sara kept count of his quotes, riveted as if she watched a magician locked in a box at the bottom of the ocean as the clock ticked away. Coming to the final quote, Carlo lowered his eyes like an actor seeking his own relationship to the text.

"David lowered his cheek to the cold flesh of Danielle's bosom. In death we are together. He collapsed on her body. The moon slipped behind the earth's shadow."

Sara gulped wine, trying not to think of Ross's suicide attempt with Lily.

Sean clapped loudly. "Bravo!' He glanced at Sara. "That's why Carlo is the only person I'll allow to translate my books into film."

"Nah." Carlo shrugged off the praise. "You write a fantastic story."

"What about doing *David and Danielle* next?" Sean asked.

Sara got a nasty suspicion that Sean had some knowledge of Ross and Lily's suicide pact and had deliberately set the stage for this moment. She watched the exuberance go out of Carlo. A visible veil of sorrow clouded his eyes. A man as intuitive as he had to associate this story with Lily, his son's childhood sweetheart. Surely he must have doubted Ross's story that he received his scar from a broken glass in a brawl with some guys. Or had he blinded himself to it, guilty because he'd been in Rome at the time, making a movie with Ilana?

"Something in me isn't ready to fully enter the darkness of that story." Carlo got up, whisked Sara's glass from her and strode to the sideboard. "How's the campaign coming along?"

"Oh," Sean whined, "do let's talk more about life and death and love. Yes, let's talk about love."

"Let's not."

Carlo's voice resonated with the steely edge of a man whose command would be final. Sean pouted. Sara grabbed the moment and brought Carlo up to date on the Thinking Woman.

"Have you cast her yet?" Carlo asked.

"No. It's between three actresses." Sara related their names but offered no biographical information as Carlo would be well acquainted with them. "The decision is up to Ross."

Carlo rattled ice in his glass. "Ross has a fantastic eye for talent. He'll pick the right woman."

"Ross has a fantastic eye for women, period," Sean said.

"Yeah." Carlo strolled back to the sideboard and topped off his drink. "And in his job, he's got an endless pool of young beauties to choose from."

"Like you used to have?' Anna sailed into the room, a welcome relief from the mounting antagonism between Sara and the two men.

"Aw, honey." Carlo swept Anna into his arms and swung her off her feet. "I've got you. That makes me the luckiest guy in the world."

Sara thought of Ross tossing her over his shoulder and carrying her into her cottage. She missed him.

"What's Ross doing in Tokyo all this time?" Sean asked.

"Adapting a TV show for the U.S. market." Carlo settled on a sofa beside Anna. "Ross speaks the language. He learned it from a Japanese girl he lived with for a while."

Sean glanced at Sara. A wicked smiled danced on his lips. "I'd love an Asian woman to live with me, all that bowing and obedience."

Carlo tossed off a laugh. "That's just in the movies, Sean. In fact, the girl Ross lived with got pregnant and when Ross said it wasn't his child, she slapped him with a paternity suit. I've got to hand it to my son." Carlo smiled. "He acted cool. He just waited until the kid was born and let DNA prove it wasn't his."

Ross's secrets brought a wave of uncomfortable power to Sara. It would be so easy to wipe that beam off Carlo's face.

"Really, Carlo." Anna interrupted the round of macho banter between the men. "It would have been kinder if Ross had accepted responsibility for the baby. Now there's a little child in the world without a father."

"Oh, honey." Carlo melted back into his Italian-papa-self. "I'm sure the real father came forward."

A black man with silver hair appeared in the doorway. "Dinner is served."

The walls of the dining room caught Sara's eye first. They had been painted with scenes of long golden beaches and gulls winging into blue skies. The sound of waves pounding against the dune brought a life-like quality to the murals. Sara imagined the room in summer with the French doors opened to the sea. Had she, years ago, strolled by on the beach with Jake, while Ross rode into the ocean on Carlo's shoulders?

They sat at a round table. Sean was on Sara's left and Anna on her right. Steamed lobsters were served. As they cracked the claws and ate the sweet flesh, Carlo quizzed Sara about her son, showing a lively interest in his studies at Stanford. They managed to avoid a straight-on meeting of their eyes, but the air grew tense with their effort, tense enough for Anna to jump in and change the subject. She spoke of how she and Carlo planned to live in Italy in the near future. Carlo would make the movies he'd set out to make—intensely personal films exploring the struggle of the human spirit. Anna gave an inspired interpretation of a script Carlo was currently working on. Husband and wife talked back and forth, revealing an intellectual compatibility that surprised Sara, considering Anna had spent twenty years in silent meditation.

Sean added lively comment on the time he'd spent in Italy. Sara displayed a well-tempered interest in him and Carlo. She hoped. All seemed very polite, but as a group they were about as sound as a house built on the fault line in the San Andreas. The first tremor came when Carlo turned his attention to Sean.

"I've had to rework the script a bit for *Love Interrupted.*"

Sara sat a little straighter as Carlo lavished praise on Sean's writing, the kind that could only lead to a big BUT.

Carlo leaned closed to Sean. "Nicky and Elizabeth are secondary characters. I've cut out the three days when Elizabeth lies dying in a coma."

Sean flung his fork on his plate. "No. No. No!"

Sara almost felt sorry for Sean as Carlo held up his hand and silenced his objections, but her world flipped over too. Intimate memories of Elizabeth haunted her. *I'll Be Seeing You* played in her head. Elizabeth's love for Nicky swelled in her heart.

Sean wrung his napkin. "You're cutting out the heart of my novel, Carlo. I won't allow it."

Carlo grimaced. "Let me explain. Let me tell you how I'll shoot Elizabeth's death scene."

Sean slumped in his chair. Sara held onto the edges of hers. She felt Carlo's attention fall on her. Sara straightened her posture.

Carlo inhaled a deep breath. "The setting is a village in Sussex, England during World War II. Ed Harroway, a fighter pilot is missing in action. Meanwhile, his best friend Nicky Hart, also a fighter pilot, and Elizabeth, Ed's wife, fall in love."

Sara nodded, indicating she understood. Carlo opened his arms like a conductor to an orchestra. Everyone fell silent. The only sound was that of the sea crashing onto the sand.

Carlo continued, "Nicky's home from the war. We see him walk through a field with his baby son on his shoulders. Across the street, Elizabeth emerges from their cottage and waves at them. Nicky grabs his son's hand. They wave back at Mommy. Elizabeth's eyes glow with the radiance of her love for them. Nicky watches Elizabeth as she dashes across the road to meet them. We see a milk van careen around the bend. We hear a thud. The van drives off. Elizabeth lies on the road, blood oozing from her head. Nicky's world blurs. We hear the baby cry. The camera pans to Nicky's face. We see a series of flashbacks from his life with

Elizabeth. *I'll Be Seeing You* plays softly, but the audience knows Nicky will never see Elizabeth alive again."

Emotion overwhelmed Sara. Tears thrashed at the back of her eyes. She struggled to control them.

Sean yelled at Carlo. "You can't cut the scenes where Elizabeth drifts in and out of consciousness. Her experiences between life and death are essential to the story."

Carlo said, "I'll convey the spiritual elements of the story through the healing woman in her dialogues with Ed. This is Ed's story. I've got to stay with him."

"I hate movies." Sean banged his fist on the table. Dishes rattled.

Anna stood. "We'll have coffee in the library. Carlo, please take Sean there now." She turned to Sara. "Come to my studio with me."

Feeling unsteady on her feet, Sara followed Anna out of the dining room. Her mind kept going back to the last time Ross had played *I'll Be Seeing You.* Although she had blanked out, she felt certain something unusual had happened when they made love. She could feel it in her bones and sensed Ross knew. She had a burning need to call him and find out.

Carlo headed down a hall with Sean in tow. Sara tapped Anna on the shoulder. "I've got a lot of work to do. I should leave."

"You bloody well can't leave." Sean marched back to Sara. "I expect you to stay and put up a fight for Elizabeth's dying scenes."

"Me?" Sara lashed out at the author. "I get a message across in sixty seconds. Three days to die? That doesn't work for me."

"Then let's see how it works for you when I tell Carlo you were out here last weekend fucking Ross on the dining room table."

Carlo appeared behind Sean. "My table?"

Sara's heart sank as she stared at his face that grew redder by the second. "Carlo, listen, there's—"

"Carlo, my darling." Anna stepped forward, smiling at her husband. "Ross is a—"

Carlo held up his hand. His thunderous look swept over Sara, and she knew his anger would prevent him from hearing any explanation. He shook his head as if too disgusted to say anything. Sean grinned. Carlo grabbed Sean's arm and dragged him off.

Speechless, Sara stared after them, holding herself back from snatching Sean away from Carlo and pounding her fists into him until he fell lifeless to the floor.

CHAPTER SEVENTEEN

Anna linked her arm through Sara's. "Let's talk in my studio."

"Anna." Sara drew her to a halt. "Ross and I did not have sex in this house."

Anna laughed. "I'm disappointed."

"This is serious, Anna. Carlo thinks—"

"Carlo's under a lot of pressure. Working with Sean is quite trying. Come on, we have other things to talk about."

There would be no escaping Anna. Sara couldn't leave without knowing she would set things right with Carlo. She followed her down a corridor and into a cavernous room with stone floors. Iron-framed windows peaked to the roof, looking Gothic and sinister. Sara glanced outside. The sand dune dropped sharply away from the house. The sea gushed around it and surged into the waters of the Georgica Pond.

Anna lit thick, black candles on a brass candelabra set in the middle of a table with pneumatic tools, chisels and knives scattered around it. Raw marble and huge uncut boulders of granite clustered in corners of the studio formed their own sporadic sculptures. The gritty metallic smell of drilled stone filled the air. Granules crunched beneath Sara's feet.

Anna glanced up from the flaming candles. Behind her, two massive wall hangings of carved black granite stood as a testament to the strength of the willowy woman. "Are you all right, Sara?"

"I'm worried that Sean's outburst will cost our agency the Lumina account."

Anna strolled to a pedestal supporting a hunk of stone shaped like a head. She swiveled the base and stared into the face. "As your healing man, did you ask Ross to give you a child?"

As much as Anna's question irritated Sara, she couldn't help but admire the way Anna went after what she wanted. "Persuasion is my business, Anna, and I'm good at it. I'll find a way to fight Lily, and I'll win."

Anna pointed to a large drawing board a few feet from Sara. "Look at that."

Sara walked over and stared at a sketch of Ross's face. It resembled an old master drawing. The muscles, sinews and fine-netting of his veins showed beneath the planes of his expression. His eyes spoke of the vague, rich world of his inner life. The slash of his scar looked poetic—a mark on his soul. "You really caught him."

"Actually, this is how I see Ross." Anna spun the black marble head around. Sara gasped. The face was blank of any carvings except for a wisp of a line representing his scar. But somehow, the stone reflected everything about Ross—all that was there and not there.

"Lily comes to Ross in his dreams." Anna caressed the sculpture. "She tells him she's trapped in hell. She cries and berates him for not keeping his promise and dying with her. She begs him to die and lead her into the light. Ross believes he owes her that. How will you persuade him otherwise?"

"I'll present him with a more desirable reality."

"How? His is true."

"Not to me, it isn't." Sara walked to the window and leaned against the frame. Since Anna seemed capable of withholding Ross's secrets from Carlo, Sara decided to speak bluntly. "I think the secrecy surrounding Lily's death has allowed Ross to cling to beliefs he created when he was a boy. His mother was an alcoholic and terrified she would loose custody of the children to Carlo. She begged Ross not to tell his father he'd been involved in a suicide pact. A boy of sixteen wants to do what's expected of him as a man. Ross was very vulnerable to such a plight from his mother. Trying to do the right thing for both parents, he made a bargain with his mother and promised he wouldn't tell Carlo, if she got sober. She got sober, and Ross kept his word. Sadly, there was no one to tell him, he was not responsible for Lily's suicide."

"Ross has been in therapy," Anna said. "He's aware of the arguments for his innocence, but it hasn't changed his feelings. Our feelings are stronger than our thoughts, aren't they?"

"Yes, they are, Anna, and right now I'm feeling that Carlo is disgusted with me. It bothers me because I'm already on thin ice with him."

Anna strolled over to the fire and poked it to life. "Unless your work doesn't measure up, Carlo will stay out of your business affairs with Lumina." She faced Sara. "Carlo and Ross had an enormous fight after your presentation. It ended with Ross telling Carlo that if he insisted on interfering with the way he ran the Studio, Carlo should consider him gone."

Sara's gut curdled. No wonder Carlo disliked her.

"But," Anna said, "blood … family ... never discount the power of that. As the eldest of eight children, Carlo assumed leadership of his siblings as a boy. When he was thirteen, he promised his father, he would create a place of opportunity for them in the world. He built Lumina Studios to keep that promise. All of his brothers and sisters work there. Carlo has passed this ethic of responsibility on to Ross." She walked back to the sculpture of Ross. "Carlo's second eldest son, Stephan, joined Lumina two years ago. Ross is grooming him to take his place." Anna leveled her gaze on Sara. "Believe me, a child of his own is the only way to keep Ross with us. Blood. His own."

"I must be missing something," Sara said. "We don't know what happens when we die. Ross can't know that he'll find Lily, and I just don't believe he would gamble his life on the unknown."

Anna bit her lip and looked away from Sara.

Sara sensed she debated whether to add something to the conversation. Sara wanted to run, but that might give Lily an edge on her. "What are you not telling me?"

Anna laid her hands on the bust of Ross. "The death process is not unknown to Ross. He actually died for a few moments before Lily's father brought him back to consciousness. He told me he saw Lily trapped in the dark planes. It was awful." She closed her eyes for a moment. "Ross feels so guilty because he introduced Lily to the book, *David and Danielle*."

"But Lily insisted they commit suicide." Sara stepped closer to Anna. "She could have forgiven him for having sex with some girl, and they'd both be alive."

"Sara, it happened as it happened, and Ross bears that guilt. To help ease his conscience, I told him something that in retrospect I probably shouldn't have."

"What?"

Anna stared into the distance. "IsMara, the woman who founded the Order I served in for twenty years, was one of the greatest mystics ever to walk this planet. IsMara knew that falling asleep was similar to the dying process. Every night as she fell asleep, she envisioned herself walking through the door of death, while retaining her illumined consciousness. She then pictured herself returning to another life and bringing her awareness of that journey with her so she could write about it and teach others. IsMara practiced that for forty years, then she died and left exactly as she had programmed. I know because I read her manuscript—a work written in her subsequent life—a work kept under lock and key at the monastery. I told Ross about that."

Sara shivered. "You encouraged him to die."

"That wasn't my intention. I emphasized IsMara's forty years of practice, but people tend to hear what they want to. I think Ross believed he could die at any time, find his way into the dark planes and take Lily into the light. You can stop him, Sara. You can have a child with him."

"Anna, there are things between Ross and me that I just can't talk about."

"I'll smooth things over with Carlo."

Sara didn't miss the note of bargain in her new friend's voice. She hovered at the edge of telling her Ross had a vasectomy, but resisted. Not so much out of honoring his secret, but because she could not afford to be associated with Carlo's discovery of that. When the pilings fell from beneath his great Italian-papa image, she could not be within firing distance of his response.

Anna's pearly gaze roved over Sara, then rested above her head. Sara trembled, thinking of how Anna had seen the story of Ross and Lily in Ross's aura. She spun on her heels and sped from the house.

CHAPTER EIGHTEEN

The door to Vicki's office cracked open. Zoey peered in, beckoning at Sara with an exaggerated gesture. Sara smiled at the executives from Xenon Oil. "Excuse me for a moment." She skimmed out of the office. "What is it, Zoey?"

"Sean Granger's in reception. He's been there for nearly an hour. He refuses to leave until he sees you."

"About what?"

"He won't say."

Sara sighed. She'd better see Sean, or God knows what he might do. "Put him in the conference room. I'll be there in five minutes."

She crept back to her seat, grateful to hear Vicki bringing the meeting to a close.

The moment the men from Xenon left, Vicki pounced on Sara.

"What did Zoey want?"

"It's personal. Something I've got to attend to right now."

"Wait a minute, you're going somewhere tomorrow, and I don't know where."

Vicki was the last person Sara wanted to know about her trip to Hawaii. "You can reach me on my cell or by e-mail."

"Meeting Ross?"

"I'm just going on a little getaway."

"Be careful. You've met your match with Ross. When the affair gets serious, he runs."

Since Vicki's trip to Lumina's offices in L.A, she had jumped on every chance to gossip about Ross. Sara always shrugged as if she didn't care. She did that now as she swept off to the conference room.

Sean sat at the far end of the long, marble table, waving a bottle of Jack Daniels in the air.

"I made myself at home."

Sara kicked the door to the liquor cabinet closed. "Tell me what you want and get out!"

"To Madam Executive Vice President." Sean raised his glass. "What extraordinary digs she occupies." He waved his arm around the room. "Everything about this place makes me feel out of date, like a puny copy of something that was never very significant. But by God," he said, gulping his drink, "how clever one must feel to be your client, to have made such a brilliant choice as to hand one's widgywoo over to you. To watch you flog the thing to us, the masses who plunk down our money, believing we shall be made thin or beautiful or whizzed along on the magic carpet of whatever you promise us the widgeywoo will do."

"Why are you here, Sean?"

"I've come to make you a proposition."

"After your performance in front of Carlo, I wouldn't trust you—"

"Ah, Carlo." Sean topped his glass with booze. "He's yesterday's bad boy transformed by the love of his healing woman."

"You compromised me in front of him."

Sean swigged on his drink, smacked his lips and lolled his head against the back of his chair. "You know, I love it that you're in this affair with Ross. You'd be bloody insufferable without that drama." He twisted his lips in a crooked smile. "I did some research on you. Sailed through Columbia … on scholarship. What a clever little girl. Tough too. Knows what she wants and how to get it. Dazzles the boys in the boardroom. Dumps deadbeat poet husband … good move that … you're not the muse-behind-the-genius type. And then this." He swung his arm around in the air. "Your very own ad agency. Balls … Christ … yours could sink a bloody fleet of nuclear submarines. But … dum de dum dum … along comes Ross, and he sits in your heart like a great big soft spot, melting you down. Yes. I love it."

"Is that it?" Sara headed for the door.

"No. Come back. I'm sorry."

A tenor of regret rang in his voice and struck an empathetic chord in Sara. She couldn't fathom why. "Five minutes, Sean."

"Thank you."

Sara yanked out a chair at the other end of the table. "What's your proposition?" She tapped her fingers on the marble table, watching Sean squint over the tops of his glasses as if trying to get her in focus.

"Fall in love with Ross. Fall to the depths of despair that only love can bring. Fall until the only return is up. Then you will have touched all of love … and all of love will be in all your moments." Sean flopped back in his chair.

"Is that something from one of your novels?"

"No."

"So, you've loved like that?"

"No, but you can. It will help you to do what I asked of you in the inscription I wrote to you in my book."

"I see." Sara recalled those words, *Return me to my soul.* "It's for you, my falling in love with Ross, is it?"

Sean toyed with his glass, then slid it aside like someone vowing never to drink again.

"I suppose you haven't read my book, *David and Danielle?*"

"No, but thanks to your little game with Carlo, I pretty much know the story."

"You probably don't know that as David and Danielle prepared to die they burned their clothes and every photograph of the two of them together. They stripped their beds, washed the linens and left their mattresses bare. They cleared out their lockers at school and wiped their fingerprints from their homes and cars. They left no visible trace of having been the children of parents whose love had turned to hate. Whose genetic pattern for infidelity had repeated itself in David, thus breaking Danielle's heart … thus making life no longer bearable."

Sean inched his drink back in front of him. "Ross and Lily did those very same things before their attempted suicides."

"Why are you telling me this?"

"When I went to L.A. to meet Ross, I had to wait for him for a while in his office. I was shocked by its emptiness. Oh, it was beautiful in a cool, minimal black slate and granite way, but there wasn't a single personal object to mark it as his. Not even a sheet of paper on the long, dark teak desk. Ross is a man ready to die."

Sara's heart sunk to her gut. "He's just a neat freak."

Sean swallowed his whiskey, let out a long sigh and leaned back in his chair. "I always knew the story of *David and Danielle* would harm someone. When Ross entered his office, the first thing I noticed about him was the scar above his eyebrow, the same scar Danielle had sliced into David's skin. It's strange, you know, but years of dread were lifted from me. I was at last face to face with my victim."

"I don't understand."

"After my first meeting with Ross, a girl named Lily began haunting my dreams. She stands at the foot of my bed, opens her black-silk kimono and shows me her thighs. They're covered with bloody cuts shaped like the one above Ross's brow. Last night, she appeared and threatened to kill you, Sara."

Sara froze. "Kill me? Why?"

Sean stood and walked toward Sara, sliding his newly filled glass along the table, guiding it around the jeweled chains that held the great slab of marble in place. He settled in the seat to Sara's right. "If I could change one thing in my life, I would not have written the story of *David and Danielle.*"

He looked suddenly haggard and terribly sad. Sara felt a rush of compassion for him. "You can't blame yourself for Lily's death.

You—"

Sean put a finger to her lips. "But I do, just as you might blame yourself if Ross met with a tragic accident tomorrow. We can't help it, Sara. It's a result of feeling important and in control, which we are to some degree. "

"But your book was fiction."

"Some stories come to me from those trapped in the ghost world, the dead who can't let go of something that happened in their lives. I'm a sick bastard, so it's usually the evil ones, those who want revenge who seek me out. In writing their story, I give them a voice. If that voice finds its victim, am I not in part responsible for the outcome?"

Sara thought of the months Sean spent in a psychiatric hospital, and tried to discount what he'd said. But Lily's ghost was real. She had felt its presence.

Sean edged his chair closer to Sara. "I told you the four main characters in *Love Interrupted* were based on real people. On the cover of the novel, you see a girl running toward Ed's crashing plane. She was Sylvia. Lily was Sylvia in her previous life. Do you remember the scene Carlo described at dinner last weekend, the one where Elizabeth, who was Ed's wife, was killed by a van?"

"Yes."

"Sylvia drove that van. She murdered Elizabeth. You were

Elizabeth in your last life. Now Lily wants to kill you again."

Sara almost laughed. It seemed outrageous, but ....

Sean pushed his glass toward her. "You look like you could use a drink."

Sara waved a dismissive hand and repeated the information like a skeptical detective interrogating a suspect. "Lily was Sylvia in a previous life. I was Elizabeth in my last life. Sylvia killed me back when I was Elizabeth. Sylvia was reborn as Lily, who is already dead, but her ghost is trying to kill me again. Is that right?"

"Yes."

Sara wanted to refute it all, but memories of the times when she had felt herself inside Elizabeth's skin wouldn't let her. "And Ross? I suppose you're going to tell me he was Nicky Hart."

"Yes."

"Phew!" Sara whistled a breath. "This is too much for me."

"Read my book, Sara. It will help you."

A soft haze floated over Sean's eyes, giving him a faraway look, a sense of belonging somewhere else. Sara wanted to ask him about his time in the psychiatric hospital but decided against it.

Sean sipped his drink. "Murder can become a habit, one that lingers in the dark planes ... a habit the murderer can bring into life after life. Sylvia and Lily are one soul. Sylvia told me the story of

David and Danielle. She bent down from the dark planes and whispered it to me day and night."

Sara laid her hands on the cool marble tabletop, wondering if Sean could no longer discern fact from fiction.

"I need your help, Sara. I need to redeem myself for having caused such harm to Ross and Lily through my novel. Here's my proposition. You do everything in your power to save Ross from Lily's attempts to pull him over to the other side, and I'll prevent Lily from taking your life."

Sara stared at Sean's outstretched hand. "How will you stop Lily from killing me?"

The author closed his eyes. "Trust me."

Trust me!

First Ross, now Sean!

Sean opened his eyes. Sorrow had faded from them. He looked as if he'd traded it in for something simpler. Simpler and steadfast. He looked completely at peace with himself. But she felt lost—so lost that she placed her hand in his. The movement seemed to take minutes to complete, but once Sean's fingers wrapped around hers, a feeling of friendship old as time itself rolled over her. Sean became someone dear. She felt grounded with him, grounded in trust. Everyone in her world might desert her, but he never would. That fact resonated with some central truth at the core of her being. But truth would bear no deception.

"I stole into your house in Telluride. I looked through your telescope."

"What did you see?"

"A small plane ripped through the skies, an old plane like the one on the cover of your novel."

"Was I flying it?
"Yes, but I called you Ed."

"Did I crash?"

She nodded. "You flew too close to the trees outside your house. A wing caught in the branches. Fire …" Sara gulped. "The plane nose-dived into the valley below. My heart …" Sara blinked tears. "My heart hurt. I drew back from the telescope. When I looked through it again there were no signs of a wrecked plane."

Sean whispered, "Thank you. That makes me whole. Never be sad you told me."

Fear and sorrow collided in Sara's heart—fear that Sean would die, and sorrow as if he already had.

CHAPTER NINETEEN

The jet skimmed over the blue waters of the Pacific, then landed at the Kona Airport on the Big Island of Hawaii. Sara tucked *Vogue* into the pocket of the seat in front of her and unfastened her seatbelt. Passengers hauled luggage from the overhead bins. The door to the aircraft opened. Sara filed down a flight of stairs and stepped onto the tarmac. She glanced back at the great steel bird, savoring the awe of flying, a pleasure missed in the usual shuffle from the jet bridge straight into the arrival lounge.

She sniffed the salt tang of the air and rolled her shoulders, freeing herself from the stiffness of travel. She had flown first class, thanks to Ross, so she stretched out in the big leather seats and slept for several hours.

The terminal consisted of a series of open-air, pavilion-styled buildings. Palm trees towered up from their midst. Sara watched her fellow passengers fall into the arms of friends and lovers. She cast her eyes down, not wanting to be caught with the worried expression of someone searching the crowd for an anticipated face.

An arm swung around her. Claimed. After two weeks apart, Ross's beauty took her by surprise all over again. She enjoyed the moment. All too soon, the complexities of their lives would set in, and she would fall blind to his looks. He ran his fingers over her cheeks as if testing to see if she was real. A gesture more precious than words, more intimate than a kiss.

He removed a lei of pink tuberoses from his neck and placed them over her head.

"Aloha."

"Aloha."

The blossoms felt warm from his body heat. She inhaled the mix of their perfume and his animal scent. He brushed his lips over hers in that sensuous way of his. A sharp pain stabbed her between the shoulders. She jumped back.

Ross tugged her toward him. "What's the matter?"

"Nothing, I'm just a little stiff after all that sitting." She felt a feathery lightness inside her back—delicate like the touch of shadow hand yanking out Lily's arrow—Sean's hand. A flush of euphoria shot through her. She was not alone.

They walked to the baggage claim. "We've made a lot of progress on The Thinking Woman campaign. I think you'll be happy with the first cut." She caught his glance. Would he say he missed her or, even better, he loved her? She flinched under the feeling of neediness—an uncomfortable and foreign feeling to her.

He grinned. "I heard you met with my father in Easthampton."

"Did you hear about the dining room table caper?"

"Anna e-mailed me. She wrote a hilarious account of Sean's antics."

"It wasn't funny at the time. Sean is a handful."

He hauled her bag from the conveyor belt. "I'm not sure I like the sound of that."

"I heard you had a Japanese lover."

"Not much is sacred."

"Come on, Ross, you're a creative guy. You can do avoidance better than that."

He steered her outside. "Maybe I have nothing to hide."

Her big soft spot for him oozed love. She kissed his cheek. He tossed her bag into the back of a Jeep, the heavy-duty kind like an army vehicle. They sped along a highway flanked with black lava. On one side, the Pacific rolled to shore in bands of sapphire and jade. On the other, the eerie black rock sprawled onto the luscious green slopes of a towering volcano.

"That's Hualalai. Can you feel the energy? The fire in the lava?"

Ross said.

"The fire? Isn't that long dead?"

"There's always fire."

She smiled, assuming he referred to them.

"This is my road." He swung the jeep onto a rough thoroughfare. They drove toward the sea through a seemingly endless landscape of black lava.

"I missed you," Sara said.

He touched her thigh. "Me you too."

The sun dropped to the other side of the world. The diamond in her bracelet glinted in the last light of day. Something rustled in the space between her and Ross. Sara closed her eyes and trickled her fingers through the air. She sensed the cold touch of ectoplasm. Her hand froze.

"Horny, huh?" Ross laughed.

"What?" She opened her eyes. Oh, God, her hand was hovering over his crotch. Sara slapped it onto her thigh. "Maybe."

Lily's voice echoed in her ear. "Ross belongs to me. Leave now."

No.

Sara crossed her arms over her chest, taking a firm stand against the ghost.

They drove between two stone posts into a richly planted area. Tall coconut palms lined the road. Giant tree ferns with fuzzy, curled fiddleheads and delicately feathered fronds spread as far as the eye could see. Yellow and white hibiscus bushes drooped over ponds afloat with lilies. Sara looked away from the lilies.

They passed a tennis court. "I guess you play well," she said.

"I'll play nice with you."

"Play your best or don't play at all."

He smiled. "You've got it." He pointed to a small house with a palm-thatched roof, hanging low over the windows. "My housekeeper, Makoa, lives there with her husband, Ali. He looks after the grounds." Ross swung the jeep to the right. "There's my house."

"Oh, it's beautiful." The sleek edifice snaked along the oceanfront, a soft blend of wood and glass—a home in perfect harmony with the landscape. She wondered if he'd built it but didn't ask. She didn't want the past to invade their time together.

Inside, they crossed a sea of blond wood floors. Massive steel-trimmed windows overlooked the ocean. Minimal furnishings in shades of ivory and white provided seating areas. Exotic plants wove in and out of the wide-open spaces.

Ross led her up a steel staircase. The master bedroom had floor-to-ceiling views of the island, a king-size bed and a minimum of teak wood furnishings. The volcano, the ocean and the rose-colored sky seemed to belong in the room.

Sara peered up a spiral staircase leading to another floor. A telescope looking like something from NASA aimed skyward.

"Your dressing room and bath are in here." Ross disappeared with her luggage through an oval portal.

Sara was about to follow him, but her eye fell to the bed. One pillow had been covered with pink hibiscus petals. She kicked off her shoes and sprawled on the white cotton bedspread, resting her head among the blossoms.

Ross returned. "Shall I let you rest?"

"No."

He stripped, then unzipped her cotton sheath dress and slid it off her. She roiled at the edges of rapture, partly frightened by how much he meant to her but at the same time, comforted by her feelings of love. A rustling sound like silk blowing in the wind ended her fervor. The competitor in Sara took over. She rolled Ross onto his back, mounted him and rode him like a crazed jockey, showing Lily who had the power.

After their love making, Ross fell asleep. Sara lay beside him, keyed up—on the lookout for Lily. The ghost remained silent, but

Sara sensed she would not be far away.

That night, they dined on a deck by the ocean. They ate grilled mahi mahi and polished off a bottle of Chablis. Sara wore a white-sequined halter-top and a silk-jersey skirt that flowed from her hips to her ankles, leaving her midriff bare.

"You're more beautiful than I remembered." Ross nuzzled her ear. "While I was in Tokyo, I thought of you every morning, the moment I woke up."

Ah, but who did you think about at night, before you went to sleep? The air above Sara began spinning.

"At night he thinks of me," Lily's girlish voice pulsed with pleasure. "He thinks of dying and spending all of eternity with me and never waking again to the thought of you."

Sara recalled her conversation with Anna about the mystic IsMara, about the way she fell asleep at night visualizing her death. She glanced at Ross, wondering if he actually did picture himself dying and saving Lily. He poured wine, obviously unaware of Lily's presence. Why could he hear her suffering in hell and not hear her now?

"Because he only sees and hears me when I want him to." Lily flapped around Sara, laughing.

Sara would not be intimidated by some homicidal teenager trapped in the dark planes. She stroked Ross's hair off his face. "I thought of you every night while you were away."

"Did we have sex?"

"Yes, and it was fantastic like it always is."

He bent over and ran his tongue over her bare abs.

Sara moaned with pleasure and upped a rude finger at Lily.

"You'll be sorry, Sara. I'll get you later when you're asleep." Lily sped off, leaving an unnatural draft in her wake.

Sara spotted Makoa, the housekeeper walking toward them. She carried a tray above her right shoulder, balancing it on the palm of her hand. Her body moved with the grace of flowing water. Her face wrinkled into soft laugh lines.

"Makoa's coming," Sara whispered to Ross, lifting his head off her stomach.

She blushed under Makoa's motherly gaze. "The fish was delicious."

"*Mahalo.*" The housekeeper bowed and cleared away their plates. "Pineapple crumble and homemade vanilla ice cream for dessert." Makoa placed the delectable looking dish on the table, beamed at them both and retreated back into the house.

They devoured generous portions of the crumble, and then Ross led Sara up to the observation deck above his bedroom. He swept the great telescope across the night sky, sharing the viewing lens with her. They gazed into the luminous stars of the Milky Way.

"Do you remember when you said yes to my being your healing man?"

"A-huh." Sara recalled the discomfort she'd felt.

"That yes is traveling among the stars. Can you see me receiving everything I need to give to you as your healing man?"

Sara pulled back from the viewing lens. "No. Can you?"

"No, but I'm sure it's coming to me." He grabbed the telescope, scanned the skies and talked about the galaxy and its three hundred billion stars and suns. They took turns staring at the gaseous lights shining back at them from millions of years in the past. Then they stared into the timeless wonder of each other's eyes and made love beneath the giant telescope.

They crept downstairs. Sara slept in Ross's arms. If Lily tried to contact her, she remained unaware. Perhaps, she was too entwined with Ross for the wily ghost to threaten her.

In the morning, they lounged over breakfast on the patio. After, they played tennis. Ross beat her in straight sets, but Sara dashed to the net at every chance and smashed several of his rocket-fast shots down the winning line. High from having played at the top of her game, she leaped onto his back and steered him to the grassy earth beneath the coconut palms. They rolled over and over, laughing, their sweaty bodies slipping and sliding in an orgy of smells.

They ate a light lunch of fresh tuna and salad greens, then snorkeled off the rocks in front of the house. Hand in hand, they glided through shoals of brightly colored fish, exploring the coral reefs. In the late afternoon, Ross gave her a massage on a table by the pool beneath a canopy. Panels of white netting surrounded them. He blended the essential oils of geranium and patchouli into a base of almond oil, plunged his hands into the mixture and kneaded her muscles. He lay naked on her back, his long legs resting on hers. A rush of heat whirled around her spine. He said it was the ying of him blending with the yang of her. She sensed the red-hot fire in the lava. She heard it gush and bubble as it gave birth to the land. The wind caressed her mind, whispering tales of times past and times future. She felt so complete, she could have died. They spent the next day doing more of the same. In the evening, Ross massaged her again by the pool, until Makoa stood outside their netted haven, saying dinner was ready.

Wrapped in white robes, they sat by the pool eating coconut crusted shrimp and drinking Muscadet. Later, they played chess on the patio. Sara won. Ross admired her skill. Sara appreciated that. Her last two boyfriends had sulked when they lost to her.

Their loving was tender that night, her last night. But after, as Sara lay beside Ross, the gates to reality swung open and the unsaid rushed at her from all angles.

"Ross."

"Yes."

"What did you mean when you said you would love me until death do us part, if that was what I wanted?"

"I'm yours, Sara, and I will be for as long as I'm here, but just as some people know they will live for a long time, I know I'll die young. Loving me means accepting that."

She propped her elbow on her pillow and gazed down at him. "How do you know you'll die young?"

"I can't turn my back on my promise to Lily. I couldn't live with myself. That's how I know."

"I'm sorry, but I still don't understand."

"A pact between lovers is the culmination of both their minds meeting on one ideal. That ideal forms its own life. It becomes their binding covenant and it must be met. What we have together is stolen. Accept that. *Please*."

He might as well have ripped her heart out with his bare hands. She flopped onto her pillow but quickly willed herself back into the fight. "I'm not religious, Ross, but every fiber of my being tells me it's wrong to take your own life."

Ross sat up bolt straight, his eyes wide with surprise. "I'm not planning to kill myself. I'll die because I'm meant to. I'm meant to find Lily and help her out of her suffering."

His belief in what he said was palpable. It emanated off him as heavy and hot as humid air. Sara looked away from him. Had Anna been right? Would Lily try to distract Ross as he piloted a small plane and pull him over to the other side? Sara heaved herself into a sitting position. "I'm about to ask you for something as my healing man."

"This isn't a good time for that."

"I doubt there's ever a good time for this sort of thing, Ross." Sara piled pillows behind her and leaned against them. "Here's my request. As my healing man, will you please give up flying in aerobatic competitions?"

"What!" Indignation burned in his eyes. "I'm committed to fly in a competition next Saturday."

"You're committed to being my healing man."

"What's this about? You can't control my life." His nostrils flared. His eyes went cold.

"So, being my healing man and saying yes to whatever I want, only applies if it's something you want to give me?"

He rolled a stormy gaze over her, doubly as thunderous as his father's after the sex-on-the-dining-room-table debacle. The competitor in her went into overdrive. She had made a pact with Sean, and by God, she would keep it.

"If dying to keep your suicide pact with Lily was the law of your relationship with her, then this healing man arrangement is the law of ours."

His eyes raked hers. He opened his mouth as if to speak but instead swung his legs off the bed and balled his hands into fists. "Don't do this to me, Sara."

"Don't do this to *you*? You roped me into this arrangement. You knew damn well I only agreed to it because I wanted your account."

He lunged off the bed and streaked up the spiral staircase—a man caught in a trap of his own making. The fight went out of Sara. She collapsed on her back. Perhaps Ross was meant to die young, and she should just let him. She tossed and rolled around in the big bed, then drifted into sleep. A grayish-blue light colored her dream world. Her skin prickled like an animal sensing an unnatural disturbance. The smoky light puffed into a cloud. A girl emerged from the vapors and stood at the foot of the bed. She had moon-white skin, light brown eyes and chestnut hair tied in a ponytail with a red ribbon. She flashed open her black silk kimono. Blood oozed from a network of small cuts on her thighs.

Sara screamed, but there was no sound to her voice. It stuck in the back of her throat.

"Ross belongs to me," Lily said. "Get out of his life, or I'll kill you."

Lily's threat sounded and resounded in Sara's head. She woke curled in a fetal position, drenched in sweat. She stumbled out of bed and paused at the foot of the stairway to the observation deck.

The events of last night came flying back. She steadied herself against the railing of the stairs, facing love lost.

She headed for the shower, dreading the day ahead. Drying off, she climbed into jeans and a T-shirt. She flung her clothes into her suitcase and went downstairs to the kitchen.

Makoa sliced pineapple and papayas. She smiled warmly at Sara. "No Mr. Ross this morning?"

"Not yet."

"He's never brought anyone here before. He's happy with you."

Sara smiled at the kind woman. "Do you think Ali could drive me to the airport? My luggage is by the front door."

"Of course, but first you must have some of my pecan pancakes with coconut syrup."

A sudden wave of nausea drove Sara from the kitchen and into a small bathroom in the hall. She bent over the toilet, wretched and threw up. Rummaging in the cabinets, she found mouthwash and rinsed the acid taste from her mouth. In the mirror, haunted eyes looked back at her. She headed for the front door.

Ali loaded her luggage into the jeep. Sara was about to climb in when Ross called to her. She turned. He stood beside a hibiscus bush, wearing a ragged shirt and swimming trunks. His arms hung limply at his sides. Dark pouches puffed beneath his eyes. The stubble of his beard glistened with sweat.

"Yes. I won't fly." He turned and strode away.

Sara longed to run after him, to gather him in her arms and hold him as she sometimes ached to be held—without words of good intent—just held. She watched him pick his way over the jagged rocks in front of his house. He stood on the end framed by an endless vista of sea and sky.

Makoa edged up to her. "Mr. Ross will be a wonderful father."

"What?"

"The morning sickness. You're pregnant."

"No. It's not that. Sorry."

Makoa beamed. "Yes. We island women know these things."

CHAPTER TWENTY

Makoa's prediction so disturbed Sara that even though she couldn't be pregnant, she would have no peace of mind until she took a test. On the way to the airport, she asked Ali to stop at the Four Season's Hotel for some last minute shopping. She found a pregnancy test kit at the general store, then spotted Sean's novel, *Love Interrupted.* She bought a copy.

This made her a little late for her plane, and after she checked through security, she had to run to the departure gate. A pretty, dark-haired flight attendant welcomed her on board and showed her to her seat. The flight was nonstop to Los Angeles. Only one other passenger sat in the small first class cabin—a man of about fifty with a sharp receding hairline. He lounged in a seat directly across the aisle from Sara, his head buried in what looked like a legal document.

Sara pulled Sean's novel from the shopping bag and transferred the pregnancy test kit to her purse. Now that she had it, her eagerness to use it vanished. She'd had a period after last sleeping with Dan, and Ross ... well, his vasectomy should eliminate the possibility. It must have been the mention of pecan pancakes and coconut syrup that made her nauseous. All that sugar first thing in the morning.

"Champagne?"

The pretty flight attendant lowered a tray of drinks in front of Sara. Her stomach did a somersault. Sara declined the drink, this time attributing the nausea to stress. She gazed at the cover of Sean's book. The plane plummeting to earth reminded her of the crash she'd seen through his telescope. A cold tremor shot through her.

"Juice or coffee?" A male flight attendant hovered over Sara.

"Nothing, thank you." A steaming towel dangled from a pair of tongs in front of Sara. She took it and laid it over her face, careful not to smudge her mascara.

Security announcements blared over the intercom. Engines roared. The plane sped down the runway. In a surge of power, the steel giant lifted off the ground and sailed into a slate blue sky. Sara wiped her hands with the warm towel and glanced out the window. She scoured the coastline of the Big Island, searching for the rich cluster of trees that marked Ross's property. Was he still standing on those rocks in front of his house? Did he hate her now? The plane leveled. The world went blue.

"Hooh, hooh, hooh." A rustle of silk swished past Sara's ear. "You'll cower at the thought of me after you've read Sean's book."

Go away, you little bitch.

"Chicken or salmon for dinner?"

Sara looked up at the smiling face of the pretty young woman. "I'm not hungry. I'm just going to read my book."

The woman sped off. Sara caught the glance of the man across the aisle and sensed he'd been watching her. She gave him an exaggerated smile, hoping to nullify any strange behavior she might have exhibited. She tapped the book. "I hear it's quite engrossing."

The man nodded. "My wife read it. She wept for days and then decided to become my healing woman." He shook his head and blew out a sigh as if totally confused.

"So that's not working for you?" Sara said.

"It's very time consuming to be wounded." The man returned to reading his document.

Sara empathized with him. Keeping Ross from Lily's clutches had become a demanding job. A swatch of black silk flashed before her, and a sense of doom dragged her down.

Get away from me.

Sara tightened her resolve not to live in fear of a ghost. If Lily had lived as Sylvia in her previous life, then the more Sara knew about Sylvia, the more prepared she would be to fight Lily and win.

She opened Sean's book.

Chapter One

I, Ed Harroway, was a rather ordinary man. I loved my family, and before the war, I aspired to little more than raising some children and working in the law practice I'd begun with my closest friend, Nicky Hart.

In combat, wing-over-wing with the enemy, or belly up beneath him, or in a nosedive black with the stench of death, I would meet my Maker with Elizabeth Sara on my mind. "Lord," I would say, "thank you for a wife so gentle and loving, and so beautiful in the morning when you shine the sun on her. Lord, look after her."

In duty to my country and with love in my heart, I assumed that should I die, the gates of heaven would open for me. That was until my Spitfire crashed into the fields of Germany. Until I did not die. Until I met Sylvia.

Sara lowered the book. She felt Elizabeth's spirit spring off the page like a spectacular burst of fireworks and fuse with her own. Her nerves twanged like the strings of a guitar in a tragic love song. Instinct told her to hold herself back a little from the story or she might lose sight of her battle against Lily. Sara crossed her legs, squeezing them together. She would maintain that posture until she finished the book.

She returned her attention to the novel. Sean's writing took her into the early lives of Elizabeth and Ed. Their parents had been close friends and lived next door to each other. Sara felt the fun Ed and Elizabeth shared as they learned to swim, ride bicycles and horses. A few years later, Sara's heart ached for Elizabeth as she ran along the platform of the train station, waving goodbye to Ed when he departed for boarding school. The great steam engine hissed and puffed smoke. Ed leaned out the window and tossed his school cap at Elizabeth. "Wait for me, E."

"Aaah!" Sara sniffled. Knowing what the future held for these innocent young people played havoc with her emotions. As she read about Ed's new friendship with the dashing Nicholas Hart, Sara all but shouted, stay away from each other! Nicky's father, a former RAF pilot from WWI, had already taught his son to fly. Ed longed to match his friend's accomplishments. Nicky invited Ed to his home in Somerset for the Easter Holidays. Ed accepted and dashed a note off to Elizabeth saying he would see her in the summer. When Nicky's father, a celebrated war ace, said, how about a go in the air, Edward? Ed's knees buckled with fear. Terror stayed with him, and as Ed took the stick for the first time, he threw up. Nicky's father tapped him on the shoulder "It's good to have that behind you, Edward. Now fly the plane."

Meanwhile, in nearby Sussex, Elizabeth locked herself in her room. At one moment, she hugged Ed's school cap to her heart and wept. In the next, she chucked it against the wall, drumming up ways to punish Nicky Hart for taking Ed away from her. A few chapters later, Sara swiped a wad of tissues from her purse and dabbed her eyes as Ed and Elizabeth met again. Both had turned fifteen, and they ran toward each other over the rolling green downs of Sussex, rain pelting against their cheeks, falling in love.

The pages flew by. Sara read about the outbreak of World War II and how Ed and Nicky joined the Royal Air Force. She kept thinking of Ed as Sean and Nicky as Ross, and her heart raced, then slowed, then leaped to the back of her throat with every turn of the story.

The scene changed to Germany, and Sylvia entered the story. Sara gritted her teeth, expecting to feel the cold rush of Lily's ghost. She heard nothing but the whir of jet engines.

Sylvia was the daughter of a high-ranking officer, a doctor in Hitler's SS forces, a man who performed atrocities on Jews in the concentration camps. Sylvia inherited her father's talent for medicine and earned her medical degree. Sara's skin crawled as Sean described her pale skin, long chestnut hair and upturned nose—the exact image of how Lily had looked when she threatened Sara in her dream last night. Sara squeezed her ankles together and read on.

After a fierce battle in the sky, Ed's plane crashed in a meadow close to Sylvia's home, just as Sylvia left her house for a walk. She ran to the aircraft and dragged Ed from the wreckage. Semiconscious, Ed talked about his love for his wife, Elizabeth. Sylvia, who had never been in love, envied this woman. Sylvia decided to win Ed for herself. Athletic and strong, Sylvia hauled Ed to an abandoned barn and told no one of his whereabouts. She stole medical supplies from her father's surgery and placed splints on Ed's badly broken legs. She kept him drugged and deliberately caused his dependence on painkillers and alcohol, all the while luring him away from Elizabeth.

Sara cringed as she read the intimate details of their sex life sprawled over dozens of pages. Soon Ed had become as hooked on Sylvia's erotic prowess as he had on the pills and booze. In his muddled mind, Ed thought he loved Sylvia and promised to divorce Elizabeth and marry her.

The next chapter switched back to England. Sara uncrossed and recrossed her legs. Nicky arrived at Elizabeth's cottage to tell her that Ed's plane had crashed in the fields outside of Hamburg. Nicky spoke of how Ed shot down three enemy bombers before he took the deadly hit that knocked him out of the skies. "He could be alive, Elizabeth. His body has not been recovered." Elizabeth wept. Then her old jealousy over Ed's friendship with Nicky raged in her breast. She pummeled her fists against Nicky's chest. "You took him from me. You made him a flyer. You killed him!" Nicky talked to her in a calm, soft voice. "Ed spoke about you all the time. Elizabeth, he adored you. He told me so many wonderful things about your childhood and your hopes for the future."

Elizabeth fell silent, remembering Ed's words of praise for his gallant friend. Both suddenly viewed each other through Ed's eyes, and the irresistible qualities he had seen in them held them spellbound. Nicky backed away from Elizabeth. "I'd better be going." Elizabeth flung her arms around his neck. "No. Please stay." She sought to kiss him. Nicky tried to resist. "Please don't do this, Elizabeth." Nicky held her at arm's length. "We must do the right thing. We both love Ed. We can walk away from whatever we feel for each other." Elizabeth laid her hand on Nicky's chest. "I can't. You see, in my heart, I feel Ed has left me." She looked up at Nicky. Passion ruled. They kissed, then tore off their clothes and …

"Phew!" The heat of the scene rose off the page and burned Sara's cheeks. She fanned her face and felt the man across the aisle looking at her. This book should be read behind a plain brown paper cover. Sara took a couple of deep breaths and returned to the story.

The war ended, and Sylvia arranged for Ed to return to England, having secured his promise that he would divorce Elizabeth and marry her. She stuffed Ed's pockets with painkillers and instructed him to take them on a regular basis, claiming he would not be able to bear the pain of walking without them. High on drugs and whiskey, Ed returned to his hometown. He hobbled up to the garden gate of the cottage he had lived in with Elizabeth, leaning heavily on two canes. Ed nearly fainted at the sight of a child crawling across the lawn—a baby that could not possibly be his. The little boy had Elizabeth's dimpled smile and the unmistakable cornflower blue eyes of his best friend, Nicky. Behind the baby, Nicky and Elizabeth gazed at each other, so engrossed in their love that they did not notice Ed.

Shock shot through Ed's addled brain, clearing his mind. He loved Elizabeth. He always had, and he always would. Little by little, he realized what Sylvia had done to him. He limped down the street, heartbroken and homeless. Lost in grief, he wrote a letter to Sylvia, expressing his anger and breaking off their relationship.

Sara turned the page. Ed moved into a cottage in a seaside village in Cornwall. He flushed his pain pills down the toilet but increased his intake of booze to numb his agony over Elizabeth. He lost his faith in God, and his journey into despair was hard to read. Sara sped through those chapters, but slowed down when the healing woman walked into Ed's life. Shrouded in a haze of golden light, the healing woman seemed so ethereal that Sara thought she must be a figment of Ed's imagination. Real or not, the golden-clad woman stood by Ed's side day in and day out. Under her loving guidance, Ed stopped drinking. Once sober, he discovered his love for Elizabeth and Nicky was greater than his sorrow. He hoped with all his heart they would be happy together. Thus, Ed transcended pain. The next morning, the healing woman walked out of his life and vanished into the light of the sun.

The story switched back to Sylvia in Germany. Sara heaved a breath, eager for her to get her comeuppance. Sylvia's father had fled to Argentina to avoid being captured and tried for his crimes against the Jews. Her mother, having found out about them, hung herself. Sylvia had just read Ed's letter breaking up with her when she found her mother's body.

Sara smacked her fist into the book. Now she felt sorry for Sylvia. If Sean kept that up, she wouldn't read anymore. She turned the page cautiously.

Sylvia arrived in England with a plan. She would kill Elizabeth, then Ed would want her back. The plotting for Elizabeth's murder-by-milk van raised the hairs at the back of Sara's neck, but she had already heard about this from Carlo during the awful evening at his Easthampton home, so it didn't hit her quite so hard.

Ed ached with sorrow when he learned Elizabeth had died. His first thoughts went to Nicky. Ed decided to visit his friend and try to help him through this painful time. Before Ed left Cornwall for Sussex, Sylvia turned up at his house and suggested they get back together. Ed slammed the door in her face. Of course, Ed had no idea Sylvia had murdered Elizabeth. Nor did he know that as Sylvia stood in the echo of the slammed door, she planned to punish Ed for rejecting her.

Sylvia stole into Nicky's house and shot him dead while he slept. His little son lay in the bed next to his dead father, howling. Sylvia bent over the child, aiming the gun at his heart.

"Oh no!" Sara covered her face with her hands and peeped

through her fingers at the page.

Sylvia pressed the gun to the baby's body, but then swung her arm up and shot her brains out. She fell on the child, and her blood ...

Oh, it was too horrific to read. Sara skipped a number of chapters and turned to the last page of the book. A new joy filled Ed's life.

He looked up at me, this little boy who bore my name, and smiled— Elizabeth's sweet dimpled smile. Sun lightened his deep blue eyes. I took his hand and thanked God for trusting me with the care of this child—this perfect combination of the two people I had loved most in the world.

Sara sunk her face into her hands and wept, mostly for the way Ed had loved Elizabeth, loved her so much that he'd wanted her to be happy, even with his best friend. She thought of the day when she had placed her hand in Sean's. She had known then that everyone else might desert her, but he never would. Dear God, why wasn't she in love with him instead of Ross?

She heaved up sob after sob, until a flash of black silk spun across her vision.

"Hooh, hooh, hooh. Do you still think you're going to get the better of me?"

The breath went out of Sara—the courage too. She sat speechless.

The ghost swooped by Sara's ear. "Now you know murder comes easy to me, so get out of Ross's life."

Sara clutched the arms of her seat. Her spine tingled with fear.

"That's better." With a rustle of silk, Lily vanished.

No, I'm not afraid of you. You're just a ghost.

Sara's stomach cramped. She clutched her purse with the pregnancy kit. The captain announced they were beginning their descent into Los Angeles airport. Sara headed for the bathroom, snatching a plastic cup from the service station on the way.

In the small lavatory, she peed in the cup and ripped open the test kit. There were two windows on the little stick: one marked PREGNANT and the other NOT PREGNANT. Sara lowered the felt part of the stick in the urine and laid it flat on the counter.

Someone knocked on the door. "Ms. Jensen, you must return to your seat."

"I'll be right there."

The second hand of her watch inched toward the minute mark. A heavier hand banged on the door, and a man's voice ordered her back to her seat.

Sara gripped the washbasin and stared at the stick.

CHAPTER TWENTY-ONE

"You're swerving all over the place!" Vicki gripped the dashboard. "Slow down."

Sara guided the car out of the Midtown Tunnel, through the prepaid tollbooth, and then floored the accelerator.

"Get over to the right!" Vicki waved her arm. "We're going to Brooklyn."

Sara cut across a couple of lanes, barely missing a car.

"What the hell's the matter with you?" Vicki asked. "You're driving like a fucking maniac!"

Sara almost laughed. What was the matter? Her pregnancy test had been positive and not just the test she taken on the plane. She'd taken two more since returning home.

"So what's up?" Vicki demanded. "Did you break up with

Ross?"

"What! No, everything's fine." Sara's life might be wobbling close to disaster, but the only person she wanted to discuss it with was Sean. His answering service said he was out of town, and they didn't know where. He did not own a cell phone. Life without a cell phone. What freedom.

Vicki flipped through the script for the Lumina commercial. "This is good. What the hell is Carlo doing poking his nose into the shoot? I knew I should never have allowed your fag friend to direct something this big."

"Carlo turning up on the set isn't Brad's fault. And *you* didn't allow him to direct the spot. Ross made that choice."

"You think he would have if you weren't screwing him?"

Sara controlled the urge to tell Vicki to get off her case. That would only fire up her interest in Ross. "Don't we get off the expressway soon?"

"Next exit."

It came up quickly, and Sara eased the Audi onto a two-lane road and filtered into traffic behind a huge semi-trailer. She swung out a little to see if she could overtake it.

"Get back in." Vicki wiped her brow. "It's bumper-to-bumper traffic."

"Oh, I don't know. I see a break—"

"Stop the fucking car. I want to drive."

"No way. You insisted on coming to the studio. I could handle this situation with Carlo a whole lot better without you bitching at me."

"I've got plenty to bitch about. You've been zoned out since you got back from your trip. I'm up to my ass talking with prospective clients and hiring people. This is no time for you to flake out."

Sara drummed her fingers against the wheel. "I'm sorry. I've been distracted. It's just ... well—"

"It's Ross, right? Which one of you wants more than the other is willing to give?"

"Vicki, we've got a serious problem with Carlo. Don't you think we should be talking about that?"

Vicki folded her arms. "Here's what I learned about Carlo and Ross during my week at Lumina. When Carlo ran the Studio, everything was about creative talent. No episode of *The Purpose* ever came in on budget. Carlo's movies ran way over projected costs. Ross, perhaps in an effort to differentiate himself from Carlo, is all about the bottom line. Everything comes in on time and on budget. Profits are up. The product is still good but not brilliant. So here we are under Ross's regime. As Executive Producer of our first commercial for Lumina, it's up to you to get Carlo the hell off the set before he turns a sixty-second spot into a fucking movie, and Ross fires us for running over the budget."

She slid the script into her briefcase. "If you're breaking up with Ross, this would be a good time to let Carlo know. It'll make him happy. Maybe get him off our backs."

Sara gripped the wheel at twelve o'clock, dizzy at the mention of breaking up with Ross. She followed Vicki's direction and turned right at the next street, dreading the thought of telling him about the baby. Her gut twisted into a pretzel. Sleet pelted against the windshield. Sara switched the wipers on. They swept back and forth, streaking grime across the glass. She drove down a road lined with dismal buildings. Car parts littered a lot beside Fred's Body Shop. Sara spotted a gray limo parked halfway down the street— Carlo's, no doubt. The driver's head hid behind a newspaper. Sara parked in the delivery entrance of the film studio.

"What's you're plan?" Vicki asked.

Sara glanced at the red brick building. "Go in and get the lay of the land."

"I just gave it to you."

Sara got out of the car. A wave of nausea worked its way up from her belly. She shoved the door to the building open and sidestepped into a cloakroom area. Digging in her shoulder bag, she found a packet of crackers and gobbled one down, hiding her mouth behind the palm of her hand.

"What the hell are you doing?"

Vicki looked at Sara as if she belonged in an asylum. Sara shrugged. "I'm hungry."

"How can you think of food at a time like this?"

"Sometimes it's the little ordinary things that keep you calm. Want one?" Sara held out the packet of crackers.

Vicki snatched them and tossed them into a trashcan. "Start thinking on your feet, Sara."

Sara shivered. It was nearly as cold inside the building as out. Her stomach felt queasy. She edged up to a wall that divided the cloakroom from the cavernous studio space, hoping the cracker would settle things.

Gray light struggled through windows covered with wire mesh. A group had gathered at the far end of the studio. They sat on wooden crates among cameras and arc lamps, gazing at a man who stood in their midst—Carlo DeLuca—grandfather to the speck of life growing inside her.

She felt Vicki's fist lodge in the small of her back, shoving her forward. They walked side by side toward the set. Sara imagined herself telling Carlo about Ross and Lily and their suicide pact. She would say, I'm the best shot you've got at keeping your son alive. I'm pregnant with his child, as your wife wanted me to be. As your wife said would be the one way to keep Ross from dying to rescue Lily from hell. She imagined Carlo's eyes drenched with remorse for having treated her so badly. Vicki jabbed her in the side, breaking up her Carlo fantasy.

"Have you got your act together?"

"Um." Sara's gaze went to Brad. Her friend perched on the edge of a crate, his slight body bent forward. An enraptured smile wavered over his hawkish features. Gone was the haunted look that had scarred his face since the death of his beloved partner, Ian.

Sara glanced at Candy McClarren, the actor who'd won The Thinking Woman role. Candy sat next to Brad, her elbows on her knees, and her face cupped in her hands, obviously mesmerized by Carlo.

Carlo's gaze wandered to Sara. He waved. Her stomach cramped. Bile hit the back of her throat. She forced the sour liquid down and fished a bottle of water from her bag.

"What are you doing?" Vicki asked. "Carlo and Brad are heading our way."

Sara downed the water and jammed the bottle back in her bag. Vicki stared at her, her eyes bulging with horror.

"You don't know what to do, do you?"

Cold terror licked at the base of Sara's spine. She conjured a smile. She was a Hitchcock Blonde. Didn't they triumph in the end? She clenched the winning fist, the thrill of adventure tickling behind her ribs. The gap between her and Vicki, and Carlo and Brad closed. Sara felt like a cowboy bound for a shoot-out, a cowboy without a gun. They all met near the middle of the room.

Carlo draped an arm over Brad's shoulder. "Whoever picked this man to direct this shoot is a genius. He's going to make the best commercial Lumina's ever had." The filmmaker smiled at Sara. "Great tan. Been in the sun?"

Sara nodded. "How are Anna and the babies?"

"Terrific … the twins are getting cuter by the moment."

Sara exchanged extravagant kisses on the cheek with Brad, while Carlo and Vicki pretended to be delighted to meet again.

Sara turned to Carlo, thinking of a polite way to ask him why he was here. "Is there a problem with the spot? The script Brad is shooting was approved by Ross."

"Yeah, well … I'll let Brad explain." Carlo spun around and sauntered back to the set.

"Isn't he divine?" Brad swished his ponytail. "He's just told us the mythology behind *The Purpose*. He's so deep. I'd like to jump into him and never come up."

"And I'd like you to shoot the script that's been approved by the client and stick to the budget," Vicki said.

Brad looked confused. "But Carlo *is* the client, isn't he?"

Sara nodded. "What's going on? Does Carlo want to change things?"

"He's been talking for a couple of hours—"

"Jesus." Vicki whipped a calculator out of her purse. "That's two hours more studio time, plus the actors, plus—"

"It's time well spent," Brad said. "Carlo has instilled the actors with the meaning of *The Purpose*, and that's important because—"

"This is a commercial, not an art film," Vicki said.

"Lumina is not an ordinary client," Brad said. "Carlo is one of the greatest moviemakers of our time. I can't ignore his ideas."

"Of course, you can't." Sara drew Brad away from Vicki, while she punched figures into her calculator. Sara hadn't told Brad of her affair with Ross. Brad loved gossip, and she didn't want to burden him with keeping a secret like that while he worked on the Lumina commercial.

"Brad, you know we answer to Carlo's son, Ross. We can't change the script, and we absolutely can't go over the budget."

"Sara, my angel, you're all caught up in the box." He formed a small square with his fingers and peered through it. "The inky-dinky, teeny-weeny, itty-bitty money box. What are you doing in there, my darling? It's so not you."

The events of the last few weeks spun through Sara's mind. She had been so distracted by Ross and his Lily-baggage that she'd lost touch with that central core of herself—the place where she would have known, out of respect, to consult with Carlo over the script before the agency ever sent it to Ross. How could she have been so stupid?

The filmmaker strode toward her. Stress tightened about Sara like a straightjacket. She asked Brad what Carlo had in mind, but before he could answer, Carlo was back.

"We need our director now." Carlo slapped a hand on Brad's shoulder.

Sara decided to stay and judge the situation firsthand. To be polite, she asked Carlo if he minded.

Carlo stroked his chin. "Candy's a hair's breadth away from a fantastic performance, and we've bonded as a group. Things will go better if it's just us. You understand, don't you, honey?"

His patronizing tone infuriated Sara. She fought the urge to argue with him. Vicki grabbed her by the arm. "Excuse us, Carlo. We have another meeting."

Vicki catapulted Sara out of the building. "I just spoke with Ross. He knew Carlo was here. It looks like they're edging us out of the picture."

Sara leaned against her car. Her stomach fluttered. "What else did Ross say?"

Vicki didn't answer. She probably didn't hear the question. She took off on a tirade. If they lost the Lumina account they might lose the other top-notch clients coming their way. And, of course, it was all Sara's fault.

CHAPTER TWENTY-TWO

Sara sat at the desk in her living room, readying herself to call Ross. She glanced at her computer and clicked on a website about the development of a baby.

For the first six weeks, the baby is called an embryo. The heart, lungs and brain are beginning to develop. The tiny heart starts beating by the twenty-fifth day. In the second month, the embryo becomes a fetus, which means 'young one.' Tiny arms and legs start to form. The head seems very large in comparison to the rest of the body because the brain is growing so fast.

She let out a slow sigh, releasing her anxiety about how Ross might react to the news of impending fatherhood. The phone rang. Sean's name appeared in the ID box. Sara pressed the instrument against her ear, got up from her desk and sank onto the sofa. "Sean." The force of her emotions filled his name. "Oh, God, Sean where have you been?"

"Why? What's the matter?"

"Everything."

"Is that all?" The author's voice rose with amusement. "Has something happened to Ross?"

"No. Ross is okay … at least as far as I know." Sara cuddled a small pillow against her heart. "I've been trying to reach you for days." She told him what had happened in Hawaii, how she'd asked Ross as her healing man to give up stunt flying and his reaction to that. Her mind jumped all over the place. She rambled on about reading *Love Interrupted* on the plane and about Carlo and her business problems. "And … I … I'm pregnant."

"Aaaah." Sean dragged the little word up and down the scale. "By Ross?"

"Yes and … well … I promised not to tell anyone, but …" She swept her hair off her face. She'd made a pact with Sean to keep Ross alive, so she would hide nothing from him. "Ross has had a vasectomy."

"I'm not surprised. In my novel, *David and Danielle*, the characters wrote into their suicide pact that if one of them should survive their attempt to kill themselves, they would never marry and never have children. To make sure they could not, they would have themselves sterilized. Ross would follow that rule."

"So, how am I pregnant?"

"Vasectomies have been known to fail, about one percent, I

believe. If all the powers of the universe are working for a child to be born, a guy might find himself among those unlucky few. Did you ever ask Ross, as your healing man, to give you a baby?"

"Never, but Anna wanted me to. She's convinced that having a child of his own would be the one thing that would keep Ross from dying to rescue Lily."

"Ah, Anna, she's got a powerful mind. Subconsciously, you probably agreed with her, and once you accepted Ross as your healing man, the universe began listening to what was said in your heart. Perhaps you said something in the height of passion."

The height of passion?

Sara's mind zeroed in on the last time Ross had played *I'll Be Seeing you,* and what she couldn't remember before, she did now. She heard Elizabeth's voice clear as the first light of dawn.

Nicky, darling, please give me a child. If I lost you, it's the only way I'd be able to go on.

Sara snapped her fingers. That's it! Ross must have experienced himself as Nicky, and for some reason, wanted to hide it from her.

"Have you remembered something?" Sean asked.

Sara told him everything about that evening with Ross. "But it wasn't me asking Ross for a child, it was Elizabeth asking Nicky."

"Yours is the heart that beats, Sara. Anna was right, and you knew it. It's great news. You've found a way to keep your end of our pact."

"But I don't want another child, and Ross—"

"Sara, when you accepted Ross as your healing man, you automatically became his healing woman. This service is indivisible between those who love each other. The baby is the universe saying yes to your quest to keep Ross alive."

"You should have explained that to me before." Sara was surprised by the anger in her voice. "I'm sorry. I didn't mean that, Sean. I wanted the Lumina account, and I blinded myself to caution."

"I've done a lot worse in my life."

Sara laughed. "You'll have to tell me about that sometime."

"I just did. I went to Bermuda for a few days, and I wrote you a letter from there. I told you about the most awful thing I've ever done."

"In a letter? Why?"

"Because I'm afraid to tell you in person."

"Oh, Sean, there's nothing—"

"I have to go, Sara. Dan's here in Telluride. We're beginning construction on the solarium. I'll be in New York next Friday. Can you have dinner then?"

"Yes."

Sara hung up. Still basking in the security of her friendship with Sean, she called Ross.

"This is Ross," he answered in a cool voice.

The calm went out of Sara. In the background, she heard the whiz of traffic and wondered if Ross leaned slightly forward, gripping the steering wheel of his car, the way he did when he thought of Lily. "When were you going to tell me about Carlo taking over the shoot?"

"Here's the deal. Sara. We'll work with your agency for the next year and run the campaign you've planned. Meanwhile, we'll be gearing up to handle our own advertising. We'll keep it quiet and make no public announcements until the last minute. That's fair … more than fair."

"You're dumping our agency because of a rift in our personal relationship, and you call that fair?"

"I don't want to hurt your business. We'll boost your image in the press, and I'll handle our separation announcement with kid gloves."

Her heart crashed to her gut. "And what about us, me? What kind of gloves are you going to wear to handle me?"

"I told you when we first met, that I want to be accepted for who I am. I told you about Lily because I thought you could understand her suffering and my need to keep my promise to her, but you can't."

"No, it's selfish. You're at the top of your field. You have power. You could make a difference in the lives of so many."

"I have a prior commitment."

"What about your commitment to the universe to be my healing man?"

"I'm asking you to release me from that."

"I'm pregnant."

She heard the screech of tires and a hoarse gasping sound like someone releasing a last painful breath. "Ross, are you all right?" She pictured him spinning off the highway. "Ross, say something."

He spoke in a harsh voice. "You know it can't be mine."

Her body hurt as if run over by a steamroller. A barrage of bitter accusations whirled into her mind. She recalled Carlo speaking of how Ross had dealt with his Japanese girlfriend, the one who had slapped him with a paternity suit. "Okay, Ross. Let's just wait until the kid's born and let DNA prove you are the father."

"I can't be a father." Ross's voice cracked with emotion.

"Why not?"

"Look, I'll take care of everything. I'll go with you for an abortion, and I'll look after you. We'll go to Hawaii after. We'll—"

"Why all that, if the child can't be yours?"

"I still love you, Sara. I just can't be the man you want. I know you don't want another child. You said so."

Sara shook her head and closed her eyes. His voice gained momentum as if he were writing a script and had stumbled onto a good plot. A tear slid down her cheek as he painted himself into a sterling character, a man who didn't care who the father was—a man who would be there for her just because he cared so deeply about her—a man she didn't recognize anymore.

Whatever doubts she had that Ross fathered the child disappeared. "Ross, here's the deal. I'm going to have this baby. If you want to be a part of your child's life, the door is open. If you don't, have a nice death."

CHAPTER TWENTY-THREE

Lily's ghost slithered out of a smoky blue light and pranced around Sara's bed. "You'll love dying." She flapped the sleeves of her black kimono. "Falling, falling, falling. Hooh, hooh, hooh. I took Red Devils and Blue Heavens and downed them with hundred proof vodka … Russian … ice cold. Hooh. Hooh. Falling, falling, falling … plummet … dash … glide, then whoosh, I entered the hell of my dreams."

The girl hovered over Sara like a hideous bird of sacrifice. Blood dripped from her scars. She sneered. "You think getting Ross to give up flying was clever? Well, I'll show you who's in charge. I'll snatch your old friend Sean. Yes, I'll snatch him right out of the sky. Hooh, hooh."

Sara lunged at the ghost's neck, but Lily darted beneath her arm, laughing.

"Sean!" Sara shouted.

The sky turned into a huge hand of light that crunched down over the ghost and tossed her into the distance.

Beep … beep … beep … beep.

Half asleep, Sara hit the off button on her alarm clock. Consciousness flooded back. Her body went limp with relief, but she quickly tensed up again. In her dream, Lily had threatened to hurt Sean. Sara sat on the edge of her bed. She should call Sean and tell him about it. She'd have to wait a while. It was 4 a.m. in Colorado.

Sara hauled on sweats and headed out for her morning jog.

Zoey sauntered into Sara's office, wearing a purple leather jacket embroidered with the lightning zigzags of *The Purpose*. "I've made the new arrangements for the Lumina shoot. Brad and the cast are booked on a flight to L.A. tomorrow. Here's the revised script." She placed it on Sara's desk.

"Thanks." Sara ignored the bundle of papers. Brad had told her Carlo just wanted to add some computer-generated fantasy shots such as they used in the TV show. They would film those at the Studio in L.A.

"You've got a three o'clock appointment with Pierre Montague. He's staying uptown at The Four Seasons." Zoey slapped a file in front of Sara. "The info you requested on his two previous fragrances for men and women."

"Thanks, Zoey."

"Are you feeling sick?" Zoey scowled.

"No. Why?"

"You're clutching your stomach."

Sara glanced at her hands. "Oh! I'm feeling bloated. I need to get to the gym." Her gaze froze on the light blinking on her phone, indicating an incoming call on her private line. She gestured for Zoey to answer the call.

"Sara Jensen's office." Zoey smiled. "Oh, hi." She lowered her voice to a sexy whisper. "This is Zoey. How are you?"

Her grin faded, and disappointment clouded her eyes. Hurt feelings palpitated off her.

Sara snatched the phone and covered the mouthpiece with her hand. "Ross is probably just in a bad mood. Don't pay any attention—"

"I don't need your sympathy." Zoey bustled from the office.

Sara pressed the phone to her ear. "Never speak unkindly to my assistant again."

"You're not answering my calls, Sara."

"What is there to say?"

"Did you see the piece in *The Post*?"

Sara glanced at the newspaper on her desk. *Page Six* quoted Carlo:

"Thinking Woman campaign is brilliantly funny, slightly tragic and full of hope. I'm awed by the creative genius of our ad agency, Hoffman Mills Jensen. Also of Brad Reese, who directed our first commercial."

"I saw it. Nice gloves."

"That's just the beginning. I'll help you build the media conglomerate of your dreams. I've worked out a business plan for you. In a couple of years, you could be flying high. Work with me, Sara."

Kill his child, and he would make her rich. Was he worth saving?

"I'll be in town on Friday. I'll show you the plan over dinner."

"I'm busy for dinner on Friday."

"Don't do this, Sara."

"What, don't see my friends?"

"Until Friday."

The phone went dead. Her neck hairs stood on end, but she had no time to ruminate on the icy tone in Ross's voice. Vicki rushed in, waving *The Post*.

Vicki flung the newspaper on Sara's desk and plunged into a chair. "This sudden praise from Carlo smells like the big kiss-off. What's going on?"

Sara met her fierce gaze. "I'm sorry."

"About what?"

"We'll talk about it later, Vicki. I've got to get uptown for a meeting."

"The future of the agency is at stake. I want to know what's going on, and I want to know now."

Sara folded her arms across her chest. "In a year, Lumina is planning to handle their own advertising. Meanwhile, they know we're lining up new clients, so they're going to keep it quiet and say nice things about us."

Vicki scowled. Sara could almost hear the cogs of her brain turning. "This is the result of your affair with Ross. I told you, he's infamous for skipping out of relationships. What happened? Tell me. Maybe we can turn things around."

"I'm pregnant."

Vicki sucked in a noisy breath. "You're pregnant!"

She glared at Sara as if grasping for the meaning of that. Sara waited for a derogatory onslaught on her character, accusations of stupidity or delusions of romantic wanderings, but Vicki cut to the chase.

"What does Ross want?"

"He wants me to have an abortion. I'm having the baby."

Vicki flew out of her chair, paced across the room and back again. "Do I know you?" She rammed her fist on Sara's desk. "Have you got religion or something?"

Sara remained silent, unflinching beneath Vicki's blazing eyes.

Vicki leaned over Sara's desk. "Do you remember when you were certain that on sight of his baby, Jack McBride would sober up and get a job?"

"I was eighteen."

"And you're none the wiser now, are you?"

Sara swayed back in her chair, distancing herself from the angry woman.

"I think I've got the picture." Vicki stood up straight. "If you do as Ross wants and have an abortion, Lumina remains here. If you have the baby, Ross will destroy us. That's it, isn't it?"

"Oh, come on, Ross isn't a vindictive person." Sara tried to convince herself of that.

"Ross is a tough negotiator, Sara. If he says he doesn't want a kid, believe him. He's probably terrified of perpetuating the misery of his own childhood. He grew up in the gory spotlight of Carlo's affair with that movie actress … the one who died. Ross is fucked up. He's broken lots of hearts. Are you going to let him break yours and destroy the agency?"

"You're being overly dramatic, Vicki. Losing Lumina won't destroy us. Handling their own advertising is a natural for them, but it isn't for any of our existing clients, or for those considering our agency."

Vicki grimaced. "Personally, Carlo annoys the fuck out of me, but he's a survivor, a legend, a hero. His quote about us in today's *Post* is priceless. A retraction would be devastating."

Sara looked away from Vicki. She couldn't refute that.

"Are you one hundred percent sure the baby is Ross's?"

"Yes. He'll be here on Friday. We'll have a face-off then."

"Think carefully about this, Sara. If you don't do what Ross wants, we'll have to do what's best for the agency."

"What's that?"

"We'll jump the gun on Ross. We'll leak it to the press that you're pregnant with his child, then—"

"No, we won't."

"Yes, we will. The media will leap all over the story and relate things back to Carlo and the movie goddess, Ilana. Remember, Ilana was pregnant with Carlo's child when she died speeding out of his estate. A good rehashing of that story always sells." Vicki licked her lips. "I know just where to place it, and this time the tabloids will have a father-son angle to play with. Ross will be exposed for the shit he is, the same shit Carlo used to be. They'll be the big bad powerful men, and you'll be the woman they done wrong."

"That's a terrible idea, Vicki. It will backfire and cause you more grief than—"

"Fuck grief. I'm talking survival. I'll deal with Ross on his level, down and dirty."

The white-hot heat of vengeance radiated off Vicki. There would be no reasoning with her. The agency was her baby. If Ross attacked it, she would come in for the kill.

CHAPTER TWENTY-FOUR

Pierre Montague stroked his manicured fingers through his mane of thin, white hair. "You must come to Paris for the launch of Monty, my darling Sara. You must meet everyone I know. I will be in love with you for your entire visit and insanely jealous of every man who tries to steal you from me." He took a step back. "*Oui.* You are perfect for my clothes. You will come in April, yes?"

Sara laughed off the Frenchman's invitation and sucked in her stomach. By April, she would be far from perfect for haute couture, but flirting with the fashion icon boosted her mood. She left Pierre's suite, thinking about the early giants of the ad industry, entrepreneurs like Albert Lasker, Ray Rubicam, Leo Burnett—men who founded some of the greatest agencies. Men who regularly met with the presidents of the companies they represented. Men who wielded power with integrity. She floated over the cool marble lobby of The Four Season's hotel. She had made it. A successful entrepreneur. No more mid-level management meetings for her.

Sara walked home, swinging her briefcase. She picked up her mail in the lobby of her building and dumped it on the sumo table in her living room. She checked her phone messages.

The first came from Anna. She had traveled to London with Carlo where he would cast *Love Interrupted.* "Call me anytime, Sara. No one answers my cell but me."

Sara would like to call her now, but she wasn't ready to tell Anna about the baby. Sometimes, in order to fall asleep at night, Sara pretended she had never met Anna, never heard her say that having a child with Ross would prevent him from dying. Sara would be just another woman who got pregnant by accident with the wrong guy. Not having the baby would be a choice.

The next three messages came from Vicki and contained a series of ongoing assaults on Sara's sanity. She ended by leaving the number of her psychiatrist. "Call him, Sara, you're losing it."

As if Vicki could possibly be the poster girl for mental health!

A sudden craving for black olives drove Sara toward the kitchen. Passing the sumo table, she spotted the blue and red stripes of an airmail envelope. Sean! Oh God, she had forgotten to call him and tell him about her dream of Lily threatening his life. She ripped the envelope open.

Dear Sara,

I'm relaxing for a few days in Bermuda, writing to you from a terrace overlooking a pink sandy beach. The sky is cloudless and powder blue. The ocean laps to shore in shimmering shades of turquoise. I glance to the horizon and imagine these waters rolling north and pounding onto the beaches of Long Island. Now you come to mind, as you were that morning when I saw you in your cottage in Wainscott with Ross. There was ice on the windows and the flush of love on your cheeks. Echoes from my lifetime as Ed Harroway tormented me. I loved you all over again. With this admission, I offer jealousy as an excuse for my often despicable behavior.

Forgive me. Please.

I feel an urgency to say this and some other things to you. For what reason I do not know, but the need will not be silenced. Perhaps I am about to lose consciousness of times past. I believe ancient memories are a gift coming forward to clear something in the present, and I must not miss their meaning. If you will listen to my thoughts on this, I will remain forever quiet on the matter—unless you should speak of it first.

I once told you if there was one thing in my life I could change, it would be to have never written David and Danielle. *That's not true. What I would change is what I did to get it published.*

David and Danielle *was my first novel. As a child, death and its rituals fascinated me. Growing up Catholic in Ireland among a preponderance of relatives, someone was always near death. I would creep up on the dying person and say, what's it like? Alas, I always got a clout about the ears from some aunt or uncle before I was answered.*

In my teens, my fascination switched to suicide. Since I could not kill myself and live to know what happened, I decided to explore that journey as a writer. The moment I took pen to hand, a young female voice began whispering in my head, and David and Danielle sprang to life.

The novel was turned down by numerous publishers. Finally, a small London house accepted it on one condition: I remove the final chapter—After Death. *In that, David and Danielle battled a terrible ride out of their earthly bodies and landed by the River of Never Ending Sorrow, which is an artery of grief in the dark planes of Hell. Their ankles were locked to an iron ring at the river bank. The waters of the river flowed with the tears of all who had loved a person who had taken their own life—every one since the beginning of time. The only sound was their grief. The only light that ever touched the land was that of souls flurrying from heaven to earth on their way into life. These looked liked snowflakes, swirling patterns of radiant light, each exquisite, each unique.*

The souls awakened remorse in David and Danielle and they began praying for forgiveness. One day, as their tears rolled into the river, sorrow went silent and the darkness turned inside out and the land lit up. Golden beings, tall as eternity itself, encircled the teenagers. They unshackled David and Danielle and offered them another chance at life. The beings warned them that suicide could become a habit, one they must not allow to develop. In their new lives, they would face similar circumstances as in their past lives—perhaps suffer even greater difficulties. They must overcome them and live until they died a natural death.

I concluded the novel with David and Danielle flurrying to Earth, radiant and beautiful among a great cascade of souls. That night, I had a vivid dream in which a golden being appeared to me. Its huge eyes were soft and mesmerizing. My heart flooded with love. The being pointed a finger in front of me and a scene opened magically. I saw a newborn child. The golden being said she had been called Sylvia in her previous life, but this time her name would be Lily.

"Lily will find your book," the golden being said. "Be careful to keep the story exactly as you wrote it or she will be influenced to follow the suicide pact of David and Danielle."

Ah, Sara, I was my family's only hope for a better life. The advance I received wasn't much, but it was a fortune to us. I could write a heart-rending paragraph about the conditions in which we lived. Truth is, no member of my family would have died without that money. Truth is, I hungered for fame and fortune.

I put up a fight for keeping the last chapter, but the publisher stood his ground, saying it removed the punch from David and Danielle's deaths. I took a couple of belts of whiskey and convinced myself my dream of the golden being was just a figment of my imagination living on in my unconscious. I deleted the chapter.

Quite unexpectedly, the book climbed to the top of the bestseller list. I consumed increasing amounts of booze, trying to blot out the memory of the golden being. I never did. I waited in agony for the day when I would hear about a girl named Lily who committed suicide.

When I met Ross and saw his scar—the exact same scar that my character, Danielle carved above David's brow, I knew the prophecy of the golden being had come true. Then Lily began haunting my dreams, telling me Ross must die and be with her as David had died to be with Danielle. I felt helpless in my plight to save Ross, until the night I opened the door of my apartment, and there you stood. I knew at once that you had been Elizabeth. Our past lives were glaringly alive in the present. I knew you would fall in love with Ross, just as you had in your last life when he was Nicky. I also knew you would do everything in your power to save Ross from Lily. I should have told you of the trade I made for success before I asked you enter into a pact with me. I didn't, because I was afraid you would hate me.

Forgive me for this, too, if you can.

Now I've drawn you into a terribly complex situation, but tilt the lens of your perception a little and consider this: a man as extravagantly blessed as Ross, who would toss it all aside to stand by a commitment he made when he was sixteen, is noble beyond any man of my acquaintance or hero of my creation. His belief that in death he will find Lily and guide her out of the dark planes is a magnificent call to love. Imagine a life shared with a man who would love you that way. Elizabeth did. Nicholas Hart had the dearest, most beautiful soul God ever implanted in a man. I've glimpsed those qualities in Ross. If you could love him through his heartbrokenness, I believe he would discover that loving you is a cause more worthy than dying for Lily. Then what a partner for life you would have.

I wish that for you, Sara, and I am here to help you in any way I can.

The words have run out. My inner sea is calm. I hope my well-being has not come at the expense of yours.

I am yours with love.

Always,

Sean

Sara handled the letter as she would a priceless, sacred document. As long as she could read Sean's words, she would not want for love, nor feel alone. She pressed the paper against her heart, awed by the immensity of her feelings for Sean and baffled as to why they did not translate into romantic love. No matter how hard she tried, she could not picture them as a couple. She lifted the phone to call Sean, but her stomach gurgled. The need for food drove her into the kitchen.

Sara fished a small container of oil-cured olives from the fridge and a wedge of fresh French feta. The soft-textured cheese and the salty, sun-drenched olives melded in her mouth. She polished them off, leaning against the sink and moaning with pleasure. She craved something sweet and rummaged a carton of chocolate fudge ice cream from the freezer. It was about a quarter full and crusted over with ice. Sara zapped it in the microwave and ate it, scraping the sides of the carton with her spoon, vowing to run an extra mile in the morning.

She plodded back to her desk to call Sean. The phone rang— Brad, calling from L.A.

"Sara darling, is this a good time for me to fill you in on

everything?"

Everything with Brad meant exactly that. Sara almost said she would call him back, but she needed to know how things were going with him. "Yes, it's fine."

Sara sat back and listened to Brad rave about life on the West Coast. "What about the commercial?" She interrupted him as he began a report on L.A. fashion. "Did you get the shots Carlo wanted?"

"Yes, and he loves them." Brad chatted on, outlining every aspect of the shoot. "It's fantastic working at the Studio … everyone is so creative." He gushed over a flurry of Studio gossip. "Darling," he lowered his voice. "Of course, Ross is rumored to be having an affair with every gorgeous young star on the lot, but I've also heard your name linked with his."

Sara laughed as if that were too ridiculous for comment. She longed to confide in Brad as she usually did but remained steadfast in her decision to spare him the responsibility of such a secret.

"I'm tired." She yawned into the phone. "I've got to go to bed."

"Oh, darling you can't do that to me. Tell, tell, are you having a thing with Ross?"

"Goodnight, Brad."

Sara hung up. Fatigue set in. She fingered Sean's letter and unfolded the thin paper. She tried to read it again. Her mind clouded. She stretched out on the bed to rest a little before calling Sean. The long hand of sleep pulled her into another world.

CHAPTER TWENTY-FIVE

Sara stormed into her office, berating herself again for falling asleep last night instead of calling Sean. She tried Sean's number for the umpteenth time this morning. His answering machine clicked on. "Hi, Sean, it's Sara again. I'm worried about you. I had a dream about Lily. Don't go flying, *please*. I'll explain when we speak. Call me ASAP." She hung up. A feeling of loss possessed her. She caressed her stomach. Could there be something wrong with the baby? No. She had visited her gynecologist yesterday. She was four weeks pregnant and in excellent health.

Zoey appeared at the door, chewing gum. "Got everything for the Xenon meeting?"

"Yes. Come in. We need to talk."

"What about?"

"Peter Marks needs an assistant. I think you'll be happier

working for him."

Zoey trekked up to Sara's desk. "Is something wrong with my work?"

"No. I just think it would be a smart move for you."

"Why? Working for Peter would be a step down."

Sara eyed the girl. It was time to come straight with her. "My affair with Ross has entered the messy stage. It might cost me my job."

"Whoa! What's with the sudden honesty?" Zoey stuck her hands on her hips. "You'll survive."

"There's a lot you don't know. My advice is, work for Peter."

Zoey spat her gum into a tissue and flung it into a wastebasket. "You leveled with me. I'm staying." She slapped a stack of message notes on Sara's desk. "Seven are from Ross. I told him you had meetings all day with clients and weren't expected back."

"Does this mean you've gotten over your crush on him?"

"This means I'm going to get a break at this agency. I'll make it happen, and I'm betting you'll help me."

"I'm trying to do that. Take the job as Peter's assistant. If I leave, Vicki might fire you."

Zoey strode to the door. "As I said, you leveled with me."

Sara shook her head. The girl had guts. She grabbed her coat and left the office.

The cab crawled uptown in the midday traffic. Sara used the time to return phone calls, even one to Dan, who had called repeatedly. She hoped to get his Voice Mail and leave an innocuous message. Dan answered.

"Sara, I'm so glad to hear from you. I miss you. I'm really sorry about Vicki. It was a terrible mistake."

"Forget it, Dan. It wasn't working between us. You know that."

"Vicki told me you're pregnant? Is it true? Is it mine?"

Sara banged her fist against her knee, furious with Vicki. "You have not fathered a child with me." She ended the call.

Her emotions fused into one big knot. She was either going to laugh or cry. Laughter bubbled up from her belly—enough for two people. She rubbed her stomach. She carried a happy little soul.

The cab stopped outside Xenon's black glass tower. The driver glanced back at Sara. His bottom teeth protruded up to his top lip, giving him the look of a boxer dog.

"You okay?"

A gentle quality to his voice surprised Sara. "Never better." She paid the fare, added a generous tip and climbed a flight of marble steps. She swung through a set of glass doors and crossed a black granite lobby, blending into a sea of black-dressed people. An elevator whisked her to the fortieth floor. Her previous meetings at Xenon had been with mid-level executives in various conference rooms. The CEO's quarters exuded an atmosphere of quiet wealth. Her heels sunk into the plush pile of slate carpeting. The panoramic views of midtown lay muted behind thin charcoal-mesh shades. Gilt-framed paintings of ships hung on the dark mahogany walls.

A slight, middle-aged woman sat behind an antique desk. Her blonde-streaked hair feathered around her face like a tulip. A pair of half-moon, red-framed glasses rested on the bridge of her nose. She held herself in the erect posture of a ballet dancer.

"Miss Jensen?" She looked Sara up and down, wrinkling her brow.

"Yes. Sara Jensen."

"I'm Miss Winters." She glanced at her watch—a Cartier tank. "You're six minutes late."

"Traffic." Sara managed a generous smile.

"Traffic is a known problem in this city." Miss Winters stood, her scalding tone lingering in the air. "Follow me."

Sara suppressed a laugh. If Miss Winters knew how Sara had met her boss, that poker up her backside might snap. Sara spotted Bob Morrow at a fund-raising event for The Metropolitan Opera on the very day one of Xenon's tankers suffered a disastrous oil spill off the coast of Alaska. Sara strode straight up to him, smiling. She handed him her card. "I've got a perfect PR solution to your problem. May I call you in the morning and tell you about it?"

The CEO, a man well into his sixties and cumbersome of girth and stride, frowned and stepped away from his wife and friends, taking Sara's arm.

"Tell me now," he said.

Sara caught the fire of interest burning in his eyes.

"If Xenon is in any way culpable for the spill, admit it. Present a plan to repair the damage to the wildlife. Tell the truth. People will forgive you."

He scratched his chin. "I like it, but my board won't."

"Well then, how about awarding us your ad account? Lumina Studios just hired us."

"So I heard. I like your spirit. Go for it."

Sara watched as he scrawled a name on the back of her business card and handed it back to her.

"Call him."

After months of perseverance and umpteen interminable meetings, Sara had landed a slice of the prestigious account. Then yesterday, Bob Morrow called, claiming he wanted to reconsider the PR campaign.

Miss Winters tapped a dainty fist against a gleaming mahogany door, pressed her ear to it and let herself in.

"Miss Jensen is here."

The stiff woman stepped inside for a moment and then returned.

"You may go in."

She ushered Sara through the door and swept away like a feather on the wind. Bob lumbered toward Sara, his big torso bent slightly forward. His eyes glowed like caterpillar lights on a dark highway.

"Sara, I'm happy to see you. I hear nothing but good things about how you're handling our account, but that's what I expected." He gestured to a seating area, and they sat side by side on a brown leather couch.

"Some of our board members are still against your ideas for the PR campaign and even more against my being the spokesman." A thoughtful frown creased his brow.

"It's got to be you, Bob. No actor can do this job. You're the conscience of Xenon. The camera will seek that out. People will trust you."

The CEO's face crinkled into a smile. "Well, I've given it a lot of thought, and I know it's the right thing to do."

"You won't regret it. People love confession. The big, rich oil company admits to negligence, shows remorse for the damage done to the land and the animals, then presents a plan to make good on all that. People will appreciate it. Believe me."

"I do."

Sara talked about the various stages of the campaign when the air about her rustled.

"Hooh, hooh, hooh. You'd better watch the news. It's just you and me now."

Sara's hand flew to her heart.

Sean!

"What's wrong?" Bob said. "Are you in pain?"

"I …" Sara yanked herself back to the moment. "I'm not feeling too well. It must be something I ate. Can we finish this another time?"

"Of course. Can I get you anything?"

Sara mustered a smile. "No thanks." She rushed from Bob's office, down the hall, past Miss Winters and into an elevator. She flew across the lobby and out onto Park Avenue, not stopping to hail a cab. Traffic jammed the streets. She kicked off her high heels, shoved them under her arms and ran flat out. Darting between taxis and trucks, she wended her way uptown and across to Third Avenue. She arrived at her apartment house without having stopped once. An elevator whisked her nonstop to her floor. She got out. A couple strolled down the corridor, hand in hand. Sara barged through them, breaking their grip.

"Sorry."

She fumbled for her keys. Her hand trembled. She dropped them. "Fuck." She swiped them off the floor, burst into her apartment and flicked on the TV.

She surfed the channels. Cartoons and soap operas whizzed by. She stopped as a BREAKING NEWS headline filled the screen.

"We repeat, best-selling novelist, Sean Granger, has died from injuries sustained in the crash of a single-engine private plane near Telluride, Colorado," the news anchor said. "The crash occurred less than a mile from Granger's mountain home. According to an unofficial source, a group of cross-country skiers witnessed the plane flying at an unusually low altitude when its wing clipped a tree branch. They allege the aircraft then caught fire and hurtled to the ground. Granger, the pilot and sole occupant of the plane, was reportedly conscious and able to speak when Search and Rescue pulled him from the wreckage. He died shortly after he arrived at an area hospital. The author first gained critical acclaim for his breakout novel, *David and Danielle*. Famed director, Carlo DeLuca is slated to film a screen adaptation of Granger's most recent book, *Love Interrupted*. Sean Granger was forty-four years old. "

A terrible wail worked its way through Sara's body. She crumpled onto the sofa, clutching her ribs. Tears welled but shock kept them from flowing. Her phone rang incessantly. The answering machine recorded one message after another. The news on Sean continued. Sara rifled Sean's letter from a desk drawer and stashed it inside her bra like a bandage over the gaping wound in her heart.

Carlo's face filled the TV screen.

"The world has lost a unique voice. A brilliant storyteller. I learned so much from Sean while working with him on the script for the movie of his novel, *Love Interrupted,* which is a magnificent and befitting last work." Carlo's voice broke, and his eyes glistened. "We'll never forget Sean. He'll live on through his books. Generations to come will be the richer for having them."

The scene switched back to the savage face of the Rocky Mountains. More details of the crash were given. Sara muted the set and closed her eyes. She would never see her dear friend again. Never hear him say, "ah," with that irreverent rise of delight. Never tell him how much he meant to her. Never tell him she understood his quest for fame and fortune, and that she too would have deleted the last chapter of *David and Danielle* to get it published. Tears gushed. She sobbed, heaving up rage and grief. Lily had killed Sean, just as she said she would. Sara should have warned Sean. She yanked tissues from a box and mopped her eyes. Her determination to beat Lily at her game rolled over her like a faithful wave. Ross was going to live, no matter what the cost.

She heard Ross's voice on her answering machine. "Sara, if you're there, pick up the phone. I need to talk with you. It has to do with Sean. It's urgent."

She grabbed the phone. "What about Sean?"

"I'm so sorry, Sara. I know—"

"What about Sean?"

"His ex-wife, Jacqueline called me. She—"

"Is she with Arielle?"

"No. Jacqueline lives in Paris. She's on her way here."

"Oh, my God, Arielle isn't alone in Sean's house, is she?"

"I don't know. I—"

"What do you mean you don't know? Arielle is Sean's daughter. You spoke to her mother. Didn't you ask her if—"

"Sara, I've never met Arielle."

"Oh, well, just kick back then. Make another movie … knock up another broad."

"I know you're angry with me, and you have the right to be, but—"

"That's so big of you. I feel so much better having you tell me what I am allowed to feel."

"This call isn't about our relationship, Sara. Sean made a dying request."

"A dying request? How do you know? What is it?"

"Jacqueline told me Arielle arrived at the hospital before her father died, and he told her he was to be cremated." Ross lowered his voice to a near whisper. "He said he wanted me to fly you over the mountains of Telluride and for you to toss his ashes onto the wind."

The phone slipped from Sara's hand. She gazed off into nowhere, one thought on her mind. Lily would try to kill her and Ross, just as she had killed Sean.

CHAPTER TWENTY-SIX

Sara flung her overnight bag into the Chevy Blazer and climbed in the driver's seat. Pulling out of the Telluride airport, she drove toward Mountain Village. A pale silver sky domed the Rockies. It was Friday. Tonight, she had been destined to dine with Sean in New York and meet Ross later. Now both men would be at Sean's house. Ross in the flesh. Sean in an urn.

She passed Mountain Village. Its fairytale blend of American Southwest and Bavarian architecture glowed in the light of the setting sun. The gondola, a cable car system that linked the Village to the town of Telluride, sailed overhead. On the slopes, skiers eked out the last of daylight.

The road wound higher into the mountains. At Star Mesa Drive, she swung the car left and skidded onto the narrow road leading to Sean's house. Dropping into low gear, she navigated the switchback turns. Her wheels crunched onto the snowy plateau in front of Sean's house. All appeared white and silent. Thin silver-barked aspens towered into the sky—traitorous trees.

She got out of the car and sucked in the cold thin air, holding it at the crest of her breath, at the point between life and death. An essence, soft as silk, brushed her cheek.

"Look into my telescope, Sara."

"Sean!" She spun around. Wind howled through the leafless aspens. A skein of birds flew into the glacial silence. Her breath caught in her throat. She searched the bay window of the master bedroom. She had to get up there.

She traipsed up to the house and pressed the bell. The door swung open. A woman smiled at Sara. She had raven hair—lots of it, tumbling to her shoulders in layers of messy curls. She was model thin and wore black jeans, an oversize black sweater and military-style boots.

"I am Jacqueline, Sean's ex-wife." She kissed Sara on each cheek. "Did Sean mention a reason to die now?"

"A reason?" Sara gaped at the woman.

"*Oui*. Sean always said he would know when he was about to die and why. He wasn't ill. Of course, he was unhappy. Sean was always unhappy, but aren't we all?"

The French woman spoke English with a cultured British accent, but her outlook was pure Gallic.

"Your coat." Jacqueline held out her hand.

Sara surrendered her jacket. "How is Arielle?"

"Devastated. She adored her papa. She's in her room. She wants to see you."

"Perhaps, I should visit her now." Sara started for the stairs, but Ross ambled into the foyer. Sara froze. Her heart flip-flopped between love and hate. His right cheek looked bruised as if he'd propped his fist against it in hours of thought. Life had gotten to him at last—probably the life growing inside her. "Hi."

"Hi."

They studied each other like boxers sizing each other up for the fight to come. Sara sensed Jacqueline's gaze shifting from one to other.

Sara faced the Frenchwoman. "Is Arielle's room upstairs?"

"I will escort you. Excuse us, Rossano." Jacqueline rolled Ross's name off her tongue like a native Italian and batted her eyes.

"Just direct me. I'll find her." Sara placed a hand on the banister.

Jacqueline smiled. "You are familiar with the house?"

"I used to date the architect who designed it."

"You attract interesting men. We have that in common, no?"

286

Sara glanced at Ross, then back at Jacqueline. "How do I find Arielle?"

"Upstairs, the first bedroom on the right."

Sara took the stairs two at a time. The spring in the thick burgundy carpet reminded her of the first time she had climbed them. Adventure did not tickle her senses now. Sorrow owned her. She stood outside Arielle's door, remembering the night at Sean's New York apartment when she'd met the girl. She recalled the fun father and daughter had making up the story of the Hitchcock Blonde and the Dark Prince, and how Sara had spoiled it by saying Sean must be the one in the love triangle to die. That she had refused to retract that statement, even under the beseeching eyes of Arielle, was despicable.

Sara leaned against the wall, shivering with regret. Worse still, the other night she had slipped under her soft, downy comforter and fallen asleep instead of calling Sean. If she had told him about her dream of Lily, he might be alive. *Ohmigod, I killed him!*

Sara rolled her back from side to side, wallowing in remorse until some better part of herself ordered her to stop and start acting responsibly. Sara gathered her senses, then knocked on Arielle's door and peeked inside.

The once bubbly girl sat by the window, staring out. "Arielle, it's me, Sara. Can I come in?"

The girl turned. Her eyes were red and swollen.

Sara moved toward her. "I'm so sorry." She hugged Arielle and rocked her like she used to rock Jake when he was little boy and frightened of the dark.

Arielle flung her arms around Sara. "Daddy loved you."

"I loved him, too."

"I thought you loved Ross."

Sara stroked the girl's hair off her face and sat on the arm of her chair. "Love comes in different ways. Your father and I were friends, very special friends, such as I've never known before. I'll miss him all my life."

"Me too."

The loss of Sara's own father welled up—raw as the day he died twenty-seven years ago. She tightened her arms around Arielle, silently promising Sean she would be there for his daughter.

"Are you sure you want me to spread your father's ashes?"

Arielle looked up. "Yes. That's what Daddy wanted."

"And he asked for Ross to fly me?"

Arielle nodded. "It was the last thing Daddy said. His voice came suddenly clear and strong. He said, you'll make sure that happens, won't you my darling girl? I promised, and then he died." The girl's voice quavered. She lowered her eyes. "But I don't understand why Daddy would want that. He called Ross the Dark

Prince, and the Dark Prince is dangerous."

Fear shot through Sara, but she didn't want to add to the girl's troubles. She struggled to sound calm. "Will you be moving to France to live with your mother?"

"No, I'm going to finish college at Georgetown."

"Can I call you there? Will you call me if you need anything?"

"Uh-huh."

"My son is your age, and he'll be home for Spring break. If you're alone—"

"Are you trying to fix me up?" A flicker of her old self sparked in Arielle's eyes.

Sarah laughed. "I wasn't, but now that you mention it ..."

The sparkle faded from Arielle's eyes. "Daddy learned to fly because he was terrified of flying. He said you must conquer your fears, or they'll diminish your life. He was very cautious. He didn't drink for eight hours before going up, and he knew the area like the back of his hand. I don't understand."

Her eyes pleaded for an explanation. Sara felt totally inadequate. "Perhaps, when they investigate the crash, they'll find something."

"Daddy would never kill himself."

"Of course he wouldn't. He wrote to me from Bermuda. He

sounded happy. We were looking forward to seeing each other."

"Did he let you read the last chapter of *David and Danielle,* the chapter that was edited out of the book?"

"He told me about it in his letter."

"Daddy never forgave himself for that. His death has something to do with that, doesn't it?"

"I don't think we can ever know."

"We can. You can."

"Why do you say that?"

"I don't know. I just know you can."

A tear trickled from the girl's eye. Sara brushed it away with her fingers. "I'll do my best to find out what happened, Arielle. I promise you that."

Arielle clasped Sara's hand and squeezed it, reminding Sara of her father's grip the day they made their pact to keep Ross alive. She kissed the girl on the forehead and left her room.

In the corridor outside, Sara grasped the railing and looked down into living room. The white presence of the Rockies loomed behind the triple-storied windows. Bach's cello suites filled the air, passage after passage of perfectly organized notes chasing each other around, exhausting form and cadence, dying, and then rising again in yet another form. Did the music echo life and death and rebirth?

Dozens of candles glowed on a table in the far end of the living room. In their midst rested a pewter urn. Sara cringed, thinking of Sean's body sliding into a furnace and crumbling into ashes.

Ross and Jacqueline sat on a couch. The French woman spread a map across Ross's lap and traced a finger over the area near his crotch. As if sensing Sara's presence, Ross glanced up. Sara moved quickly on.

She marched into the master bedroom and went straight to the telescope in the bay window. She rested a hand on its cold, tubular body and pressed her eye to the viewer. The lens had been trained onto the valley where Sean's plane crashed. Searchlights lit the area. The official yellow tape of a crime scene surrounded the charred remains of a fuselage. A wing stood on end, serene as an Indian burial mark. The scene appeared slightly out of focus as it had been the last time she'd looked through this instrument. Sara didn't adjust the lens. She watched and waited.

The focus cleared, and the scene magnified, bringing everything up close. A form like that of an ancient warrior stood beside the wreckage. He wore a suit of silver armor and carried a great sword with a diamond studded handle. Bright hazel eyes moved behind the slits in his face mask.

"Sean! Where are you?"

"I'm working on returning to my soul."

"What do you mean? Come back. I need you."

Sean swung his sword skyward. Inky clouds parted, and a pair of massive iron gates appeared. *River of Never Ending Sorrow* flashed over them in crimson lights, diffused slightly by a dark mist.

"What are you doing?" Trembling, Sara leaned on the telescope to steady herself but knocked it askew.

God, no. Not again!

The scene blurred. She lost sight of Sean.

Stupid!

She twisted the lens this way and that, begging Sean to come back.

"Who are you talking to?"

Sara spun around. Ross sat on the edge of the bed holding the urn. Her jacket lay beside him.

"How long have you been here?"

"We have to go."

Sara pointed to the small pewter vessel. "Is ..."

Ross stood. "That was nothing ... what you saw with Jacqueline."

"I don't care what you do."

His eyes bored into Sara, peeling through the layers of her mind, pleading for something. Probably for her to understand his love for Lily. Sara huffed. She would be bound to the *River of Never Ending Sorrow* before he gained any ground on that front.

The doorbell chimed and reverberated through the house like a gong calling an order of monks to prayer.

Ross stepped closer to Sara. "That will be Sean's brothers and sisters. Jacqueline doesn't want to have to explain us to them. We can leave by a side door."

They tiptoed along the corridor, down some back stairs and outside. Their escape eased the angst between them, but not for long. Ross opened the passenger door of her rental car, taking control as usual. Sara bit back her annoyance and climbed in.

Ross handed her the urn. She balanced it between her knees, wondering if the lid was secure. They rode in silence, the weighty silence of unhappy people trapped in a small space. She fingered the button that opened her window. They traveled high in the mountains. She could dump Sean's ashes here and avoid that plane ride with Ross tomorrow. Sara shivered. A dying request could not be refused—least of all Sean's.

Ross gripped the steering wheel and leaned slightly forward in the tense way he did when he thought of Lily. A prism of light flashed off the diamond in the clasp of Sara's bracelet. A rustling filled the air. Lily! Sara waited for the girl's ghostly laughter, but she heard a different Lily. This time, she wept and spoke in a pitiful little voice.

"Help me, Ross." Sob, sob. "It hurts. I can't bear the pain. Please, Ross, you promised. Help!" Sob. Sob.

Conniving little bitch.

Sara watched a tear roll down Ross's cheek.

"Ross, *please.*" Lily continued begging and pleading, her voice laden with agony.

Ross's hands trembled on the wheel. Sara almost reached out to comfort him. The impulse scared her. She still loved him. She could feel that love surging through her, an untamable force she would likely endure for the rest of her life. She caressed the urn. Slowly, the burning need to avenge Sean's death took precedence.

They headed down the steep drive to the Peaks Hotel. The valet greeted Ross with a big smile and handed him a ticket for the car.

Crossing the stone-flagged floors of the hotel lobby, Sara wished she could be among those gathered around the fireplace— rosy-cheeked skiers—drinking and laughing. The rich aromas of massage oil drifted up Sara's nostrils, the essence of rosemary and the clean clear scent of orange peel. The hotel hosted a great spa. She'd love to be headed there, to sink into a hot whirlpool and relax her weary body.

"I checked you in earlier." Ross steered her toward the

elevators.

"Thank you, but I made a reservation. I want my own room."

"You've got it. It adjoins my suite."

Sara walked beside Ross, too tired to argue. Or did hope hold her back? Hope he would suddenly want his unborn child. Oh, God! Her emotions swung from anger to optimism like a pendulum in the hands of a lunatic.

People filed into the elevator, exchanging ski stories. A pretty brunette nudged her girlfriend and swung her glance in Ross's direction. The girlfriend looked at Ross and gasped. When the elevator thinned out, the brunette thrust a small pad of paper at Ross and asked for his autograph. He scrawled his name on it without saying a word.

As the girls left, Sara said, "You weren't very nice to them."

"I'm saving nice for you."

"When does that begin?"

"Give me a break, Sara. I'm—"

"No sad stories from you, please." Sara pressed the urn into the crook of his arm. "Look after Sean. Think about all the people who will miss him ... forever."

They got off the elevator. Ross glanced at his watch. "I've ordered dinner for eight-thirty in my suite." He opened the door to her room.

"What am I eating?"

He cocked an eyebrow.

Sara swiped her bag from his hand and slammed the door in his face.

The room service waiter lifted metal domes off their plates with an exuberant gesture, then left. Sara stared at blackened chicken covered with red peppers and corn relish. She ate a small piece, hoping it would sit well on her stomach. Ross poured her a glass of wine as if in total denial of her pregnancy. She almost snatched the glass from beneath the flow of burgundy liquid, but resisted. Before she tackled the subject of the baby, she had to deal with business.

She eased into the subject. "Carlo put it eloquently when he described *The Thinking Woman* campaign as brilliantly funny, slightly tragic and endlessly hopeful. That's a unique voice created by our agency. You can hire very talented people, but they won't be able to copy it." She munched on a piece of chicken. "To take the account away from us is to flirt dangerously with customer loyalty."

Ross set his fork down. "You're right, we shouldn't run your campaign at all."

"Ross, *please*, don't let our personal problems affect our business relationship. It's not fair."

"Is it fair that I have no say in the matter of becoming a father?"

"No, and it's not fair for me to find myself pregnant. I had unprotected sex with you because you had a vasectomy. What happened? Have you seen a doctor?"

He downed a glass of wine. "I'm leaking sperm. I had the operation in Mexico when I was eighteen." He stood, then charged over to a seating area by the window and sank onto a sofa.

Sara moved slowly across the room and sat beside him, horrified that any doctor anywhere in the world would perform such a procedure on a teenager.

"Don't do this to me, Sara. You're breaking my heart."

"I thought it was already broken."

"Don't be cruel."

"Cruel? How do you think I felt when you said this baby couldn't be yours?"

"I'm sorry. I was beside myself. I can't believe you would have a child. This is not who you were when I met you."

"No, it's not, but it's happened, and you need to face the fact that your life is no longer just about you."

"I can't. I don't have that to give. I've never been anything but honest about that."

"I'm four weeks pregnant, which means I conceived this child the last time you played, *I'll Be Seeing You*. I've remembered what happened. It was just like the first time we played that song. I felt as if I'd been overtaken by a woman named Elizabeth, and I think you knew that because you were similarly affected by a man called Nicky. You—"

"Where's this going, Sara?"

Ross stared at her as if he had no idea what she was talking about. It disturbed her. He might claim she was unstable as a way of weaseling out of their business contract. It no longer mattered. She continued. "Sean told me the main characters in his book were based on real people … that he had lived as Ed Harroway, and I as Elizabeth. You were Nicholas Hart. I think you know that."

"Sean's novel is fiction. F-I-C-T-I-O-N."

Sara shivered beneath his glowering look.

He tapped a finger on the table. "Let's stick to the facts."

"The facts? Okay. I'll give them to you." Sara flung caution aside and plowed ahead. "On that last night when you played *I'll Be Seeing You,* it tripped a memory from our past lives. I, as Elizabeth, asked you, Nicky, for a baby. When you agreed, the universe took that as you, Ross, saying yes to me. This child is a result of the healing-man experiment *you* insisted we try."

Ross smacked his fist into his hand as if at the end of his wits. "I've explained, I'm leaking sperm. The tubes severed in a vasectomy do sometimes reattach. It's very rare, but it does happen. It's happened to me."

Sara calmed her breathing. "I read that it sometimes occurs, but usually during the first year following the operation."

Ross stood, exuding the restless energy of a man used to getting his way. He strode down the room, picked up a file from a dresser and paced back to Sara. "This is what you really want." He dropped the blue vinyl folder in her lap.

She stared at the shiny cover. Her gut knotted up. "What is it?"

"A business plan for your agency. In two years, you'll be acquiring other media properties. I've listed those prospects and how to get the financing. You can meet your goal, Sara. You can be a woman of capital before you're forty."

"I don't need you to make that happen. I have my own plan."

Moonlight glowed on his face. He resembled Anna's drawing of him. The sinews of his finely chiseled features showed through his skin. His eyes burned with the fleetingness of him.

"Ross, we're talking about a baby, yours and mine."

"It's early. It's not a baby."

Emotion caught in her breath. It should have been anger, but it was love, love for her unborn child. She thought of the beautiful young man Jake had become and how empty her life would be without him. She flung the folder at Ross's feet and started for the door.

Ross yanked her back, then picked up the file and held it against her chest. "This is a great plan, Sara. It's what you want. I know it is."

She shoved him away. "The price is too high."

He crushed his lips onto hers. She struggled for a moment, but her nerve endings caught fire. Half hating herself, but thinking he might soften toward having the baby, she caved in to him. She felt herself riding beside him in the rhythm of his stride—floating in a dream—being unfurled onto the bed.

He peeled off his clothes. She rested her head against the curve of his neck. The warmth of his torso radiated on hers. He turned her on her side and ran his tongue down her spine to the small of her back.

"Ross, a child is—"

"I love you, Sara." He caressed her slightly swollen breasts. "You're the only woman for me."

She shivered beneath the thrust of him entering her body— beneath the promise of his words. Their moans of ecstasy rose and fell together. The heat of him poured into her. He collapsed, burying his head in her breasts. Their heartbeats raced in the thin air, keeping time together.

Lily's pathetic little voice filled the silence. "Ross," she whined. "All I think of is you. Come soon. I can't stand the pain. Help me. HELP!"

Sara felt something splash between her breasts. Tears—Ross's tears.

"Don't listen to Lily, Ross."

His body sagged, and his weight sunk heavily on her. She shook him by the shoulders. "Ross." She rolled him off her. "Ross, wake up." She leaned her ear against his heart. The beat was strong and his skin warm, but his eyes seemed sealed as if never to open again.

"Ross, wake up. Lily is a fickle bitch. I know she had a hand in Sean's death, and she plans to kill me too."

Sara shook him again, but he remained asleep, probably dreaming he was in the dark planes looking for Lily.

Lily's taunting voice sounded in Sara's ear. "Hooh, hooh, hooh! Who's got the power now?"

CHAPTER TWENTY-SEVEN

The small plane Ross had rented to toss Sean's ashes looked like a bug from another planet. The wings glistened blood red, and the cockpit perched between them like a giant Perspex bubble. Sara settled in the passenger seat and tucked her feet back to avoid the foot pedals on her side. She hugged the urn against her chest, keeping her arms clear of the control yoke.

Ross sat in the pilot's seat, studying the dashboard where needles wavered over dials marked volts, amps and RPMs. Sara had never worked on an aircraft account. If she had, she would have done enough research to at least have a rudimentary understanding of these instruments. She eyed the door. She could leap out now, ride the cable car up to the highest peak and release Sean's ashes onto the wind.

"We'll take off in a minute." Ross adjusted a knob. "The engine's idling, warming the oil temperature to a safe level for the cold conditions."

Nothing about flying with him felt safe. Sara gazed at Lumina's Gulfstream parked to their right, waiting to whiz Ross back to L.A. She scrutinized the purple zigzag on its tail, wondering what logo she might one day choose for her media empire. In the brittle light of day, it seemed stupid not to have at least glanced at Ross's business plan. Her stomach cramped. She sensed her unborn child telling her she'd done the right thing. The pain passed. A flicker of joy shot through her. Lightning fast, but it made an indelible mark on her mind, the kind that would spark back to life at odd times, perhaps upon the sound of her child's laughter.

Ross reached across her and touched a latch on her window. "This opens from the bottom and tilts up. When you're ready to toss the ashes, wedge the neck of the urn into the rear corner so they fly out behind us."

Sara nodded. His face moved close to hers. He smelled of shaving soap and fresh air. After her encounter with Lily last night, Sara had dashed back to her own room to sleep. When she awoke this morning, she found a message from Ross saying he had gone skiing and would meet her at the airport at noon. Since then, he'd been occupied with renting the plane. Their conversation of last night remained unfinished.

Ross placed earphones over his head and spoke into a microphone on a little arm. "Alpha Foxtrot four five zero, requesting clearance for takeoff."

Foxtrot. Nicky and Elizabeth would have danced the foxtrot.

The plane taxied onto the runway and came to an abrupt stop. Ross fiddled with the instruments. Wing flaps flipped up and down. The engine roared. The little propeller spun, its silver blades flashing like swords in the sun. The plane sped down the tarmac. Ross gripped the control yoke, pulling it back. Sara gazed at his long fingers—fingers that had once held hers the whole night through.

The little craft rose into the air and wobbled as it crossed the mountainous gorge beyond the end of the runway. They climbed, banked and leveled off. She gazed at snow-drenched mountains, pine forests and the great blue dome of the sky. She caressed the urn, and the loss of Sean flowed through the passages of her life— twisting and turning like a river fated to follow her to her dying day. She touched his letter tucked inside her bra. She knew it by heart. She recalled the paragraph where he asked her to tilt the lens of perception and view Ross's devotion to Lily as a magnificent call to love. Hard as she tried, her perception just wouldn't swivel that far.

The plane plowed through low-flying clouds, bumping about like a rubber ball. Her stomach met her throat, but there was nothing in it. She'd thrown up last night's dinner earlier this morning and hadn't eaten since for fear of vomiting in the air. They rose above the clouds.

Ross banked the plane. "This is as good a place as any."

Hands shaking, Sara unscrewed the lid of the urn. She dipped her fingers into finely sifted whitish powder. The grains of Sean's body stuck to her skin. She felt something crisp like the remains of a bone. She wretched a dry heave and jammed the lid back on.

"Ready?" Ross said.

"No."

In an impatient gesture, Ross leaned over and opened her window. A blast of arctic air stung Sara's cheeks. Sunlight flashed on the diamond in the clasp of her bracelet. Lily's laughter filled the cabin.

"Come on, Sara." Ross nudged her. "Toss the ashes."

Sara couldn't move. She listened for the silken rustle of Lily's ghost. Ross tried to pry the urn from her. "Stop it!" Sara yelled. Then a rush of black silk swirled and flapped around her like a raven over the dead.

"Hooh, hooh, hooh, plummet … dash … glide."

Lily's shivering mass of ectoplasm glistened before Sara, youthful and supple. Powerful.

Obviously blind to her presence, Ross kept telling Sara to dump the ashes, but as Sara stared at the ghost, his voice faded. Lily's features filled the whole world—her moon-white skin, her chestnut hair swept up in a ponytail, her light brown gaze.

"Hooh, hooh." Lily pointed at the urn. "Sean was easy to kill.

BORING. I hope you're going to be a bit more of a challenge."

Rage overwhelmed Sara. She lifted the urn, mustered every ounce of her strength and whacked it down on Lily's head. The container shot straight through her shadow-form and crashed onto the control yoke. The aircraft jack-knifed on its side with one wing tipped to the heavens and the other to earth.

Ross was now directly above her. He seemed to be shouting at her, but Sara couldn't fathom what he said. Wind gusted through the open window. She dropped the urn. The lid fell off. Sean's ashes showered through the cockpit and floated around her like a snow scene in a glass container. She screamed. Ashes flew into her mouth and coated her tongue. Her eyes burned. She tightened her throat, stopping herself from swallowing Sean's remains. All the while, Lily flapped about, laughing and trying to grab Sara's control. Sara kept her arms ramrod straight in front of her. Her hands welded to the yoke.

"Hooh, hooh." Lily's laugh thundered in Sara's head. "This is fun. Ross thinks you've gone crazy."

"I don't care!" Sara shouted.

"For Christ's sake, Sara." Ross gripped her wrist. "Let go of the control."

Never. Lily was probably inside his thoughts begging him to die and save her.

Ross's fingers tightened around her arm like a vise squeezing the blood from her veins. "Stop it!" she yelled. "You're hurting me."

"Don't make me break your arm."

She glanced up at him. From her blurred, sideways view, she glimpsed Sean's ashes dusting his hair giving him the look of the older man she had been determined he would live to be. She blinked. Her vision cleared a little—enough to see a cold glint in his eyes—a steely cast that told her he would, without a doubt, break her arm if necessary. She released her grip on the control.

Ross leveled the plane and closed her window. Eyes stinging and streaming with tears, Sara scanned the small cabin, searching for Lily. No sign of her. All fell calm. The little craft swept through the raw blue sky. Sara yanked tissues from her purse and mopped her eyes. She offered one to Ross. He declined. She caught the emotion in his eyes. His sadness touched her soul. She rested her hands in her lap—a gesture of surrender.

Ross squeezed her shoulder. "It'll be all right."

Sara dusted ashes off his cheek. He stroked her hair off her face. The swift black rustle of Lily's ghost swept between them. Lily grabbed Sara's yoke and plunged the plane into a nosedive.

Sean's ashes pelted against Sara's face as if flying back at her through a wind tunnel. She sensed Ross trying to shield his eyes while attempting to gain control of the plane.

"Hooh, hooh, hooh." Lily's mocking laughter filled the cockpit.

The hard face of the mountains zoomed closer and closer. Blood rushed to Sara's head, and her heart beat so fast she thought it would break out of her chest. "I'll fight you to the bitter end!" She wrestled the ghost for the control yoke.

She heard Ross coughing—choking—gasping and yelling at her to let go.

The world spun in kaleidoscopic patterns of white, green and blue. Then everything went black.

"Sean, help!"

A diamond studded sword floated before Sara. She reached for it, but something smashed into the side of her head. She gazed into an ocean of stars. Her body went limp. Up, up, up. She rode on a roller coaster cresting its highest peak. Petrified, she waited for the fall. It never came. She floated into the sky, then flew like an eagle, her wings spread wide and even—gliding on a golden wind. If this was death, bring it on. Ah, but she lived. She heard Ross talking to the tower. He confirmed they were not in distress. They would be landing soon.

A fierce pain shot through Sara's temples. Her eyes flickered open. The plane sailed through a cloudless sky. Her mouth tasted dry and bitter—the taste of Sean's ashes.

The baby! She felt her abdomen. No pain. No thick wetness

between her legs.

She glanced at Ross. Gray rivulets stained his cheeks, a mix of his tears and Sean's remains. Why hadn't Lily killed them both while she had the chance? Had Ross perceived her presence? Had he reasoned with her, saying he couldn't take Sara's life along with his? Sara took a deep breath.

"Lily was here, Ross. She tried to kill us, just as she killed Sean."

Ross turned slowly and met her gaze. It felt as if he looked straight through her and into some far away place. She hung in the abyss of love gone wrong, waiting to see how wrong.

"You were hysterical, Sara. You were hell-bent on crashing the plane. I had to knock you out." Ross combed his fingers through her hair, shaking out ashes. "I guess I didn't realize how much Sean meant to you."

Sara caved into fate. Lily had hidden herself from Ross. He didn't believe a word Sara said. He never would. He only heard the pitiful girl suffering in hell, and his determination to rescue her superseded all else, even the life of his unborn child. Did that mean Lily had won the battle against Sara? No. Sara would never break her promise to Sean—never give up the fight for Ross's life, but she did, at long last, accept Ross for who he was. She rested her head on his shoulder, listening to the resonance of his voice as he talked to the tower.

The wheels of the aircraft bumped onto the runway. They

taxied to the hanger. Ross cut the engine. Sara buried her head in his chest, not wanting to face what must be faced. He wrapped his arms around her, rested his cheek on her head and held her.

Questions about their future spun in her head. Flashbulbs exploded.

"Are you in love?" A female voice shouted.

"Are you getting married?" A male reporter asked.

"Is it true you're having a baby?" Two women with microphones pushed through the throng of reporters.

Vicki had jumped the gun on Ross.

Sara pulled out of his embrace. "What now?"

A cool clarity crossed his eyes. "I love you, Sara. I want to spend what time I have with you. But if you have the baby, you'll never see me again."

CHAPTER TWENTY-EIGHT

On a crisp, bright October day, Sara sat on a bench in Central Park, watching the sun blaze gold on the towers of Manhattan. Mothers strolled by, wheeling their babies. Young children chased after each other, their shrieks of delight carrying on the wind. Leaves flurried to the ground in shades of amber, orange and red. Sara rested her hands on her belly. In two weeks, the little boy inside would be born. True to his word, Ross had disappeared from her life. The ache of that blistered on her heart, but Ross lived on. At least, she had kept her pact with Sean.

A stocky, middle-aged woman jogged by, the wings of her Thinking Woman's shoes sparkling at her heels, her face a smudge of dreams. Sara recalled the first time she had laid eyes on the shoes. The vision she had of herself running in them played again in her mind. How intrigued she had been by the faded images of two men—how certain that the shoes would take her to them. Not in her most heightened state of creativity, could she have imagined the men would be Sean and Ross—men she had loved in a previous life. Sara still found it hard to believe she had lived as Elizabeth—a woman so totally preoccupied with love. On the plus side of things, The Thinking Woman campaign had caught fire like a match to a forest in a hot wind. Women of all ages related to her. They snapped up the shoes and ran for their dreams. The Thinking Woman became so popular that Lumina had written her into *The Purpose*. The show's audience tripled. Lumina had not withdrawn their account from HMJ, but whatever expectations Sara had of success did not exist. Sean's death existed. His plane crash had been ruled pilot error. Lily had gotten away with murder.

Lily had been quiet since her failed attempt to kill Sara and Ross in the small plane, but Sara would not underestimate her again. Her ear remained ever alert for the sounds of Lily's ghost.

Sara rifled *The New York Times*, looking for *The Arts* section. She checked her watch and glanced toward Fifth Avenue. Four in the afternoon, and right on cue, the one person Sara had come to depend on sailed toward her. She wore a pair of oversized tortoiseshell sunglasses, a red beret and matching pea coat. Mousy curls frothed around her face. Who but Anna, trying to pass unnoticed, would don such a flamboyant disguise?

She swaggered toward Sara, the buttons of her coat straining over the portly body suit she wore beneath it. A bemused smile wavered on her lips, giving her an air of someone on the brink of discovery, which seemed to be the norm for Anna. Despite her padded girth and brazen clothes, an undisputed grace courted Anna—a lunar radiance that could slow the slant of the sun.

The mystical woman stopped in front of Sara, hauled a man-size handkerchief from her pocket and sneezed into it.

"Hay fever. Mind if I sit for a moment?"

"Help yourself." Sara pretended to read *The Times*. Her attention fell on a recipe for *Soffretto*, the dish Ross had cooked on their first date in her beach house. She released a shuddering breath of grief.

"Stay in the present, Sara. Everything's perfect in the now." Anna yanked *The Enquirer* from a tote bag slung over her shoulder.

"Are you reading my aura?" Sara asked.

Anna opened the tabloid. "I don't have to. Pain showers off you like shards of glass."

Sara relaxed into the relief she felt from being with Anna, who had become the most reliable person Sara ever knew. She managed a career as a sculptor, traveled the world with Carlo and their three small children, and ministered to a number of strangely wounded people like Sara.

"Are we safe?" Anna asked.

Sara scoured the scene, searching for anyone lurking with a camera. Her dose of fame had long since come and gone. After the media photographed her with Ross in the small plane, she endured days of such headlines as: *ROSS DENIES PATERNITY. ROSS DUMPS SARA*. Then just as Vicki had predicted, or more likely arranged, the spotlight fell on father-son comparisons between Ross and Carlo. Finally, it landed once again on Carlo's affair of years ago with the ill-fated Ilana. Anna had been caught in the sweep of that, measured in every which way against the movie goddess—all seemingly to her amusement.

"No one's interested in the fat ladies." Sara glanced back at *The Times*. "How was England? Has Carlo finished filming *Love Interrupted?*"

"Yes, he'll edit it at the Studio." Anna peered at Sara from behind her paper. "Ross is in town. He came to dinner last night. It was very strained. He talked about business the whole time. At one point, Carlo asked him about you and if the baby was his." Anna lowered her voice. "Ross did exactly what Carlo used to do when he was asked why he never married Ilana when she was pregnant with his child. Ross ignored the question and kept on talking about business. Oh," she said with a sympathetic gasp. "It was terrible. My poor darling Carlo was devastated."

Ross was in town. Sara couldn't move past the hurt. He must have been in the city dozens of times in the last seven months. Ross no longer worked directly with the agency, and Sara had not known when he came to New York—had not wanted to know.

Anna shook her head. "Ross looked gaunt and tired. He was very careful not to be alone with me. He also ignored Claire

314

Michaela whom he used to adore. She kept tugging at his leg, begging to be picked up. It was heartbreaking."

"Didn't Carlo at least try to find out what was wrong with him?"

Anna sighed. "No. Carlo was like Ross when I first met him. It wasn't long after Ilana had died. The tabloids pointed the finger of blame at him, and he just closed down emotionally and buried himself in work. He thinks Ross is doing the same, but that he'll come out of it when ... well ... soon." Anna lowered her head closer to the paper.

When he meets the right woman, Sara thought. Carlo had not warmed up to Sara, and she doubted he would be in favor of Anna's friendship with her—if he even knew the extent of it. Sara had overheard several of Anna's phone conversations with Carlo. Anna handled Carlo with the ease of a courtesan.

"Oh, look!" Anna shifted *The Enquirer* so Sara could see the page. "Look, it says that Ilana's ghost climbs into bed with Carlo and me at night, and that I've told Carlo it's either her or me." She snorted a laugh. "How funny. That would be true if it were about you and Ross and Lily's ghost? I wonder how they got it wrong."

"They just make up stuff to sell papers." Sara stared at Anna, amazed that she would give credence to such nonsense.

Anna thumbed the page over. "Not entirely. All this information is floating around in the ether. The reporter probably felt a ghostly presence, and since he or she was writing about Carlo and Ilana, just guessed it was Ilana."

Anna's casual acceptance of things floored Sara.

"My goodness!" Anna moved the paper closer to Sara. "Look at this." Among old photographs of Carlo and Ilana, Anna's finger rested next to a picture of Ross at Lily's funeral. The headline read: *GIRLFRIEND OF CARLO DeLUCA'S SON COMMITS SUICIDE.*

Sara cringed. Even though it referred to the death of her nemesis, the headline horrified her. How awful it must have been for Ross to see Lily's life demeaned that way. She stared at the photo of Ross, a lanky youth gazing into Lily's grave, the toes of his shoes perched over the raw hole in the ground as if ready to jump in and join her.

Anna lowered the paper. "Isn't it strange that in all their prodding and digging into Ross's life, no reporter has asked why he was wearing that bandage above his eye?"

"Anna, reporters are all about selling papers. Ilana sells papers. Ross is but an avenue to Carlo, and Carlo is the main highway to Ilana."

"Really?"

"Yes, really. Most of us don't get the love we want. That Ilana with all her beauty, talent and girl-next-door-niceness didn't get it either, makes us feel better."

"Oh, you're so cynical, Sara, but that's not true about Ilana. Carlo loved her. The problem was Ilana had a dream of the way love should be, and at that time, Carlo couldn't fit into her dream, and Ilana couldn't change it."

"Um … well, until Carlo explains why he couldn't fit into her dream, he's going to look like the bad guy."

Anna closed the tabloid. "Carlo will never speak of his relationship with Ilana. It wouldn't be fair. She's not here to tell her side of the story."

No wonder Carlo adored Anna. She viewed him as a heroic figure.

Sara asked, "Do you think if we imagine someone to be a certain way, that affects them and they become it?"

"It doesn't really matter how anyone else is. What we see in others is but a reflection of that very thing in ourselves. You could be blissful all the time if you wanted to be. Just look at the light in the other person's eyes … the light of your spirit … your life force. Look at that and nothing else, and soon you'll feel the power of that love in them and in yourself."

"Anna, for those of us who haven't spent twenty years in a monastery, that seems beyond reach."

Anna lowered her sunglasses. Her eyes glowed like exotic gray pearls, and her face seemed hardly big enough to contain them. Sara felt an energy exude off Anna and wrap around her. Pain and confusion evaporated. Life went into a freeze frame. Runners suspended midstride. Leaves hung on the air. The sun paused in a long golden ray of Indian summer.

"What's happening?" Sara asked.

"I'm looking into the light in your eyes, and you're looking into that same light in mine. You're feeling the love of your soul. If you focus your whole attention on that love, you'll begin to become conscious in the awareness of the soul."

"What's that like?"

"Like a grand field of knowing, like living in your immortality. You are the absolute perfection of everything. You are creation, and it's simple and exquisite." Anna folded her hands in her lap. "When Carlo came to the monastery to research IsMara's life for his movie, an immediate attraction developed between us. It terrified me." She twisted the whopping diamond on her finger. "I tried to ignore my feelings for him, but my soul awareness told me it was time for me to live a worldly life, to interact with others and test my abilities to love and accept them as they are."

"You're good at it." Sara realized more fully the enormous transition Anna had made from one life to another.

"The loving is easy, Sara. The hardest thing for me is not to inflict my knowledge on others. I'm often tempted to tell Carlo that

Ross planned to die with Lily, but in my soul I know it is not for me to decide what Carlo should know about Ross. That's their journey."

Looking into the light in Anna's eyes, Sara understood. She also realized that without her heartbreak over Ross, she would never have experienced this moment with Anna—never felt this love. It presented a force so strong, she barely remembered the agony she felt when Ross walked out of her life—nor even her grief over Sean.

"I must go now, Sara." Anna blinked.

Leaves scattered into action. The sun sank lower in the sky. Bliss receded into some distant and inaccessible place. Anger at Lily resurfaced. Exasperated, Sara asked, "Is it possible to see any good in Lily?"

"You're a warrior angel, Sara. You're capable of extraordinary compassion."

"What makes you say that?"

"You asked the question. That means you know how to love Lily."

"Love her! As they say, hell will freeze over first."

Anna smiled. "We're going to Los Angeles tomorrow, but I'll be back before the baby comes."

"Two weeks, Grandma."

They laughed.

Anna stuffed *The Enquirer* into her bag and stood. "Take care, Sara." She tossed her wig of mousy curls and strode off.

Sara watched Anna until she faded from view. A little later, Sara left the park. She strolled up Fifth Avenue, admiring the city from a laid-back place behind the baby.

A group of young men with cameras slung about their necks ambled close to her. They had broad Slavic features and the rosy-cheeked look of mountaineers. They spoke a language Sara didn't recognize, but their male-buddy laughter told her they discussed a cute girl running by in shorts and a tank top. As if catching their spirit, her unborn son kicked a gentle thrust of his foot.

Sara placed a hand on her stomach. *You've got a long wait before that sort of thing.*

Memories of Jake as a baby rushed to mind. The smile on his little face when he first looked at her in the morning. The warmth of his young legs as they snuggled against hers. The feel of his silky hair on her cheek.

A prism of light flashed off the diamond in her bracelet. The breathless breath of Lily puffed at the edges of her mind. Sara's heart raced. Lily got to her through the diamond!

Hands trembling, Sara wrestled with the claw-type clasp of the bracelet. It was stiff, and she couldn't get a grip on the tiny gold lever. In her peripheral vision, she glimpsed the swirling black force of Lily winging through a gust of leaves.

The wind picked up, and huge as Sara was, she almost lost her balance at the curb. Traffic whizzed by. The whirling force of Lily drew closer. Sara tugged on the clasp of her bracelet. It came unhooked, but not before Lily crashed into her back.

Sara's feet sailed off the pavement. She heard the dull thud of her body as it collided with the yellow blur of a passing taxi. An excruciating pain ripped through her. The cab skidded to a stop. Sara bounced onto the hood and smashed her head against the metal frame of the windshield. A bomb exploded in her temples. She was falling, falling, falling. Time slowed. She floated in streams of swirling black silk. "Get away from me!" She thrashed her hands around in the tangles of Lily's darkness.

The ghost circled above her, laughing. Sara heard the chink of her bracelet as it landed on the road. Male voices shouted in a guttural language. Rosy cheeks faded in and out of focus. Arms shot up, swaying, reaching through the waters of life.

"Hooh, hooh, hooh. Let go, Sara. You've lost. You're as good as dead."

The reaching arms vanished. Voices went silent. "But I'm free of you." Sara waved a fist at Lily. "The bracelet's gone."

Lily swished back and forth, dipping her arms like a bird of prey. "You never had the right to that diamond. Ross promised it to me for my engagement ring. Anyway, I don't need it now. You're on my side of the world."

Sara kept moving her arms and legs, treading water, fighting the downward tug of fury. "You killed Sean, and I'm not letting you get away with it."

The ghost shot off like a bat-wing jet and zoomed into a dark distant sky.

Sara paddled hard, thinking of the love she had felt while looking into Anna's eyes. The air got lighter and lighter and turned into a soft golden haze. "Help!"

"Hello, beloved, Sara."

The voice sounded low and haunting like the sound of a muted cello. Sara spun, searching the golden mist. "Where are you? Who are you?"

"I'm inside you. I am your wisdom voice."

"Where am I?"

"Your spirit was knocked out of your body when you hit the taxi. Thinking of Lily has drawn you to the murky planes between heaven and earth."

"Good. I've got to destroy Lily. Where is she?"

"By the *River of Never Ending Sorrow*, but it is not wise to go there. It will be hard to hear me above the sounds of the river."

Sara remembered how Lily had flitted off when she threatened to get even with her for killing Sean—as if she had been frightened. "How do I get to the river?"

No sooner had Sara asked than she found herself outside a set of massive black gates, the same fortress she had once seen through Sean's telescope. *River of Never Ending Sorrow* flashed above them—pulsing crimson against the inky sky. An awful cacophony of sobs and moans filled her ears. She strode the length of the iron gates, wondering how to get inside. When she'd seen Sean through his telescope, he had pointed his sword toward the area.

The sword! Images swirled in Sara's mind, images of her, striding through time, wielding a diamond-studded sword—a sword of just cause.

You're a warrior angel, Sara.

Was she? Sara stopped, and out of a memory so old that she could not locate its origin, she raised her right hand above her head. "My sword, please."

The great weapon slid into her hand. A tremendous surge of power ran down her arm. She became aware of herself inside a light body—a luminous duplicate of her physical form. She curled her fingers around the diamond handle of the sword and swiveled the blade. The whole purpose of her existence, mortal and immortal, centered on one objective—to avenge Sean's death.

CHAPTER TWENTY-NINE

Sara touched the tip of the blade to the gates. They parted, making a grinding sound that jarred her nerves. She gritted her teeth and marched into the darkness.

Her sword created a beam of light, which she used to pick her way through swarms of black-hooded ghosts. Most bent over the River of Sorrow, sobbing. Others waved their fists, shouting obscenities. A few laughed, obviously amused in the hell of their choosing. It seemed just as Sean had described it in his letter.

"Mercy! Free me." A black-draped woman flung herself before Sara. She clutched the hood of her robe close to her face, hiding her hollowed features. Hundreds followed her, spilling into the light of Sara's sword, pleading to be forgiven.

Sara told them the story of David and Danielle, as Sean had written it in his letter. "Golden beings answered the teenager's prayers and offered them another chance at life. Pray to them." She described Lily and asked if they knew where she might be.

The ghosts cowered deeper inside their robes and trudged back to the river, their chains clanking behind them.

Sara strode on, swishing her sword from side to side, trying to think above the sounds of misery. A ray of light landed on a bend in the river. Sara's heart pounded. Lily stood at the water's edge. She neither cried nor wore a hood. Her chestnut hair swept up in a ponytail tied with a red ribbon. Her black silk kimono swayed in the breeze. She sniffed the air and turned her head from side to side, smiling as if inhaling a divine fragrance.

Sara swung the sword behind her, hiding its light, and crept up behind Lily. The girl seemed so engrossed in her own actions, she appeared oblivious to all else. Lily withdrew two arrows from a wooden box by her feet. Parting her kimono, she rolled the point of one into blood oozing from the wounds on her thighs. She used it to write Sara's name on the second arrow.

Sara squeezed her fingers around the handle of her weapon. Lily inserted the arrow bearing Sara's name into a bow and drew back her arm. Sara lunged forward, aiming her sword between the blades of Lily's shoulders. But before she could slice it into Lily, a figure shot up from the river like a rocket firing into space. Water sluiced off his suit of silver armor.

Sean!

"Sara!" Sean shouted. "Don't use your sword on Lily."

The urgency of his voice struck home. Sara's arm went limp. Lily's arrow soared through the air. Sean leaped higher up from the river and slashed the arrow in half with his sword.

Lily swung around and glared at Sara. Her young face contorted with anger.

Thrilled as Sara was to see Sean, she trembled beneath the tension of her unfulfilled mission. She pointed the sword at Lily's throat. "You'll never harm Ross now."

Lily smirked. "Go on. Kill me." She spread her arms wide like a willing victim.

"Don't do it, Sara." Sean waded up from the river. "If you strike her out of anger, she won't die. Anger is never just. Anger will only give her more power. I know. I tried. That's how she got past me and pushed you into traffic."

Light from Sean's bright hazel eyes shone through the slits in his mask. Emotion choked in Sara's throat. "What are you doing here, Sean?"

"Keeping my end of our pact, trying to stop Lily from taking your life."

"My God, you didn't crash your plane on purpose, did you?"

"Hooh! He's not that brave." Lily threw her head back laughing. Her hideous cackle rolled over the river, mingling with the sobs and sorrows of those chained to its bank.

Sean staked his sword into the ground at Lily's feet. The ghost fell silent—frozen with her arms outstretched, her head thrown back and a sneer on her lips.

Sean withdrew his hand from the sword. "I'm not supposed to use my power unless provoked, but then I'm not a very obedient angel."

"Provoked! Lily killed you, didn't she?"

"Angels hold no grudges."

"Well, I do. After Lily killed you in your plane, why did you put Ross and me in the same danger?"

"Aaah." Sean dragged the little word into a rise of pleasure. "Lily caused my death, but Ross is a champion stunt flyer. Where I could not keep control of my plane against Lily's powers, I thought he could. I sent you flying with him because when Lily attacked you, as I was certain she would, Ross would have to choose between dying for Lily and saving your life. He chose you, Sara."

"What kind of logic is that?" Sara shook her head in disbelief. "Anyway, it didn't work. Ross left me. He said if I had the baby I would never see him again."

"But he is alive. You kept your end of our pact, and that helps me."

Sara touched his arm. "I guess I'm dead." Her voice broke. "My baby …"

"You're not dead. On earth, you've only been unconscious for a few seconds."

"And my baby?"

"You can look through the light of your sword and know what's happening on earth. Just think of the exact location and time before you lost consciousness."

Sara tightened her grip on the sword and pictured herself at the corner of Sixty-Ninth Street and Fifth Avenue. The area lit up. She lay unconscious in the arms of those rosy-cheeked young men she had passed on the street. It looked as if they had caught her as she flew off the cab.

Sirens wailed. Squad cars raced down Fifth Avenue with an ambulance in tow. Traffic parted. A few blocks north, Anna stopped suddenly and dashed back to the scene of the accident. She shouldered her way through the growing crowd.

"I'm the baby's grandmother. Let me through."

A police officer shooed her off. Anna whacked him on the arm with her tote bag and swept off her sunglasses. "You let me in that ambulance, or you'll find yourself burning in hell."

Something in her eyes must have terrified the cop, because he stepped aside, his eyes blinking like a broken traffic light. Anna climbed into the ambulance.

"Sara." Sean's hand covered Sara's. The scene faded. "I've been told to tell you something."

"Not now. I don't know if my baby is all right."

"Now, Sara."

She looked up him. "What is it?"

"Because you have stayed true to the universe, true to what you took on when you accepted Ross as your healing man, you may use your sword to heal one person. You may free them of anything that ails them. That includes you. While you do this, Lily must stay mute under the power of my sword. I can't hold her there for long, so act swiftly."

"I can heal anyone of anything?"

"Yes, but you must do it within an hour, and it must be someone you know. Remember, the beam of your sword will not find them unless you can visualize them in their exact location." Sean squeezed her hand. "The hour starts now."

Questions hammered at Sara, but time ruled. She lowered her eyes to the sword and envisioned herself on Fifth Avenue. The scene came back into view. The ambulance sped away. Inside, Anna held Sara's hand. A team of medics bent over her.

"We've got the baby's heartbeat," one said.

Sara breathed a sigh of relief. That would have to do for now. The ambulance would be at Lennox Hill Hospital within minutes.

She would use that time to consider whom she might heal. Ross. Oh, to exorcize Lily from his life. Sara ignored a tirade of inner backtalk demanding to know why she would consider healing a man who made her pregnant and dumped her. She guided the sword to the penthouse suite of The Meteor Hotel. Empty.

Sara slanted a beam of light into her mother's room in the Queens Hospital Center on Long Island. The cancer had returned and devoured her bones. Aunt Alice sat by her side, stroking her hand. Sara tilted a light beam on her mother's face. Olivia's eyes opened.

"Sara, is that you?"

"Yes."

"I'm afraid. I've been a terrible mother."

Sara clasped the sword with both hands. She could take away her mother's cancer. Should she? A circle of tall golden beings surrounded Olivia, their eyes huge and soft like pools of clear water. One looked directly up at Sara.

"It is your mother's time to leave."

All the bitter scenes between Sara and mother passed before her. She mustered the words she needed to say. "I love you, Mom."

"Sara … I changed your names on your birth certificate. I …" She gasped a breath. "I didn't … your father … I didn't understand him. I just wanted you to be you."

"Oh, I see. Thank you, Mom." Sara wished she could hug her mother and tell her that was the best gift she could have possibly have given her, but the golden beings gathered Olivia in their arms. Olivia seemed mesmerized by them.

"You're so beautiful," Olivia whispered. Then, in the reflection of the golden beings, age and illness fell away from her, and the radiance of youth lit up her face. Her spirit slipped from her body—a glorious ray of light, speeding toward a diamond-bright sun.

"Forty-five minutes." Sean tapped Sara's hand.

Sara's heart ached, but at the same time, she felt uplifted by her mother's passing. Uplifted to know she would be in the safekeeping of the golden beings. Sara leveled her sword on the ambulance. The vehicle had not yet reached the hospital. She redirected her sword to Stanford University. Jake sat in his room, writing an e-mail.

Hi Mom, how's my baby brother treating you? Arielle said her Dad's house in Telluride has sold. The new owners take possession December 1st. She asked me to go there with her, help her pack her things and say goodbye to that part of her life. We would leave right after Thanksgiving. Is that okay with you? Love you lots, Jake.

Jake and Arielle—she must remember to tell Sean they were dating. Sara glanced into her son's heart. The wounds of his childhood scarred him, but they did not rule his life. Jake had been powered by his goal to become a lawyer and help others. He did not need healing.

"Forty minutes, Sara."

Ross flitted in and out of her thoughts like a moth against a light. Sara veered her sword through Lumina's New York offices. No sign of Ross, but Carlo left a conference room with a phone pressed to his ear. He talked to Anna. His face paled as Anna told him about Sara's accident.

"Oh, honey … I don't know where Ross is but I'll find him." Carlo checked his watch. "I'll be there as fast as I can."

Sara lanced the sword's beam back on the ambulance. It pulled into the hospital. White-coated people whisked her onto a trolley. Running alongside it, they stuck stethoscopes on her belly, shone lights in her eyes and spoke in rapid medical shorthand. The only word Sara understood was C-Section. Steel doors swung open. She rolled into a bright, cold room filled with instruments as foreign to Sara as a space command center.

Robed people lifted her onto an operating table. Doctors, nurses and technicians surrounded her. Techs inserted needles into her arms. Scissors ripped open the front of her maternity dress. A nurse swabbed her belly. Monitors beeped. The baby's heartbeat registered low, dangerously low.

Sean nudged her. "Twenty minutes."

Sara aimed the sword into the reception area where Anna waited. Anna talked on the phone with Vicki. Sara looked through the light of her sword into Vicki's apartment. Vicki sat at her desk in the room she used as an office. Looking into Vicki's heart, Sara saw a woman plagued by a sense of worthlessness, a dreadful despair that distanced her from all intimate relationships. Frayed as their friendship was, it was all Vicki had left. Sara watched a cast of horror cross Vicki's eyes as Anna told her about Sara's accident. But Vicki didn't need a miraculous healing. Vicki needed a better friend than Sara had been of late. Someone to validate the qualities she hid behind her aggressive behavior. If Sara lived, she would be that friend.

She angled the sword back on Anna at the hospital. Carlo charged up to her and threw his arms around her. "Ross is on his way."

Ross. The seesaw of love and hate swung wildly in Sara's heart, but steadied as Brad arrived in the waiting area. Brad's hawkish features appeared drawn and his eyes swollen. She wanted to stroke his brow and tell him she would be all right. But would she?

Vicki stormed in, weeping like a Jew at the Wailing Wall. Zoey followed her, carrying the suitcase Sara had kept at the office in case her water broke.

Sara's wisdom voice emerged. "Act soon. While Lily is under the power of Sean's sword, he is subject to the vibrations of Earth. If you take longer than an hour, he will be pulled into another life.

He will take with him the same desire for fame and fortune as he had in his last life. Then Lily will find him and wreak havoc again."

"Sean didn't tell me that."

"But it's true. Hurry!"

"Where's Ross?"

"He's coming up the steps of the subway at the corner of Lexington Avenue and Seventy-Seventh Street."

Sara shot the beam of her sword to that location. Ross emerged onto the street, his face twisted in anguish. He crossed the road, weaving through traffic with athletic grace. As if intuiting him, Anna rushed to the hospital lobby. As she guided Ross down a corridor, Sara raised her sword to look into his heart. At that moment, Sean tapped her on the shoulder.

"Five minutes."

Her baby! Sara levied a light beam inside the operating room. Her belly had been slit from her navel to pubic hair. Gloved hands moved deftly inside her, easing her organs apart, reaching for the baby. Blood splattered onto goggles. Her infant son was raised into the world. He made no sound. Anxious eyes met other anxious eyes. A doctor cut the umbilical chord. Her little boy cried. Shoulders sagged with relief. Across the room, a group of grim-faced doctors studied a panel of X-rays, pointing to the lower part of Sara's spine.

"Three minutes," Sean said.

Sara gulped. What condition would she be in if she got off that table alive? She might be brain damaged or crippled. With a swipe of her sword she could heal herself.

"Look at Sean," her wisdom voice said.

Sara glanced up from her sword.

Sean's eyes danced behind his mask. "Quick. Choose! You know how you love to win."

Time evaporated. The moment spun on and on, weaving in and out of itself. Sarah held it like a precious pearl in the palm of her hand. Dear Sean. He would sacrifice a lifetime for her and double his problems with Lily. She felt the love that held all time—the love of the eternal second. In that clarity, Sara realized whom she would heal. She met Sean's glance. "Free Lily from the power of your sword."

"Sara, you're badly injured. Heal yourself."

"Eight seconds, Sean."

He reached for his sword and looked back at Sara. His eyes misted. "Sara, please."

"Four seconds. One. Two."

Sean swiped his sword from Lily's feet. Her ugly sneer came back to life. Her laughter cackled above the sounds of sorrow rising off the river.

Sara touched the tip of her sword to Lily's heart. A force surged into Sara's—a welling of love so grand that it felt as if all the oceans of the world met inside her.

Lily's sneer faded. She lowered her arms. Murderous images oozed off her, hideous scenes of violence and bloodshed. Zillions of tiny flames spun off a wheel of fire spinning around her heart, burning them up. The steely hardness in Lily's eyes softened. A sunburst of white light surrounded her.

Sara looked into Lily's eyes and met her own reflection. She shone with love, pure and rich with infinite knowing. She blended with the stars, galaxies and planets. Then, space itself. One. Identical to Lily.

CHAPTER THIRTY

With every dark image purged from her heart, Lily grew taller and taller until she matched the height of the tall golden beings flocking around her—until she transformed into one herself. Her huge eyes glowed. Her shimmering golden body flowed through eternity, swaying gently like the substance in a lava lamp.

She bowed to Sara. "This is the grace I had fallen from. You have returned me to my true nature. Thank you, my beloved friend."

Her voice floated over Sara as mellifluous as the silk-spun timbre of an alto sax. Sara gazed at her, so awed by her transcendence that she couldn't speak.

"Whatever did you do to fall so far?" Sean asked.

"Are you sure you want to know?" Lily said.

"Never mind." Sean rolled his shoulders as if guarding against some demonic force. "What happens to us now?"

Lily closed her eyes for a moment, then smiled at Sara. "You have a choice, Sara. You may reenter your earthly life, or under my guidance, pass on to the high realms of your soul. This is a rare gift. Consider it wisely."

The life or death choice sent shockwaves through Sara. Her mind shut down and blinked like a curser on a blank document, waiting for the touch of a writer's hand.

"What about me?" Sean asked

Lily tapped a finger on Sean's head. A sphere of luminosity shone around him. It encompassed Sara, too. Delicate as gossamer, the glow radiated for as far as her eye could see. Infinitesimal lines of light wove in and out of the sphere, crisscrossing like a billion arc lamps. A sound, as pure and mellow and grounded as middle C floated into Sara's heart. A sense of well-being enveloped her.

"This is your soul," Lily said to Sean. "The perfect pattern for everything in creation lies within its sound and light. Now you may return to it and absorb the knowledge of your choosing. Years hence, you will be reborn on Earth and teach what you have learned."

Sean turned to Sara, his hazel eyes brilliant with light. "This is what I felt when I wrote that inscription asking you to return me to my soul. I didn't know what it meant then, but I knew it was meant to be. Amazing isn't it, the way things happen?"

Sara's feeling of well-being vanished. She thought of Sean and Arielle making up the story of the Hitchcock Blonde and the Dark Prince, and of Arielle begging Sara to rescind her statement that Sean must be the one to die in the deadly love triangle. She clutched Sean's arm to tell him she was sorry, but the sheen of his armor tarnished beneath her fingers. Horrified, she watched the cloudy substance crawl up to his shoulder.

"Don't look at the past." Sean knocked her hand off his arm. "Everything is perfect as it is." He tilted her head back until she looked up at Lily. Rays of Lily's light seeped into the crevices of Sara's mind. She felt her friendship with Sean weaving through the tapestry of her eternity like a current of healing waters. Guilt vanished, as did the tarnish on his armor.

"You have unfinished love between the two of you," Lily said. "Love interrupted." She smiled at Sean. "In the future, when Sean is reborn as a teacher, you too Sara, will be alive on Earth. You will meet and know each other upon sight. You will be conscious of your history together."

Sean squeezed Sara's hands. "That's something to look forward to."

Sara thought of the passage from Sean's book describing the teenage Elizabeth and Edward running toward each other on the rolling green fields of Sussex, falling in love. Sara determined they would meet as young children, as Elizabeth and Ed had. They would unravel the world through the eyes of innocence and wonder—a magic upon which they would build their future. A flurry of pleasure swept through her.

Sean released her hands. Sara sensed an unspoken communication pass between Sean and Lily, which made her uncomfortable.

Sean looked back at Sara. "You have unfinished love with Ross too." He dropped his voice to an earnest tone. "If you choose to return to your life, work out your differences with Ross and do it as quickly as possible."

At the mention of Ross, Sara sank into a quagmire of emotion. Ross's last words to her dominated her thoughts.

If you have the baby, you'll never see me again.

Her body convulsed with pain. She lost her balance and tumbled backward, falling away from Sean. She flapped her arms and struggled to stop her descent, but it proved useless. She spun downward like a diver in an endless series of backward flips—over and over, faster and faster, her plea for more time with Sean lost in the roar of a cosmic wind. She shot into the golden haze, the place where she had first met her wisdom voice. She flailed her arms again, trying to slow her fall. She plummeted straight through the gentle mist. Her body slowed down as she entered the heavier atmosphere of the dark planes. She drifted through the black-hooded ghosts, their cries deafening her.

Sara covered her eyes with her hands until the sparkle of

starlight shone between her fingers. She floated among the glittering stars of the Milky Way and gazed at the blue-green globe of Earth revolving in space. The oceans melted against the great continents of the world, and the sun rose and set, bathing the different lands in rays of pink and gold. The planet looked breathtakingly beautiful and frighteningly vulnerable. She spread her arms of light around the globe and vowed to do all the little everyday things she could to keep it alive and well.

A cascade of lights swept past her, soft and intricate as snowflakes, filling space with the same constant note she'd heard in Sean's soul. The lights fanned out over the earth—new lives, new beginnings.

Sara traveled in the wake of the souls and descended toward the East coast of the United States. The brilliant towers of Manhattan pierced the night sky. She zoomed over the Hudson River, sailed on a scattering of leaves across Central Park, then sped through a window of Lennox Hill Hospital—a spirit in search of her physical body.

She glided down a long, white corridor. A janitor swabbed the floors, his floppy mop splashing pine-scented cleanser over the tiles. The hums and bleeps of medical machines penetrated the stark silence. Sensing the closeness of her physical form, she passed through a half-open door and quivered at the sight of her body lying in bed. Her head had been bandaged, and a livid bruise stained her left cheekbone. She slipped inside her body once again, a spirit waiting to be remembered.

Sara opened her eyes. Her vision appeared dense like a fog. Her head throbbed. Her stomach hurt as if trampled by a herd of elephants. Her legs felt numb, dead as if no longer a part of her. Ice-cold fear trickled down her spine but stopped at her lower back. Terror seized her. Paralyzed! Visions of life in a wheelchair bombarded her. How would she work? Her baby! Where was he? How would she take care of him?

Her time with Sean and Lily seemed like a distant dream. As she struggled to remember the love she'd felt with them, a golden glow appeared in her mind. The towering Golden Lily stood in its midst. Her voice floated in Sara's ear.

"In return for your miraculous healing, I am likewise empowered to help you."

Sara's pulse quickened. Life loomed glorious on the horizon. "Could you heal me so I could walk and run and do everything as I did before?"

"I could."

A voice tapped at Sara's conscience—a small voice suggesting, she ask for a different kind of healing, perhaps to be rid of her anger at Ross, or her need to win at all costs. But the joy of being able to romp around with her little son, and the thrill of charging about the world doing business overrode it. She spoke with absolute certainty, "I wish to be healed of my injuries."

"So be it." Lily slid an arm down Sara's spine. At the touch of her golden fingers, tingling sensations prickled at the bottoms of Sara's feet, then shot through her limbs and up her spine. Sara wriggled her toes and kicked her legs. "Oh, thank you, thank you," she whispered over and over, swearing it would be her life's mantra from now on.

"Be careful what you tell people," Lily said. "The nerves in the lumbar section of your spine were injured when you hit the taxi, and now they're badly swollen. From your x-rays, the doctors were not able to predict if the damage would result in a complete or incomplete paralysis. Your sudden healing will cause a stir."

"I understand."

Lily smiled. "I will return in twenty-four hours. Is there anything you would like to ask me before I go?"

So many questions leaped to mind that Sara couldn't discern one over another. "What advice would you give me?"

"Beware of the unforgiven."

Lily vanished. The warmth of her glow and the chill of her warning lingered. Sara told herself everything would be all right. She mused on the turn of events that transformed Lily from her enemy into her guardian angel.

Her vision cleared. She felt an immediate need to locate herself in time. She glanced at a large, black-framed wall clock. Eight-forty. She eyed a window facing north up Lexington Avenue. Puffy charcoal clouds floated beneath the stars, dimming their light. She had met Anna in the park this afternoon around four. The sun had been setting when Anna left, which meant they spent about an hour together. A little more than three hours had passed since Lily's once-murderous ghost shoved her in front of a passing taxi.

Sara discerned a white-clad figure at the foot of the bed. She blinked. Ross stood beside the doctor. A long, cold shiver trickled down her spine, as long and cold as the months of their separation. The tiny utterances of an infant caught her attention. She glanced to the right of her bed. Her baby lay in a crib, less than an arm's length away. Sara's heart swelled like a parachute in a full and gentle wind. The baby faced her. Wisps of dark hair feathered his scalp. His wide, newborn gaze roamed over her, still luminous with the light of his soul.

She ached to hold him. "What's your name?" she whispered.

Nicholas flashed to mind, the man Sean had described as the kindest, gentlest soul God put on this earth. That fit her little boy. She reached through the bars of his crib and stroked his forehead. "Hey, Nicky."

Ross rushed to her side. "You're awake. He shifted his eyes to the baby. "Isn't he amazing? I wanted him to be the first thing you saw when you opened your eyes."

Sara scanned Ross's expression, searching for signs of remorse for having left her alone and pregnant. She found none. He appeared exuberant, fizzing with pride. He spoke of how Carlo said the baby looked exactly as Ross had when he was born, and he beamed like a man expecting to be admired for having sired such a beautiful child.

How dare he be so happy, he who had tried to bribe her to abort his child?

Ross lifted the infant from his crib. "Time to meet Mommy." He plastered kisses on the baby and smiled at Sara. "Thank you for the most beautiful little boy in the whole world."

But for the nearness of her baby, Sara would have demanded an on-the-spot apology for Ross's disgraceful behavior. Avoiding his eyes, she lifted her arms to receive Nicky. Ross laid the infant in them, leaning so close to her that his cheek brushed hers. She nudged him away with her elbow. He would grovel on his knees before he ever attempted such an intimacy again.

A fragrance wafted off her newborn son—a perfume as sweet as wild strawberries. He gazed at her from blue eyes, deep and fathomless as space itself. She traced a finger over his brows and long, glossy lashes. "Welcome to the world."

Ross fondled the infant's tiny hand. "Let's call him Rossano

Giancarlo. Carlo would love it if we gave him his name too."

His presumptuousness exasperated her.

You said, if I had the baby, I'd never see you again. Go away. I hate you.

She stifled her anger, remembering Sean's advice that she work out her problems with Ross. "His name is Nicholas Sean."

Ross looked confused. She wondered if Lily's miraculous healing had somehow affected him too, perhaps causing him to feel blameless of any wrongdoing. Anna might know. She really needed to talk to her.

Ross rested a hand on her leg. She watched a piteous expression fill his eyes.

"Nicholas Sean, it is."

Sara gripped the sheets ready to kick him off the bed, but Lily had cautioned her to be careful what she told people. She needed time to think about that.

Sara glanced at the doctor standing at the foot of her bed. "How am I doing?"

The doctor smiled. "You're in stable condition." He scribbled on a chart, then left the room.

Ross stroked the baby's cheek. "The hospital staff is stressed out. Since my father arrived, the lobby has buzzed with reporters. They claim four young men caught you as you were thrown off the hood of the cab. They saved you from a disastrous fall. What happened, Sara?"

"It's all a blank to me." Sara shifted Nicky in her arms. She thought of her mother and cuddled Nicky closer, sad that Olivia hadn't lived to see him. Her mother must have felt the same boundless love for Sara as a newborn as Sara did for Nicky. Enough to go behind the back of the man she adored and alter Sara's names. *I just wanted you to be you.* Sara smiled at Nicky and passed the message on to him. Her thoughts went to Jake. Ohmigod! Had anyone called him?

"Is Anna here?"

"Sara." Ross tucked the baby's hand inside his blanket. "We need—"

"I want to see Anna."

He sighed, then loped from the room.

CHAPTER THIRTY-ONE

Anna had changed from the fat-lady disguise she wore earlier for their meeting in the park. She now wore jeans and a pastel pink sweater. She hugged Sara and kissed Nicky, then sat on the bed and opened her arms.

"Grandma wants to hold him."

Sara laughed. "Is he really going to call you Grandma?"

"Absolutely."

Sara handed Anna the baby, a pang of separation anxiety tugging at her heart. "Do you know if anyone has called Jake?"

"Brad did. He called him last night. Jake will be here tomorrow." Anna smiled. "Don't worry. I'm sure Brad handled things in a calm and positive manner."

"Yes, he would. Brad has been like a father to Jake. We formed a funny family. Brad and his partner Ian looked after Jake like a second set of parents."

Anna laughed. "Love is grand."

"Yes." Sara leaned against a stack of pillows, eager to tell Anna about Sean and Lily. "So much has happened to me, I don't know how to tell you."

"You don't have to. I followed your journey. I saw everything."

"You did? How?"

"Through the beam of my sword." Anna's eyes shone with that mischievous look of hers. "It takes a warrior angel to know one."

Sara wagged a playful finger at her. "You should have told me more about that."

"But you wouldn't have believed me. Then you would not have been receptive to the subtle planes of higher consciousness. You would not have received the extraordinary gift of choice Lily offered you."

Sara shifted uncomfortably in the bed. She hadn't even considered Lily's offer of guiding her into the higher realms—into her soul. "I can't die now, Anna. I can't leave Nicky. I had to resume my life here. Lily understood. She healed my spine. I guess you knew that."

A tender expression crossed Anna's face—an almost

unbearable kindness. It deepened Sara's discomfort. "What would you have done? I mean ... could you leave Carlo and your children?"

Anna stroked her fingers through Nicky's hair. "I think the choice Lily offered would bring a field of knowing with it ... knowledge from my soul. If I veered toward dying to my mortal life, it would reveal something about my family that would make it possible for me to leave them."

Sara released a slow breath of relief. "Nothing like that happened to me, but I did stand with Sean in the light of his soul. Oh, the peace I felt. When I think of that, as opposed to how I feel around Ross, I wish ..." She clutched at the sheets. "Ross is so different, so damn cavalier. He sailed in here and never said a word about the way he left me."

"He's so happy with Nicky that he probably can't remember not wanting him, at least for the moment. Give him a chance, Sara."

Sara squeezed her fists under the blankets. She wanted to shout, what about me? Why should I always have to consider *his* needs? "You know, if Lily really wanted Ross dead, why didn't she just shove him in front a car?"

Anna shook her head. "Lily wouldn't do anything as obvious as that to Ross. After we die we review our life. We find out what a gift it was and what we were meant to do. If Ross discovered Lily had deliberately killed him and cut that short, he wouldn't have felt the same way about her. Ross had to be willing to cross over and rescue her. You really messed up her plans."

Anna snorted a little laugh, then talked in that abstract manner of hers about how everything was perfect—about staying in the moment and letting the perfection rise up and greet you. All the while, she rocked Nicky and smiled at him. The baby stared back at her, wriggling his little fingers as if he grasped the meaning of her words.

Sara plumped up a pillow. Tears welled in her eyes. "Did you see my mother with the golden beings?"

"Yes. What a blessing to heal your differences with her."

"Um, but I do so wish I'd had more time with her. My father died when I was ten. Recently, I learned something about him that bothers me. I would like to have asked my mother about that."

"Perhaps you don't need to know that about your father."

"Yes. I do." Looking at Anna, Sara felt a flicker of hope. "Maybe you could help me."

"What is it?"

"Did you know the main characters in *Love Interrupted* were based on real people?"

"Yes. Sean told me all about that when he stayed with us in

Easthampton. By eleven at night, he would have worn Carlo out, then Sean and I would talk for long hours." Anna smiled. "How wonderful to know about your life as Elizabeth. You must feel most fortunate to have met Sean and Ross again, to have a chance to resolve painful issues that stem from that lifetime."

Sara's heart raced. "Does Ross know he was Nicky Hart?"

"I have no idea. Why don't you ask him?"

"When I brought it up, Ross acted as if I was crazy."

"There you are then. It doesn't feel real to him."

Sara resisted telling Anna she suspected Ross of hiding from the truth. Anna took people at their word. "Are you suggesting I just drop the subject?"

Anna looked surprised by the question. "Of course. Ross will work things out in his own way."

"Oh, Anna, I wish I had your casual acceptance of people."

"You do have it, Sara. You also have a highly developed intellect, and the intellect likes to look at things from one angle and then another. It's fun, you learn a great deal, and you need that knowledge to function in your work. Acceptance lives in a quieter place in the mind. I'm used to living there. It's easy for me."

"So I'm too busy thinking—"

"You're perfect, Sara ... perfect for your life's journey, just as

Ross is for his."

Sara bit her lip, catching herself on the verge of arguing the matter with Anna. "About my father."

Anna rubbed Nicky's back. "Yes?"

Sara told Anna of her father's childhood visits to his aunt in Sussex. "His aunt was some sort of a medium. Apparently, she channeled Elizabeth's spirit. My Aunt Alice, my mother's sister, told me my father formed a deep attachment to Elizabeth. Even as a man, he longed for Elizabeth to appear to him again. The night my mother told him she was pregnant with me, Elizabeth came to my father in a dream and asked him to come to England and be with her. My father took off for Sussex. He stayed for three months. It bothers me. I adored my father." Sara reached out and stroked Nicky's shoulder. "Now that I know what it's like to be left when you're pregnant, I hate to think my father did that to my mother." Tears rolled down Sara's cheeks. She wiped them with her fingers. "Why would he?"

Anna swiped a cloth from the side table and mopped drool from Nicky's chin. "I don't know the answer."

Sara stared at Anna. "But you know something. I can feel it."

"If I tell you what I know, I need you to promise me that you won't just believe it. Belief is a double-edge sword. It can be beautiful or dangerous. Look at what happened when I told Ross about IsMara's writings on the death process. A great deal of your suffering resulted from his belief that he could die, find Lily and lead her into the light. I have suffered, too. I cannot make that mistake again."

Sara dabbed her tears with the bed sheet. "Oh, Anna, I'm so sorry. I would never ask you to do anything that would hurt you. I'll get over my feelings about my father."

Anna chuckled. "No, you won't. You are the proverbial dog with a bone."

Sara's pulse quickened as she looked hopefully at Anna.

Anna switched Nicky to her other arm. "IsMara also wrote about the journey of the human spirit as it enters life. What she said might help you resolve your feelings toward your father. I will tell you that, if you promise to test IsMara's knowledge against your own. That is, meditate upon the matter until it is clear to you. You don't have to be an avatar to do this. Find a method to silence your mind. Using your breath works well. Simply breathe and watch your breath. Eventually, your mind will fall silent, and then your feelings will tell you the truth."

Sara sat up straight. "I will do what you ask. I promise."

"Very well. This is IsMara's truth. She wrote that the spirit does not enter the fetus for the first three months. The spirit takes at least that time, and sometimes four or five or the whole nine months to decide if the mother and father will provide the right journey for that spirit's soul growth."

Sara's mouth gaped open. "Three months … so my father …" She shook her head. "Sorry."

Anna laughed. "Good catch."

Sara's feelings told her right away that Elizabeth—the person Sara had been—had called her father to see if he would be the right father for her— Sara, the person she needed to become. Sara's body trembled with excitement. She forced herself to stop thinking about this. She must stand true to her promise to Anna. She took a couple of very deep breaths. "Thank you, Anna. That really helps me to understand my father."

"Good. So, back to your journey to the other side."

"Yes, where was I?"

"You healed Lily, and she turned into a golden being."

"Did you see that?"

Anna nodded. "I was outside in the waiting area with Carlo and Ross when you touched your sword to her heart. Right after that, Lily performed her first act as a golden being."

"I don't recall that. What was it?"

"She reached a golden hand into Ross's memory and erased his guilt over her. Imagine how wonderful it must be for him not to feel the pain of her death anymore."

Sara's shoulders sagged, and her anger at Ross returned. Why hadn't he told her about that? His teenage pledge to die with Lily had been the root of all their problems. "Did Ross see Lily?"

"I don't know, but I'm sure he felt her presence. He left the waiting area, saying he wanted to be alone in the chapel. Carlo was worried about him and followed him there. When they came back, Carlo said Ross had told him about his suicide attempt with Lily. I expected my poor darling to be plagued with guilt, but he wasn't. Once he was convinced Ross was all right, he faced a dread that had been so deeply entombed in him that he'd dared not acknowledge it … a deadly premonition that Ross would die before him. Oh!" Anna gasped. "I knew Carlo suffered from that, and I was so relieved to see him free of it. Then your doctor arrived and told us the baby was born and in good health." Anna stroked Nicky's cheek. "We all rushed to the nursery. Ross was beside himself with happiness. He couldn't stop talking about all the things he was going to do with his son. Carlo wept upon sight of his first grandchild … wept for joy." Anna curled her fingers around the baby's. "When you healed Lily, you healed us all."

It pleased Sara that Anna had benefited from the miraculous healing. Carlo still irked her, but she'd get over it. Anna had been such a faithful friend, she wouldn't allow anything to mar their relationship.

"Ross has spent hours on the phone, searching for the best doctors and physical therapists for you, Sara. He looked sad when he came to get me a few minutes ago. Did you tell him you can walk?"

"No."

"Shall I ask him to come in so you can cheer him up?"

The thought of Ross making needless calls appeased Sara's appetite to hurt him. She felt buoyed up, riding on a rush of justifiable pleasure. Sara glanced away from Anna, hoping she wouldn't notice. Of course she did.

Anna squeezed her shoulder gently. "Sara, you gave Ross a child to save his life. You love him."

"Um, but he's made it impossible for me to feel that right now."

"I understand."

Sara doubted that, doubted Anna would let anyone suffer if she had the power to prevent it. She felt a little ashamed for her retaliatory ways, although not enough to rise above them. But she did want to wipe the slate clean of secrets between them. "Since you were so certain Ross could father a child, I guess he didn't tell you he had a vasectomy when he was eighteen."

"No, but after I read *David and Danielle,* I presumed he would keep the promises of his suicide pact with Lily." She propped Nicky up against her shoulder and stroked his back. "The first night you visited me, as we sat in the atrium room of my apartment, as the snow splashed against the windows, I saw Nicky in your aura. He told me you were to be his mother and Ross his father." Her eyes danced with delight. "I knew then something would go wrong with any procedure Ross might have had to prevent him from having children."

Sara's nerves twitched. That Anna had known she would give birth to Nicky and not told her, frightened Sara, but not nearly as much as the way Anna looked at her now—her brow frozen in a frown.

CHAPTER THIRTY-TWO

Sara lathered her body with Kiehl's coconut soap, a gift from a basket of toiletries sent by Brad, and luxuriated in the shower. Hot water pummeled her shoulders. She remembered the first shower she'd taken with Ross. What might her life be like had she not stripped and stepped boldly into the water with him? Ross would probably not have granted her another chance to pitch him for the account, and without Lumina the agency might have failed. And she wouldn't have Nicky. A year ago, the thought of having another baby horrified her. Now Nicky lit up her future.

A nurse's aide flung a towel over the shower rod. "You okay in there?"

"Yes, thank you." Sara snatched the towel and dried off.

"Your son Jake is here. He's outside in the waiting area."

"Oh, great." Sara heard the bathroom door close. She wrapped the towel around her and hurried into her room. She pulled on a gown and robe from the suitcase Zoey had brought to the hospital, then opened the door to the hallway.

Jake charged in, his hair straggling to his shoulders beneath a baseball cap, his face shaded with stubble. Gone was the languid boy who possessed an air of owning all the time in the world.

"Mom." He wrapped his arms around her. The tremble in his voice revealed how scared he must have been by her brush with death.

Tears flooded Sara's eyes. She buried her head against his shoulder and ran her hands over his back. "I'm fine, darling ... really."

Jake took a step back. "But Mom, I don't understand. How could you fall off the pavement and in front of a cab?"

"Look at me." She smiled, blinking tears. "I'm not hurt. Hardly a bruise on me. Isn't that all that matters?"

"I guess, but—"

"No buts. Come and meet your little brother."

Sara led him to the crib. Jake smiled at the infant. A dizzying smile, just like his father's—an expression that had once knocked Sara out of her senses and into love with Jack McBride. Jake also had his father's eyes—sea green and flickering with the light of surprise. But his mouth was full and firm like Sara's. She glanced at

Nicky. Would he inherit Ross's chiseled beauty, or would he resemble her?

"What a cute little guy." Jake bent over the crib. "What's his name?"

"Nicholas Sean. Nicky."

"I'm glad you didn't name him after Ross. He doesn't deserve you. I hope you've kicked him out of your life. We don't need him."

Jake stuck his hands on his hips and thrust his head forward—a mannerism that told Sara he stood ready to combat any argument to the contrary.

Sara chided herself for having aired her grievances over Ross with her son. She had infected him with her anger. "Jake, listen, darling, I'm not without fault in what happened between Ross and me. I can't explain it to you. I'm too confused about things right now."

"You, confused? Cool."

Jake let out a roar of laughter—deep, rich, mature laughter. It seemed like he'd grown from a boy into a man in a few short months. Sara suspected it had a lot to do with Arielle. Jake had been the mainstay of her life since Sean's death.

"Please be civil to Ross," Sara pleaded. "For Nicky's sake."

"Okay, but if he ever hurts you again, that's it. He's out. I'll be around for Nicky. I know you worried a lot about Dad not being there for me, but you know, I always thought it must be great to be him. To live in the spur of the moment, to catch that wave, any old wave, and ride it to wherever. I'd like to be able to do that … sometimes," he added quickly.

Sara scooped Nicky up from his crib and handed him to Jake. "Then do it before you have one of these. And after you've finished college."

Jake rocked the baby. "He's amazing. I'd be terrified to look after something so tiny. Were you scared when you had me?"

"I might have been, but for Grandma Gracie. Have you talked to her lately?"

"This morning. She can't wait to see the baby. She's coming to Olivia's funeral." He swallowed hard. "I'm sad about Grandma O but … well … it was hard to watch her suffer."

Sara nodded. She hoped one day to tell Jake of the moments she had shared with Olivia before she died, but this didn't feel like the right time.

"I'm helping Aunt Alice with the funeral arrangements. I called Dad, too. He seemed really sad about Olivia." Jake paused. "Dad asked if he could say a few words at the funeral. Do you mind?"

Sara's old frustrations with Jack surfaced. "It's okay with me.

Just remember, he might not show up."

Jake shrugged. "Whatever."

Arielle dashed into the room and threw her arms around Sara. "Oh, look at the baby … he's so adorable." She eased him from Jake's arms into her own. "He's handsome like the Dark Prince." She smiled. Her father's humor rang in her voice. "Last night I dreamed you found out the truth about Daddy's plane crash."

"I did, Arielle. Your father is in a wonderful place. I want to tell you all about it, but at another time … when we're alone."

Arielle's eyes clouded with disappointment, but then she smiled. "Yes, at Thanksgiving in Wainscott. In my dream, you told me about him as we walked by the sea. I can't remember why, but for some reason it had to be then."

"What about the sea?"

Vicki swept into the room, jeweled scarves flying, shopping bags dripping from her arms. Brad followed, lugging a camera and a tripod. They greeted Jake and Arielle and fussed over the baby. Well, Brad fussed over the baby. Vicki took control.

"We're going to take mother and baby pictures." Vicki dumped the shopping bags on the floor. "There's champagne and caviar in the brown bag. That's from Jonathon. He called from Monte Carlo and told me to get something for the baby from him."

Jake sauntered over to Vicki. "How's my wicked aunty?"

"Wicked. Very wicked." Vicki flashed her eyes, then smiled. "Look at you." She whisked the baseball cap off Jake's head. "You're not bad looking." She tugged on his hair and screwed up her nose. "Shampoo, kid. Comes in a bottle." She shoved Jake aside. "Start opening the champagne."

Vicki selected a Victoria's Secret bag from her stash and dragged Sara into the bathroom. She kicked the door closed. "What's going on with Ross?"

"I don't know. We haven't really talked yet. I saw him once, but the doctor was with us most of the time."

"He told the press having a son was the greatest thing that's ever happened to him." Vicki's eyes bulged. "Is he fucked up or is he fucked up?"

"He's one of those." Sara eyed the skimpy scarlet gown Vicki withdrew from the shopping bag. "I'm hardly in shape to wear that."

"While you've got big boobs, flaunt 'em. Here, it's got a matching robe."

"What's happening at the office?" Sara discarded her comfortable chenille gown.

Vicki gaped at the scar on Sara's stomach. "Jesus! Cover that up." She hung her head over the sink as if she were about to throw up.

"Still squeamish, I see." Sara pulled the negligee over her head. The filmy satin stretched awkwardly over her swollen stomach, ruining the drape of the bias-cut gown.

"Here." Vicki helped her into the robe. "The office? Everyone was really upset about you. They probably wished I'd gotten hit by a cab instead of you."

Vicki lowered her eyes, a habit Sara often associated with deception, but which she now thought might be to hide her feelings of unworthiness. Sara touched her lightly on the arm. "Show people who you really are, Vicki. They'll respond differently. Start with Zoey. While I'm on maternity leave, I'm going to let her handle more of my work. She's smart. She'll work day and night. Help her. Will you?"

Vicki slashed a dismissive hand through the air but lowered it slowly. Her eyes softened. "Last night, when Anna DeLuca came out of your room, she asked me, Brad and Zoey to stay for a moment. She sat between Carlo and Ross and told us your paralysis had been temporary and you would have full use of your legs." Vicki paused. "I don't remember what anyone said or when they left. I was so relieved I couldn't move."

"Oh, Vicki." Sara hugged her. "I'm—"

"Okay, enough." Vicki wriggled out of her embrace. "I just didn't want to get stuck at the office without you."

Sara pushed on. She had vowed to be a better friend to Vicki.

Now was the time. "Remember how green I was when you first met me? Remember how you showed me the city? You took me to Off Off Broadway plays, to hear jazz in Harlem, to visit artists who painted so far off the page that I thought I was somewhere else in time."

"Yeah … well, someone had to knock the girl from Queens out of you."

Sara tied the sash of her robe. "The first time you took me home to meet your family, your father asked me if I liked opera. I didn't know. I'd never heard one. He played a recording of Maria Callas singing Tosca. That changed my life. These things are bigger than any differences we've had."

"Bigger than my fucking Jack McBride?"

"Yes. We're still friends. I love you."

Vicki grunted, dug into the shopping bag, withdrew a plastic case and slapped it on the sink. "Makeup, you're going to need it to be photographed."

Sara laughed and patted foundation on her face. "This is the best, I-love-you-too I've had for a long time."

"So, am I also forgiven for Dan?"

"Dan who?"

"Yeah, really." Vicki stood beside Sara. "When will you see

Ross again?"

Sara glanced at their images in the mirror over the sink. "Why, are you worried about the account?"

"Fuck the account. Do what's best for you."

"Fuck the account?" Sara's voice rose in disbelief.

"Uh-hum."

"Are you sure?"

"I'm sure."

They stared at each other in the mirror. Their eyes sparkled with amusement. Laughter bubbled up. It was quiet at first as if coming from a new place, one they didn't want to exhaust too soon. Then it gathered momentum. Laughter—irrepressible—like them— people who had wounded each other deeply but who traveled on to a better place.

Brad peered around the door. "Anna's here, and we're knocking back the champagne pretty good."

Vicki bolted from the bathroom.

"Got her." Brad grinned. "Oh, darling!" He flung his arms around Sara. "You're all right, that's so fabulous. What happened? One moment we heard you were paralyzed, and the next that you'd be okay. These doctors … really ..." He rolled his eyes. "Anyway, because you almost died, and because I don't know how I would have lived without you, I'm going to forgive you for not confiding in me about Ross. Not that I wasn't hurt."

"I thought it best for you not to know the intimate details about Ross and me. You've really hit it off with Carlo, and that's great for your career, but I'm not exactly his favorite person."

"You're wrong about that, darling. Carlo admires you. He thinks you're brilliant and very responsible to your clients."

"That's nice." Sara stopped herself from saying anything about Carlo's icy attitude toward her relationship with Ross. Carlo hovered near the top of her forgiveness list, so she'd better start thinking about him in a positive way.

"Oh, darling!" Brad took a step back and wrung his hands together. "Look at your hair!" He dug into the shopping bag, produced a tube of styling gel and trailed globules through her locks. He painted her lips pale pink and brushed gold dust on her eyelids and her cheeks, all the while chatting nonstop about Marty, a young, male model he'd hooked up with in L.A.

"There." He took a step back and appraised his work. "Now you look like an Aegean goddess."

Sara gripped his hand and held it against her cheek. "I'm so glad you've found someone."

"It's not love, Sara." A bereft looked filled his eyes. He blinked. "But it's fun. I'll enjoy it for as long as it lasts."

She smiled, thinking back to when she had thought the same about having an affair with Ross.

Brad laid a hand on her shoulder. "I feel like I've let you down, that you felt you couldn't trust me enough to tell me about Ross. How did that happen between us? I promise you, Sara, on my beloved Ian's spirit, that if you had asked me, I would never have repeated a word of what you told me about Ross to anyone."

The desolate look on Brad's face ate into Sara's heart. "I thought I was having a fling with Ross, but before I knew it I was so deeply involved with him that I didn't know what hit me. I had your best interests in mind when I didn't confide in you, but I also hid behind that. I hid because there's a metaphysical side to my relationship with Ross … a spiritual connection that I found threatening. If I'd spoken about it to you, I would have given it a place in my life, and I resisted that with all my might."

"You mean like karma, darling? Like you've lived with Ross before and you've discovered that you're with him now to finish something you started in that previous life?"

Aghast, Sara stared at Brad as if seeing him for the first time.

"I know, darling, you think I've gone all L.A., but that's not true. Ian and I knew we had lived together before."

"And you kept that from me!"

"So I'm right. That's it with you and Ross."

Brad's gaze bored into Sara, emitting his need to be trusted. If she told him anything but the truth it would destroy their friendship. She squared her shoulders and faced down doubt. "Yes, that's it."

Brad swished his ponytail. "Then forgive him and love him, no matter what."

In a flash, Sara knew Ian had not contracted AIDS via a blood transfusion, as in the complex story they had told her. Ian had cheated on Brad, and Brad had forgiven him unconditionally. She flung her arms around her friend. Had she shown some intolerance for Ian that didn't permit him to confide in her? No. Some things needed to remain secret. Even in this new closeness to Brad, she did not want to tell him to read *Love Interrupted* and learn all about her previous life as Elizabeth Harroway. Stillness settled between them. She felt their friendship rooting into deeper, richer soil.

Brad held her at arm's length. "You look marvelous, darling, imperative, commanding. Unbeatable. Come on, let's join the party."

Her hospital room buzzed with the sound of friends having a good time. Nicky lay in his crib, moving his arm and legs. Sara kissed him on the forehead, then crossed the room and stood by Anna.

"Scarlet becomes you," Anna said.

"I bet." Sara laughed. "How did Ross react last night after you told him I could walk?"

"He looked stunned, then ... oh, I'm sorry I don't remember. Carlo flung his arms around me, and we hugged and hugged, so grateful that everything had turned out well." Anna linked her arm through Sara's. "Carlo had to go to Los Angeles this morning, or he would be here. He asked me to give you this." She withdrew a manila envelope from her shoulder bag and offered it to Sara.

Sara's hand froze. Was it some sort of legal document, perhaps a petition for custody of Nicky? Suspicious thoughts about Carlo whizzed through her mind. Her heart banged in her chest. "What is it?"

"Nicky's shares in Lumina."

"Oh!" Sara whispered, breathless with relief. "I never expected—"

"The stock is Nicky's birthright. Blood. Family." Anna eased the envelope into Sara's hand.

"That's most generous of Carlo, but I don't know if Ross and I can make it together."

"That makes no difference. Nicky is our grandchild, and you're his mother, so put the stock in a safe place and say no more about it."

"Then you'd better look after it until I get out of the hospital." Sara handed the envelope back to Anna, having no curiosity about the worth of the gift. It was indeed the thought that counted. Carlo's thought.

"You were supposed to go to L.A with Carlo. I'm all right, Anna. You don't have to stay in New York for me."

Anna's eyes fluttered, giving her an appearance of falling into a trance. She remained like that for several moments. "I'm exactly where I'm meant to be."

Sara's throat tightened. Had Anna looked into her aura and seen something bad? Something about Ross? Did Anna think she might need to help Sara pick up the pieces of her life? Sara opened her mouth and then shut it as Jake strode up.

"Anna, hi, I'm Jake." He offered his hand.

Anna gripped it. "I've heard so much about you."

"And I've been reading about your art. I checked out your sculptures online. They're fantastic. I'm amazed by the feeling you convey with granite."

Sara brimmed with pride. Jake was so at ease with Anna and had obviously done considerable research on her. She wondered if Arielle ignited his sudden interest in art. A pang of jealousy hit her. She sighed inwardly. It was time to release Jake into a world even further away from hers.

"Come and visit me in my studio in Easthampton this summer." Anna smiled at Jake. "Bring Arielle and stay for a while. I mean ..." She darted a glance at Sara. "I mean visit me when you're at your mother's house." Anna giggled and mocked herself, saying she sometimes invited people to stay without thinking. "Oh, my goodness. Poor Carlo, he never knows who he will find at the breakfast table." Anna swept across the room and started talking to Vicki.

Sara felt a little disturbed by this flighty side of Anna but tossed it off. Anna could be enigmatic, to say the least.

Arielle swung a tray of food in front of Sara. "I love Vicki." She widened her eyes. "She is so her own person. Who else would give a newborn four pounds of Beluga caviar and a case of Cristal champagne?"

Sara laughed, remembering her college days with Vicki and how enchanted she'd been by her. "Yes. Vicki is very special."

Arielle raised the tray of appetizers. "So, want some grub?"

Sara eyed the caviar surrounded by finely chopped egg white and onions. "No, thanks."

"Let's do pictures." Brad took Sara's arm. "First, I'll get some of Sara and the baby, then shots of each of you with her and Nicky. Then I'll time the camera, and we'll get a group portrait."

Sara sat on the sofa holding Nicky, feeling more like a hooker than a mother in her scarlet peignoir. Brad posed each person beside her, fussing with hair and clothes, but the more they drank the sillier they got. Finally, he gave up and snapped picture after picture as they jumped up and down on either side of her like kids playing musical chairs.

"Now for the group photo. Everyone smile on the count of three. One!" Brad dashed from the camera to the couch and squeezed in between Sara and Vicki. Jake and Arielle perched on the arms. Anna sat crossed-legged on the floor in front of Sara.

"Two. Three!"

The flash went off. The shutter opened and closed. Sara imagined herself looking at the photo years from now. The people she loved surrounded her. She had just turned thirty-eight. Her shares in HMJ certainly qualified her as a woman of capital. She had met her goal with two years in hand.

Everyone laughed and blinked in the aftermath of the flash. The door opened.

Ross stood on the threshold.

CHAPTER THIRTY-THREE

With a whirlwind of hugs and kisses, everyone left the room. Sara sat with Ross on the sofa. Nicky lay on his lap with his head at his father's knees, gazing back at them as if pondering why he had landed at the mercy of these strangely mismatched people.

Ross rubbed his thumbs on the soles of Nicky's feet. "I've got so much to account for I hardly know where to begin."

He raised a brow. Sara looked away from his hopeful expression. Hurt feelings would not allow her to ease the way for him.

He spoke softly. "Being a father has given me a new perspective on life. After Lily died, and after I failed to die with her, I lost all sense of belonging in this world. Having this beautiful little boy has restored that. I do believe what goes around comes around, but I can't think of anything I've ever done to deserve you. I can't believe I was so self-involved that I expected you to understand my pledge to die and rescue Lily. You, of all people … you, with your feet so firmly entrenched in life."

He paused, his breath seeming to catch in his throat.

"I've not closed my eyes without remembering how you looked when I told you that if you had the baby, you'd never see me again." Tears trickled down his cheeks. "I'm so sorry."

Sara waited for love to rise up. He had said the words she ached to hear, and grief stained his face. Still the sensual flurries of love lay frozen somewhere inside her. Unnerved by her lack of feelings, she tried to think of something appropriate to say. Nothing came. Was it too late? Had love died?

She studied the soft weave of Ross's jacket—cashmere, no doubt—muted in hues of brown and amber, fading into each other like autumn into winter. A fragrance wafted off him—an earthy, hemp-like smell—his animal scent. She inhaled it, sucking it deep into her lungs, certain it would arouse her. It didn't. An embarrassing amount of time had passed since his apology. He looked like a man caught at the scene of an unspeakable horror. The sweep of their history passed before Sara, and her many mistakes with him pounded on her conscience.

"I'm sorry too, Ross. I could have been more understanding of your promise to Lily. Sometimes I can be so competitive that it blinds me to all else. With Lily … well … she threatened your life. I had to get the better of her."

"Your strength always attracted me, Sara. I knew you would survive no matter what I did." He inched closer to her. "But it seemed Lily would suffer forever unless I helped her. I just couldn't live with that."

Sara felt her perception shift a little. Perhaps that was a magnificent call to love.

Ross touched his hand to hers. "I want to talk about Lily before we go on. Is that okay?"

Sara nodded, eager to hear his rendition of what Anna had told her.

"Yesterday, I went to the chapel to pray that you would be all right, and I had a vision of Lily. She appeared as a tall golden being. I felt that angel presence about her that I sometimes felt when we were kids. She said someone had helped her out of the dark planes … that she had returned to the beingness of her true nature. She touched my head. It was amazing. The awful sounds of Lily's suffering vanished. I can't even remember them now." His eyes misted over. "I asked Anna if she had helped Lily. She said no, but then Anna wouldn't admit it if she had. She once told me that when she did things anonymously, her soul rewarded her by increasing her ability to help others." He paused. "So, I wonder, do you know anything about Lily's transformation?"

His eyes dug into the substance of Sara's soul. Suddenly, nothing seemed more important than guarding the secret of Lily's miraculous healing. To speak about it would open a vein of inquiry that would be hard to close. Also, she sensed words would diminish the wonder of it all. "Me?" Sara slapped her hand against her chest. "Me, with my feet so firmly on the ground?"

"Yeah, but your accident presents some inconsistency to that. Your doctor told me you must have lost your balance ... become disoriented, but that doesn't sound like you. I wondered if you had an out-of-body experience."

Nicky whimpered. Sara leaned across Ross and stroked the baby's cheek. "My doctor got it right, I lost my balance."

"What about this huge gust of wind that supposedly came out of nowhere?"

"I was knocked unconscious, Ross." She adjusted the blanket around Nicky. "Lily's free, isn't that all that matters?" She could tell by his frown that his mind churned with questions. Silence hung between them. Nicky gurgled. They both shifted their attention to him. He lulled his head to the side with his mouth slightly open. Drool trickled onto his chin. Ross scooped it up with his little finger and wiped it on the sleeve of his jacket. A gesture so tender it melted the last of her resistance to him.

"You're all that matters, Sara. You and Nicky."

She trembled. What would come next? What did he want? What did she want? Could they make it together? What would that be like for them? He lived on the West coast, and she on the East.

They both had demanding careers. She lifted the baby off his lap and cuddled him against her breast.

Ross stroked her cheek. "There's something I've got to tell you."

The pulse at Sara's throat quickened. She hated that kind of announcement. She steeled herself. "What is it?"

"That first morning when you followed me into the park, I saw you before I left the hotel. I was in the swing door as you approached the building. A prism of light shone off the wings at the heels of your shoes. I felt dizzy. My heart sliced down the middle. You, a complete stranger, suddenly owned one half of it, and Lily the other. I backtracked into the hotel and collapsed in a chair in the lobby. What occurred next was even more bizarre. Everything that has happened to us passed before me then. Fragmented. You know flashes of times when we made love. Dancing with you in your house in Wainscott. Flying with you over the Rockies. My eyes even stung as they did when Sean's ashes blew in my face. Then everything went blank."

Sara felt the blood drain from her cheeks. "You knew Sean was going to die, and you didn't do anything to prevent his death?"

He shook his head. "I was like a guy on an acid trip. A never-ending collage of events spun before me. It was bigger than life ... more than I could process. All I really knew was that I loved the woman I had seen in those shoes, and that I had no right to love her because my life belonged to Lily." He rubbed his eyes with the heels of his hands.

Sara could think of nothing but Sean trapped in his small plane, fighting for his life against Lily's murderous ghost. She got up and laid Nicky in his crib before she could contaminate him with the pain burning in her breast.

"Sara." Ross followed her and stood beside her. "I—"

"Please." She held up a hand. "I need some space." She walked to the window and pressed her palms against the panes. Traffic lumbered down Lexington Avenue. People strode along snapping their fingers to music that pounded into their ears from headphones and iPods. The lights of restaurants and shops glowed against the dark of the night.

She was ten years old again. She heard the cold metallic click of the front door closing. She ran to her bedroom window. Her father hurried down the street, a suitcase in his hand. That morning, he had told her he was leaving to chase his dream. "I'll be back for you, Sara." Perhaps, her mother's constant degrading remarks about him foreshadowed a certainty that she would not see him again. Or, maybe it came from a childlike foreknowledge, that with love there would be loss. It didn't matter. She decided right then, nothing would ever hurt her again as much as the loss of her father. It would be the bass note of her suffering and when it rang, she would flee. That had worked until Sean died. Now Ross had added to that sorrow, and Sara could not flee from the father of her child. She recalled her mother's drugged ramblings about what love might do to Sara. Would it eat away at her bones or would it kill her as it had her namesake?

Her namesake … Elizabeth Sara … she must have been the bass note of her mother's suffering. Sara trembled, remembering her mother's dying words. *Your father … I didn't understand him.* Sara tried to imagine her father telling Olivia he spent three months in England with Elizabeth's spirit because Elizabeth wanted to check him out to see if he would be the right father for Sara. Ohmigod! Olivia must have gone berserk. As far as Sara could determine, her mother had never let her father back into her life. She had destroyed her own chance at happiness rather than accept him for who he was. A long-forbidden memory surfaced in Sara's thoughts. Another woman had died in the car crash with her father—a young woman who met death clutching his hand. Sara had overheard Aunt Alice breaking the news to her mother, but Sara had stuffed her fingers into her ears and pretended not to hear.

The skin at the back of her neck prickled. Ross had said a part of her was locked up in her childhood, that she was angry with men, that she didn't trust them. He had seen straight through the elaborate guise with which Sara had fooled herself. She blew out a soft breath of relief. Facing the truth about her father did not diminish him in any way. If Olivia had denied him her love, he had the right to look for it elsewhere.

As Sara ruminated on her childhood, it struck that her father had come back for her as he had promised. He came a year ago—in a haze of golden light—on the day she found the note with her forgotten goal.

Everyone you will meet on the way to your goal already waits for you, Sara.

Yes! Sara clenched a happy fist. Her life felt balanced for the first time. She sensed Ross standing behind her. His quiet, slow-burning energy seeped into her heart. She thought of the time he had lured her into the healing-man relationship. Her newfound balance wavered. Dear God, she had just recovered from the effects of that. Now he confessed that he had foreseen Sean's death! Hallucination or no hallucination, he should have told her about it long ago.

Her nerves trembled. Her body smarted from head to toe. Her heartbeat fluctuated wildly. She felt dizzy, probably from the stress of her accident and giving birth. She lowered her head. The dizziness passed. She removed her hands from the windows. A thin imprint of her palms clung to the panes. As they faded, she felt a new urgency to let go of her grievances and claim the riches of life being offered to her. Her eye went to the reflection of the wall clock higher on the windowpane. Almost twenty-four hours had passed since Lily's last visit. She would be back soon. Sara thought of Sean telling her to work things out with Ross and to do it quickly. She wished she'd heard his reason for that. Instead, she had obsessed over the way Ross had left her, which had hauled her away from Sean and back into her body.

Beware of the unforgiven.

Shock racked her brain, and a new understanding of forgiveness unfolded. It was not for her to forgive Ross. What did she really know of his life? She barely understood the complexities of her own. No, she needed to forgive herself for her own misunderstandings—for her ignorance.

The mellow tone of her wisdom voice resonated in her thoughts. "That's right, Sara. Forgiveness is the something precious you chased in that vision you had of yourself in the Lumina shoes. But you've always had it. Forgiveness is literally fore-given … a grace bestowed before birth. It is the unstoppable power you've felt driving you forward, thrusting you into this relationship with Ross … driving you to this understanding."

Sara shifted her weight onto the balls of her feet, ready to run for a new start. She glanced back at Ross. He bent over the crib, twining his fingers through Nicky's, passing his quiet energy on to his son.

"Ross."

He looked up and smiled—his wide-open wonderful smile. He came up behind her and circled his arms around her waist. "Am I good for another chance?"

She remembered the day he had given Brad a second chance and agreed to let him direct the Lumina commercial. Déjà vu had come full circle. Her sense back then that Ross would do something awful to her had been valid, but she would not let that rule her life. She would grab love for all its worth. "Yes. You deserve another chance."

"Does that mean you love me?"

"Yes."

"Yes, you're sure?"

"Yes."

The little word hung between them like the last chord of a symphony, and love, like music, never died. Love lived in the pauses between each breath. If she listened hard enough, she could hear where it had come from and where it went. Sara rested her head on Ross's shoulder, loving him as she would until the unfinished love between them had been finished.

A soft thud sounded in her chest—a noise like that of a book closing. She glanced out the window. A shimmering golden glow shone through the clouds.

Lily emerged, tall and flowing, filling the whole world with her light, walking toward Sara—her arms outstretched.

CHAPTER THRITY-FOUR

Lily sailed through the window. Her long translucent form floated past Sara and Ross and towered behind them. Looking up into Lily's light, Sara felt a sharp sensation shoot through her temples like a blade slicing her head in half. Part of her consciousness drifted into a dreamy state and hung weightless above her body. The other remained rooted in logic. She struggled to keep her thoughts there, in the more familiar realm of reason. She leaned heavily against Ross. He stood behind her with his arms locked around her waist, nuzzling her cheek.

"I want you to become all that you've dreamed of becoming, Sara. Everything will fall into place with us. I'll be here for you and Nicky. Always."

Always, she thought, what a beautiful word. It rang of comfort and continuity. Yes, always was her new favorite word.

Lily reached her arms around Ross and Sara, engulfing them in her golden light. Her love flooded into Sara's heart, and she drifted back to the dream state. The soft essence of her soul shivered in her cells. Sara watched its radiant luminosity weave in and out of her and over the planet and throughout the whole galaxy. She heard sound waves melting into one another. At first, one note, then one chord, then all the notes and all the chords of the scale, quavering on top of each other—a dazzling complexity of music waiting to be heard by the human ear—to be arranged and rearranged—to touch the hearts of all people. Maybe when she returned to her soul she could absorb the language of music. Perhaps in that future lifetime when Lily said she and Sean would be together, she would be a composer. She would transcribe these sounds into symphonies and operas. This view of eternity elated Sara and increased her determination to live this life to the fullest. She would keep on challenging herself so she'd be worthy of such an artistic calling.

The light of her soul wove around her eyes, and recent fragments of her life flashed to mind. Laughing with Vicki and healing old wounds. Discovering the profound nature of Brad's love for his unfaithful partner. The tender way Ross had scooped drool from Nicky's chin. The moment she noticed Jake had grown from a boy into a man, and the pride she'd felt over his instant rapport with Anna.

Sara recalled Anna's words:

I think the choice would bring a field of knowing with it—knowledge from my soul. If I veered toward dying, it would reveal something about my family that would make it possible for me to leave them.

A surge of panic pulled Sara back into her mortal mind. Surely she was not dying. She had not chosen to die when she was with Lily, and she did not choose it now. She must be misinterpreting things.

The image of Anna and Jake talking together lodged in Sara's thoughts. Goose bumps crawled up her arms. That was no innocent slip when Anna invited Jake to stay with her at her Easthampton home. She'd said it so Sara would know she would watch over Jake.

Ohmigod! Yes, literally. Dear God, I can't die, not now.

The glorious glow of eternity turned dark and scary. What about Nicky, her darling little baby? Anna would not mother him. She would leave Nicky's welfare entirely up to Ross. After all, she believed having a child of his own was the one thing that would keep Ross grounded in his life.

Death's sting flew off the pages of mythology and stabbed Sara in the heart. Ross kept hugging her close to him, but he was quiet now. The future he dreamed for them danced in the silence. She ached with every fiber in her body to share it with him. She would go to any ends to love him. How foolish she'd been to worry about where they would live or even if they could live together.

Her heart pounded furiously as if running for life, running to win—to beat death, and if not that, then to at least punch it square in the face before it claimed her.

She glanced up at Lily, conveying her thoughts in silence. *I can't leave Nicky. He needs me.*

With a touch of Lily's hand, Sara floated back into the dream state. Gazing down on her herself, she watched a large artery near the base of her brain balloon out. Blood seeped into the crevices of her brain. Her birth date appeared, then a dash, and then the date of her death. Yesterday! The gift Lily had spoken of was another day of life—twenty-four hours to set things straight. Sean must have known. He'd urged her to hurry up and work things out with Ross.

Sara glanced down from the dream state. Blind to her impending death, Ross continued to hold her in his arms and speak of the life they would share. Longing to be with him, Sara slipped into the pits of despair.

Lilly hoisted her back into her higher mind. "Look into the future, Sara."

Sara gazed in the direction of Lily's finger. Ross sat by a pool reading a script with six-month-old Nicky on his lap. He had his father's deep-blue eyes and dark hair, but his little face was all Sara's.

The vague outline of an unknown woman loomed behind Ross. She had been shaded in shadows—the fog of Ross's grief. Nicky, unknowing of sorrow, could see the woman, and he reached his hand out to her, gurgling with delight. Then Anna arrived. She gathered Nicky in her arms, walked through the shadows and introduced him to the mystery woman. Nicky squirmed and reached his hands out, wanting to be with her. Anna placed him in her arms. Nicky laid his head on the young woman's shoulder and smiled as if looking straight back at Sara in her soul. Sara blew him kisses on the wind. Nicky caught one and smacked it against his mouth. His laughter filled the world.

Anna took the mystery woman's hand and led her out of the shadows of Ross's grief and into the light of day. She appeared to be about twenty-two, with a golden tan and silky, sugar-brown hair. Her energy field touched Sara's. It was deeply loving and filled with the light of her soul. Anna introduced the girl to Ross. He studied her in a long, slow glance. The allure of the young woman broke through his sorrow. The girl met Ross's glance straight on, offering her heart to him. Ross raised his eyes and gazed into the distance beyond her. He listened with all the powers of his concentration until the vibration of his question echoed in Sara's soul. "Should I love her?"

"Yes," she whispered back to him.

In an instant, Ross fell in love with the girl. Two months later, they married.

Lily released her grip on Sara. Sara crashed into her mortal mind and immediately forgot the largess of her soul. Jealousy ravished her. How could Ross forget her so quickly?

"He may not," Lily whispered. "That future is but a possibility. Only you can grant him the freedom to live it."

Sara thought of asking Lily what other possibilities there might be for Ross. Perhaps nothing so devastating as dying of sorrow over her death, but also not quite so ecstatic as marrying that beautiful girl. But she did not. Love represented the price of her future life with Sean. Love without measure.

Her head throbbed with pain, and strength ebbed from her body. She fell limp in Ross's arms.

"Oh, my God!" Ross tightened his grip on her. "What's the matter?"

The force of his alarm sped through Sara like an electrical current.

He scooped her up and laid her on the bed. "I'll get the doctor."

She caught his arm as he reached for the call button. "No. Just hold me. Please. It's my time to go. It's written on my soul."

"No!"

The leaden hue of agony darkened his eyes.

"No! That can't be. You're just tired." His voice choked. He stroked her brow. "I'll get help. You'll be fine."

"Just hold me, Ross."

His tears splashed onto her face. She licked their salty, warm wetness, cherishing the taste of him. He slid his arms beneath her, sobbing and begging her not to leave him. "I can't go on without you."

"You have to. You've got to look after Nicky. As my healing man, I'm asking you. Will you please live a long and happy life and look after our child?"

Tears gushed down his cheeks. He searched her eyes as if looking for some sign that this was not happening. She met his gaze with solemn assurance.

He gulped and struggled for breath. "Yes." He buried his head in her shoulder and sobbed.

Sara pictured herself gripping the diamond handle of her great sword—the sword of just cause. A rush of energy ran down her arm. Her voice came strong and steady. "Ross, you're meant to love again. I want that for you. Nicky needs a mother. Promise me."

"No, Sara. Don't ... please ..." He pressed his heart against hers and rocked her back and forth as if trying to infuse his life into her.

"For Nicky. For me," she whispered. "I'm counting on you."

Lily floated between them and entwined Sara in her light, lifting her above the pain of Ross's heartbreak.

When Sara could feel his grief no more, the perfection at the center of all things shone brilliantly around her. The future opened. She saw that Ross and the young woman would be happy together. They'd have three more children, and their marriage would last until Ross died—at the age of eighty-six. Lily would appear to him as he released his last breath, and he would realize the perfection of all that had happened in their lives. Sara could see the light of that revelation dancing in his last glance.

As for Vicki, she would help Zoey move up the career ladder. She would force herself in the beginning as a tribute to Sara, but the rewards of watching Zoey flourish would touch a talent long asleep in Vicki. Vicki would sponsor a program for troubled kids— high school dropouts and recovering drug addicts. As these kids filed in for their first session, Vicki would write on the blackboard:

A dream come true puts hope in the world.

She would tell the story of how her best friend had believed in that, and how Vicki had become their mentor because of her, which made them the hope she hoped to put in the world.

Ross would invite Brad to be Nicky's godfather—a role Brad would relish. He'd infuse Nicky with the same joy for life that he instilled in Jake as a young boy. Ross would also invite Brad to direct an episode of *The Purpose*. Brad would excel and move to Los Angeles.

At Thanksgiving, Sara would appear to Arielle in a dream. They would be walking on the beach at Wainscott. Sara would tell Arielle the story of her father's journey back to his soul.

Sara would be with Jake and Nicky whenever they needed her, as a part of her would be alive in them—always.

Years from now, after Anna's children graduated from college, Carlo would die. Anna would return to the monastery in the Isles of Scilly where she had lived for twenty years before she met Carlo. Anna would live in silent meditation until she died at age ninety-four. She would walk through death's door and straight into her soul. Anna would not stay long. She would return to another life, bringing an enormous field of illumined consciousness with her. She would revise and publish the book written by the beloved mystic, IsMara centuries ago. Many would read it, Sara among them. Sara would cross the world to meet Anna. They would know each other upon first glance.

These became the people Sara had been meant to meet along the way. They had taught her about love and forgiveness, and she reflected those qualities back to them. Never in her whole life had anything felt so right or as complete as this, her last moment.

Sara released a final breath and placed her hand in Lily's.

EPILOGUE

They left their primordial perfection at exactly the same moment, joining a cascade of lights as brilliant as heaven itself and as soft as snowflakes—souls migrating to Earth. A hundred years had passed, a mere blip in eternity, and Sara and Sean, conscious in the heartbeat of joy, found each other at once.

"Where are you going, Sean?"

"Wherever you're going, Sara."

Sara laughed. "Do you remember our last lifetime?"

"I remember everything, just as Lily predicted. Do you?"

"Yes, and I'm already in love with you."

"I love you too. I always have and I always will."

Sara drew closer to Sean, mingling her light with his. They floated among the stars of the Milky Way and then perched on the rim of the Earth. They listened for the sound vibrations of their parents to be. When they heard the murmurings of two couples, each deeply in love, friends who lived next door to each other, they swept toward them, passing over land and sea and through sunsets and sunrises. Laughter trailed in their wake and touched the hearts of all who waited to meet them.

Also by Christina Greenaway:

WRITTEN IN RUBERAH
The first book of the *Age of Jeweled Intelligence* trilogy

www.christinagreenaway.com